a little too

WILD

WALL STREET JOURNAL & USA TODAY BESTSELLING AUTHOR

DEVNEY PERRY

A LITTLE TOO WILD

Copyright © 2022 by Devney Perry LLC

All rights reserved.

ISBN: 978-1-957376-22-6

This is a work of fiction. Names, characters, places and incidents are the product of the author's imagination or are used fictitiously. Any resemblance to actual events, locales or persons, living or dead, is coincidental.

Editing & Proofreading:

Elizabeth Nover, Razor Sharp Editing

Julie Deaton, Deaton Author Services

Judy Zweifel, Judy's Proofreading

Cover:

Sarah Hansen © Okay Creations

OTHER TITLES

Jamison Valley Series

The Coppersmith Farmhouse

The Clover Chapel

The Lucky Heart

The Outpost

The Bitterroot Inn

The Candle Palace

Maysen Jar Series

The Birthday List

Letters to Molly

Lark Cove Series

Tattered

Timid

Tragic

Tinsel

Timeless

CHAPTER ONE

CREW

"The plane is crashing. I gotta go."

"Crew." I could practically hear Sydney's eyes roll on the other end of our phone call. "Stop being over-dramatic."

"What if it really was crashing? And your last words to me were an insult?"

"You're not even on a plane," she barked as the whirl of my wheels on the highway's pavement hummed in the background. "Focus."

No, I didn't want to focus. I wanted to skip the lecture she'd started five minutes ago, then turn my army-green G-Wagon around and drive back to Utah.

"You need to be back in Park City on Monday for that photo shoot with GNU."

"I know." This was the fifth time she'd reminded me about that photo shoot. "I'll be back in time."

"You cannot be late. They are flying in from Washington just for this shoot."

Also something she'd told me five times. "Don't worry. I'll be there. Trust me." The last place in the world I wanted to be this weekend was Colorado.

"This trip couldn't fall at a worse time." Sydney sighed. "This sponsorship is huge. I don't want to risk anything happening to screw it up."

"Relax, Syd. It'll be fine. I'll be there Monday."

"Is this trip one hundred percent necessary?"

"What would you like me to do? Skip my brother's wedding?"

"Yes."

I chuckled. "You are ruthless."

"Which is why you love me."

"True."

Sydney had been my agent for the past three years and had made it her personal mission in life to make me, Crew Madigan, the face of snowboarding in America. So far, she'd done a hell of a job.

Her ruthlessness padded my bank account. As well as her own.

This Mercedes was my latest purchase, thanks to my recent sponsorship contracts. Syd had spent her commission on the same model, but in black.

"I'll see you Monday." There was no chance I'd linger in Colorado. My only obligation was the actual wedding tonight, and first thing tomorrow morning, I'd be on the road.

"Expect a phone call on Monday morning," Sydney said. "Early. I don't trust you to set your alarm."

"One time, Syd. I was late for one photo shoot."

She'd scheduled it for six in the morning because the photographer had wanted a sunrise shot, and when I'd set the hotel alarm the night before, I'd accidentally chosen p.m., not a.m.

Though Syd loved to rub that in my face, the shoot itself had worked out fine. The photographer was cool, and instead of worrying about a morning shoot, we'd just spent the day together, freestyling the Big Sky slopes in Montana.

With nothing staged or faked, the photos he'd taken had been epic. He'd captured a picture of me as I'd come off a cliff and bent for a grab, the afternoon sky at my back with mountain ranges and clouds in the distance.

That photo had landed on the cover of *Snowboarder Magazine*.

"Be on time, Crew."

"I cross my heart."

"And hope to die if you disappoint me."

Why did I always feel like saluting Sydney at the end of a phone call? "See ya."

She hung up without a goodbye.

I sighed, shifting my grip on the wheel. The drive from Park City was seven hours, and with every passing minute, the throb behind my temples intensified. For the past hundred miles, I'd begun to squirm.

Nagging as it was, at least Sydney's call had been a brief distraction from the anxiety rattling through my bones. I had been in knots for weeks, dreading this trip.

Why couldn't Reed have gotten married in Hawaii or Cabo?

My stomach churned as I neared the outskirts of Penny Ridge. For twelve years, I'd avoided returning to my hometown. Over a decade. After all that time, shouldn't this be easier? After the life and career I'd built, shouldn't twelve years have dulled the painful memories of home?

I was no longer the eighteen-year-old kid who'd run away from anything and everything in his life. Except as the speed limit dropped, the town coming into view, it was like being blasted into the past.

My heart beat too fast as I approached a sign with an arrow that hadn't been there when I'd left.

Madigan Mountain

A new access point to my family's ski resort. The entrance to a place I would have happily avoided until the end of my days.

The turnoff to town approached, so I slowed, hit my turn signal and pulled off the highway to Main Street. Buildings with red-brick faces sprouted up on both sides of the road, like walls—or jail-cell bars.

Another sign came into view, this one familiar and built into the median of the road.

Welcome to Penny Ridge

Located seventy miles from Denver along the ridgeline from Keystone, Penny Ridge had been my family's home for generations. But the day I'd left town, I hadn't looked back once. Not for friends. Not even for family.

As a professional snowboarder, there was no way to entirely avoid Colorado, not with its famed ski slopes and resorts. But I'd limited my time in the state, spending the bulk of it at alternative mountains.

Park City had become home. Montana was a favorite vacation destination. So were Canada, New Zealand and Japan. I'd travel anywhere in the world, especially if it meant distance from Penny Ridge.

Maybe I should have skipped my brother's wedding. Except I hadn't seen Reed in years. Hell, I hadn't even met his fiancée. Weston and I hadn't caught up lately either, and the only time I'd seen his fiancée, Callie, had been over FaceTime.

When both of my brothers had called about the wedding, asking me to come, I'd had a hard time finding an excuse not to show.

There was a suit in the back seat, pressed and ready for tonight's ceremony and reception. My overnight bag was packed with a single change of clothes, limited toiletries and nothing more. I'd do this wedding, make an appearance, then disappear from Penny Ridge for another decade. Maybe two.

As I drove down Main, I took in the changes as I rolled down the blocks. Flip's Gold and Silver was now Black Diamond Coffee. The Dive Bar was gone, replaced with a craft brewery. Mom's favorite bookstore was a Helly Hansen franchise.

The coffee shop and brewery, she would have loved. The demise of her bookstore, not so much.

Her ghost walked these sidewalks. Mom haunted this town, these streets.

Tomorrow. I only had to stick this out through tomorrow. Then I'd get out of Penny Ridge.

People meandered the sidewalks. Half of the parking spaces were taken. It was fairly quiet this afternoon, something I suspected would change when the resort opened for the season next weekend. Then downtown would be clamoring with tourists.

As much as I longed to retreat to the highway, I headed

for the winding Old Mine Road and started up the mountain.

My ears popped as I climbed and weaved past towering evergreens. With the new access point, I doubted this old road got as much traffic as it had in years past. Probably a good thing. It was too narrow for decent shuttles, and on icy days, the drive down could be treacherous.

Mom had always hated this road in the winter, given the sharp drop-off. She'd love that Reed had put in a safer road.

My oldest brother had been working hard for the past two years to expand Madigan Mountain. The new access road. More terrain. New residential and commercial properties. Not that I'd seen any of it firsthand, but Weston had told me that it was becoming a next-level resort. He'd even moved home last year to help Reed by starting a heliskiing operation.

They had more plans, some of which they'd shared, but whatever they had in store for the mountain was not my problem. I was here for one night and one night only.

I turned one final corner and the lodge and hotel came into view. The mountain stood tall and proud at its back.

It looked the same. It looked different.

It was home. Yet it wasn't.

"I don't want to be here," I muttered as I drove past the parking lots.

The signage was new, branded with mountain goats. Beyond the hotel, a condo development hugged the mountain base. The new chairlift stretched toward the summit, leading to new runs that snaked white through the trees. And past the lodge, in a forest clearing, was a helipad. Weston's helicopter was likely stowed in the adjacent hangar.

I pulled into a parking spot outside the hotel and hopped out, breathing the mountain air as I stretched my legs. It smelled like my childhood, snow and pine and sunshine. It smelled like good memories. And bad.

With my bag looped over a shoulder and my suit bag draped over an arm, I walked toward the hotel's stone entrance. My grandfather had constructed this wooden A-frame in the fifties as the original ski lodge. Years later, a new lodge had been built and this had become the lobby to the connected three-story hotel.

At least with all the changes Reed had made lately, he'd left the red shutters on the windows. Mom had loved those shutters.

I dropped my eyes to the sidewalk. The less I took in, the better. The more I looked around, the more I saw Mom.

"Good afternoon, sir." The bellhop opened the door, waving me inside.

The lobby smelled like vanilla and cedar. Tall, gleaming windows along the far wall gave guests a sweeping view of the mountain. As a kid, my brothers would chase me around the lobby in the summers, when there weren't many guests and my parents were busy. The long-time front desk clerk, Mona, would snap at us when-ever we got too loud. But Mom would always laugh it off, telling her we were simply testing the acoustics, then shooing us outside to play.

More memories.

"Excuse me."

A man walked past me, snapping me out of my stupor. I unglued my feet from the floor and walked toward the front desk, passing a couple as they came out of the bar. The woman was dressed in a black gown. The man was in a gray suit. Each was carrying a cocktail.

They were most likely going to the wedding. There was a good chance Dad was in the bar, holding a tumbler of his favorite whiskey, and since that reunion was one I'd delay for as long as possible, I headed for the reception desk.

"Good afternoon, sir." The clerk smiled, her eyes flaring slightly. She was young. Pretty. Blond hair with big hazel eyes. If this were any other resort, any other mountain, maybe I'd let her flirt. Maybe I'd get an extra key to my room and hand it over with an invitation.

But I was leaving first thing in the morning and had no time to play with my brothers' employees.

"Crew Madigan," I said. "Checking in."

"Madigan. Oh, um, of course." She stood taller, a flush creeping into her cheeks as she focused on the computer's screen. "You're in a suite, staying for two nights."

"No, just the one." I dug out my wallet from my jeans pocket, fishing out a credit card.

"There's no charge, Mr. Madigan." Reed's doing, no doubt. "You're on the third floor. Room 312. It's the Vista Suite. How many keys would you like?"

"Also just the one." This trip wasn't pleasure. It wasn't business either. It was family.

She worked quickly to get me my key card, sliding it across the counter. "Can I help you with anything else?"

"No, thanks." With a nod, I walked away, heading straight for the elevators and the third floor.

The hallway greeted me with fresh paint, clean carpets and the scent of laundry soap. These hallways used to be racetracks for us. Reed, Weston and I had played hide-and-seek throughout the hotel until the time I'd hidden in a storage closet for an hour. By the time Weston had found me, every staff member and my parents had been in a panic.

That was back when Dad had actually cared about his kids' whereabouts. When he'd been more than the cold, heartless widower who'd forgotten his three sons had just lost their mother.

I unlocked the door to my suite, letting it close behind me as I strode into the living room, plopping my things on the leather sofa.

The updates from the hallway extended into the rooms, making them feel up-to-date with that rustic ski resort vibe. It was a nice room, with a fireplace and sprawling view of the mountain. Perfect for one night and one night only.

I unzipped my bag, wanting to take a quick shower to wash off the road trip before the wedding started in an hour. But the moment I had my toiletry case in the bathroom, a knock came at the door.

Probably someone with the last name Madigan. Hopefully a brother, not a father. I checked the peephole, grinning at the man wearing a black suit on the other side.

"Hey," I said, opening the door.

"Hi." Weston smiled, pulling me into a hug and slapping me on the back. "About time you got here. I was starting to worry you weren't going to show."

"Tempting, but I figured you'd bust my ass, so here I am."

"How are you?" he asked, coming inside.

I shrugged. "All right. It's good to see you."

"Yeah." He put his hand on my shoulder. "You too."

Weston was two years older, and when our family had fallen apart after Mom's death, he'd been the one to see me through the darkest days. Instead of moving away to start his own life, he'd stayed in Penny Ridge until I'd graduated high school. He'd made sure that a fourteen-year-old kid hadn't drowned in his grief.

He'd done what Dad should have.

Those four years, I couldn't repay him for that. For all he'd done. I wasn't here because Reed had called, even though it was his wedding.

I'd come because Weston had asked me to.

Not that I didn't love Reed. But our relationship was different. After Mom, he'd gone away to college. He'd left us behind. For those first few years, I'd blamed Reed for abandoning us. But over time, that resentment had faded.

We'd all been devastated. We'd all needed to escape.

But unlike my brothers, I had no intention of returning home.

"You look good," I told Weston as we moved into the living room, each taking a chair in the sitting area next to the windows that overlooked the mountain.

He seemed . . . lighter. Happy. There was a twinkle in his brown eyes.

"I am good," he said. "Glad you're here. Nice to talk to you face-to-face for a change."

Conversation between us had been limited over the years. He'd been busy with his career in the military. I'd been consumed with professional sports.

Mostly, we'd talked via voicemail. The last time I'd actually seen him in person had been three years ago. Our travel schedules had coincided and we'd met for dinner in the Seattle airport.

"How do you like living here?" I asked.

"It's been good. Retirement took a bit of an adjustment but I've managed to keep myself out of trouble."

"Saw a helipad on my way in."

He grinned. "This expansion has been amazing. The new terrain is insane. We've got decent snow already too. The base is solid. If you want to go up tomorrow—"

"Can't." I cut him off before he could talk me into it. "I've got to get back to Park City. There's a sponsor flying in for a meeting."

"Oh." His smile faltered. "Thought we'd get you for a couple days at least."

"Not this time." *Not any time.* "Besides, I didn't bring a board," I lied.

I didn't go anywhere in the winter without a snowboard, not that I'd be tempted to ride here. The memories . . .

The hotel, the lodge, the town were bad enough. I wasn't sure I could handle being on the mountain.

"We do have snowboards here," Weston said. "A whole rental shop full of them, in fact."

"Next time." There would be no next time.

Weston studied my face, undoubtedly spotting the lie. Once upon a time, he'd been both brother and keeper. When I'd told a bullshit lie to do something stupid, like go to a party or skip school to ride, those lies had gone to Weston, not my father.

Disappointment clouded his gaze as he dropped it to the floor before standing. "I'd better let you get ready. And I need to go pick up Callie and Sutton."

"I'm looking forward to meeting them."

"Yeah." His face softened. "They're excited to meet you too. Just to warn you, Sutton is going to ask you for your autograph.

She found one of your old Olympic posters at a shop downtown. She wants to take it to school next week to show her friends."

"I'll sign whatever she wants."

"Appreciate it." Weston clapped me on the shoulder again, his version of another hug. "See you in a bit? I'll save you a seat."

"Sounds great." I forced another smile, then waited for him to leave before I returned to the bathroom, taking a long look in the mirror.

Damn, I didn't want to be here. But it was just one night.

I'd congratulate Reed and meet Ava. I'd meet Weston's fiancée, Callie, and her daughter, Sutton. I'd ignore my father and his new wife, Melody. Then come dawn . . .

"I'm getting the hell off this mountain."

After a quick shower, I styled my hair and dressed in my black suit. With my shoulders squared, I headed to the main floor, following a stream of people through the lobby.

"Crew."

I turned at my name. Reed crossed the space, wearing a tux and an ear-to-ear grin. "Hey."

"Thanks for being here." He closed the space between us, pulling me into a hug, holding me so tight it took me off guard.

"Congratulations."

"Thanks." He gulped, then fussed with the boutonniere pinned to his lapel.

"Nervous?" I asked.

"Yes. No. I just want everything to go smoothly. But I'm more than ready to make Ava my wife. And I'm glad you could be here."

"Me too." It was even slightly true. For Reed, I was glad to be here. "You'd better go. I'll be here afterward. We'll catch up. Have a drink."

"There's a lot to talk about." He laughed. "So I'll hold you to that drink."

He strode past me for the entrance to the ballrooms, greeting people as he walked.

I followed, in no rush. I fell in line with the other guests, shuffling into the ballrooms, taking in more of the changes. Structurally, the hotel was exactly as I remembered. But with the updated décor and style, it rivaled larger, glitzier Colorado resorts.

A new crystal chandelier illuminated the foyer between the ballrooms. The old industrial tile had been removed and replaced with a plush burgundy carpet. The elk and moose mounts had been swapped for wall art.

The line filtered through double doors to a room decked out in flowers and glimmering lights. An aisle, flanked by two sections of white chairs, led to an arched altar adorned with greenery and roses.

Reed stood chatting with Pastor Jennings, the man who'd busted me at thirteen for making out with his daughter at a middle school dance.

Familiar faces jumped out from all directions, including one that wasn't all that different from my own.

Dad stood not far from Reed, laughing with the woman on his arm. She was tall and thin. Pretty, with a big smile and graying blond hair.

It wasn't fair that she was here. Mom should have been here on her oldest son's wedding day.

I clenched my teeth, my molars grinding, as a hand smacked my back.

"Hey, man."

"River." I relaxed instantly, letting my best friend from high school pull me into a quick hug. "How are you?"

"Can't complain."

River was one of the few people in Penny Ridge I'd kept in touch with over the years. Mostly because he was good about texting and had met me a few times to ride.

We'd both grown up with dreams of professional snowboarding. While I'd gone on to become a world champion, his career had fizzled. But there'd been trips when I'd invited him along. River was always good at providing levity in heavy moments and irritating the shit out of Sydney and my manager.

"What's new?" I asked.

"Not much. Looking forward to another season. Think this is gonna be my year."

It wasn't. But I didn't have the heart to break it to River that he just wasn't good enough. Maybe he could have been, but he didn't have the discipline to hone his skill and take it to the next level.

"I'm sure it is," I lied. "Did you come with a date?"

"Nah. I'm here with my sister."

"Raven's here?"

"Yeah." River searched the crowd. "She's around here somewhere."

But before he could find her, another man appeared at my side. "Crew."

Fuck. So much for avoidance. "Dad."

"How are you, son? Glad to see you."

I nodded, holding his gaze for a moment. He looked . . . different. Maybe because he was missing his standard scowl.

"Oh, hello!" The woman he'd been standing with earlier swept past him, coming straight into my space for a hug. "Crew, I'm Melody. It is so good to finally meet you."

"Uh . . ." I looked down at her, then to Dad, who just beamed at his new wife.

"You must sit with us," Melody said. "The front row is for family."

Family. That word felt like a knife to my spine spoken from a woman who hadn't been around when my real family had disintegrated.

"Actually, I'm sitting with River." I took my friend's elbow, practically shoving him out of the line. "Nice to meet you."

Melody's smile faltered.

Dad put his arm around her shoulders, hauling her into his side. He bent to murmur something in her ear, but I didn't stick around.

I pushed River along toward the middle of the groom's section.

"Take it you haven't talked to your old man lately?" River asked.

"No." And I didn't plan on changing that tonight.

"I got you. I'll run interference."

"Appreciated."

River knew all about what had happened in high school. He'd had my back then and still had it now.

We lingered beside the aisle, standing between huddles of people all chatting before the ceremony started.

A swish of black hair caught my eye. I did a double take and the air was sucked out of my lungs.

Raven.

River's sister had always been pretty. When I'd left here, she'd been a sophomore. Twelve years later, she'd grown into a woman who wasn't pretty.

She was devastating.

Long, silky hair fell nearly to her waist. A handful of freckles dusted her nose. Her soft lips were painted a sultry red. A sleeveless, black dress hugged her lithe body.

The dress had a swath of leather around her torso, giving it a sexy edge. That and the slit that ran up her thigh. She had mile-long legs accentuated with a pair of strappy heels.

Goddamn. She was stunning.

Then again, she'd always snagged my attention.

There wasn't much that River didn't know about me. Mostly because we'd been friends for so long, but also because he'd been my confidant in high school.

But not once had I let it show how much I'd crushed on his sister.

"Raven." He jerked up his chin, waving her over.

"Oh, there you are." She smiled at him, then turned to me, flashing me those arctic-blue eyes framed by sooty lashes. "Oh." Her smile dropped. "Hey, Crew."

"Hey, Raven."

"I'm going to go find a seat," she told River.

"'Kay. I'm sitting with Crew."

Without another word, she walked away, taking a chair on the bride's side of the room.

Twelve years and all I got was a *Hey, Crew.*

Why did that surprise me? Raven had never seemed

even slightly interested. The only girl at Penny Ridge High I'd wanted was the only girl who couldn't have cared less. I was a world champion, an Olympian, and she still stared straight through me.

Maybe some things around here had changed. But not enough.

I needed to get the fuck off Madigan Mountain.

CHAPTER TWO

RAVEN

"Oh. My. God." Halley's jaw dropped.

"What?" I followed her gaze across the ballroom, instantly spotting the man who'd caught her eye.

Crew Madigan.

Snowboarding legend. World champion. Gorgeous. Rich. Famous. Every woman's dream.

Well, except mine.

I tore my gaze away from his handsome profile and took a sip from my champagne flute. "Meh."

Halley blinked, refocusing on me. "Meh?"

"You know I've sworn off athletes. Besides, he's not my type."

"Right." She deadpanned. "So if he was some geeky guy with an awkward streak who wouldn't know what to do with a pair of skis to save his life, you'd be drooling over Crew like the other single women in this room."

I raised my glass. "Exactly."

Halley narrowed her eyes. "Seriously?"

"Seriously."

"Lies."

I giggled and raised a hand, palm facing out. "I, Raven Darcy, do solemnly swear that I've never once had improper thoughts about Crew Madigan."

She reached out and pressed the back of her hand to my forehead. "Are you feeling okay?"

I laughed and swatted her away. "He's River's best friend."

"So?"

"So . . ." I shrugged. "I've just never thought of him that way."

Crew had always just been River's buddy. In elementary school, he'd been the boy who'd come over to our house and played video games with my brother. In middle school, those two had been inseparable, always snickering over their inside jokes. In high school, they'd been partners in crime, giving my mother premature gray hairs. Then he'd left town after graduation and hadn't been back since.

"He's a lot hotter in person than he is on TV," Halley said. "And that's saying something because he's pretty hot on TV." She shook her head, picking up her own champagne flute. "I question your taste in men."

You and me both.

After my latest disaster of a relationship, I didn't trust my judgment.

"Is this about Thayer?" she asked.

My lip curled.

"Never mind." She waved it off. "I shouldn't have brought him up."

"It's okay." Maybe one day, hearing his name wouldn't

sting. Not that anyone brought him up often, including Halley.

The two of us had been friends for years, ever since she'd come to work for the resort, tending bar in the hotel. There weren't a lot of Madigan Mountain employees who lived in town full-time. The seasonal staff came and went with the snow, so those of us who called Penny Ridge home stuck together.

"That was a pretty wedding," I said, changing the subject.

"I'm happy for Ava." Halley smiled at our friend on the dance floor in the arms of her now husband.

"Me too."

It had taken us all some time to warm up to Reed after his history with Ava, but as we'd gotten to know him over the last couple of years, it was impossible not to admit he was a good guy. And he worshiped the ground beneath Ava's feet.

That's all I wanted.

Undying adoration.

Another reason to stay far away from professional athletes. I knew firsthand just where I'd fit in the scheme of their priorities—below anything and everything related to their sport. Not even a wife and children could outrank a powder day. Certainly not a regularly paying job.

"Well, if you're not going to chase Crew, then I am." Halley downed the rest of her champagne and stood, smoothing out the skirt of her plum dress and tucking a lock of her brown hair behind an ear. "I haven't had a decent orgasm in way too long and there's no way a man with that swagger isn't good in bed."

I glanced over my shoulder as Crew strode across the ballroom.

The swagger *was* hot. Really hot. So was that chiseled jaw and those broad shoulders wrapped in an expensive suit.

"I saw that."

My eyes shot up to Halley. "Saw what?"

She pointed at my nose, smirking. "I knew it. You think he's hot."

"Well, I have eyes." To demonstrate, I rolled them. "But that doesn't mean I'm interested."

"I love you, Raven." Halley gave me a sad smile. "But I have never met a person who is so good at convincing herself of what she doesn't want."

"What?" I gaped. "What's that supposed to mean?"

"Did you register for those competitions we talked about?"

No. A string of excuses came rushing forward, but I couldn't voice them. I knew exactly how trivial and spineless they'd sound.

"That's what I thought." She put her hand on my shoulder, giving it a squeeze. "We need more champagne."

I waited until she was gone before slumping in my seat.

The music changed, from a slow-dance song to a fast-paced beat that had a swarm of little kids rushing to the dance floor.

I smiled as Sutton tugged Weston to the floor, making him twirl her in circles. That man was wrapped around that girl's pinky, and from the smile on his face, he wouldn't have it any other way. Neither would Callie, who was standing off to the side of the floor, watching with hearts in her eyes.

Finishing the last swig of my champagne, I took in the

room. Every table was draped in white with a stunning floral centerpiece of bloodred roses and snow-white camellias. Lights had been strung across the ceiling, similar to how they'd decorated the ceremony room, and their glow cast the space in gold.

This was a dream wedding. Elegant and classy. There was a crush of people but it still felt intimate and cozy.

I shifted, about to stand and join Halley at the bar, when a towering figure sank into her empty chair.

"Hey." Crew handed me a fresh champagne flute.

"Thanks?" It came out as a question. What was he doing? I searched the room for my brother. "Were you looking for River?"

He chuckled. "No."

The laugh accentuated the sharp corners of his jaw and the straight bridge of his nose. His eyes met mine, and maybe it was just the lights above us, but they had more flecks of gold than I remembered.

Not that I'd spent a lot of time in my youth staring into Crew's eyes.

"River left," he said.

"What?" I whirled, scanning the crowd for his dark hair and coming up empty. My shoulders slumped. "He was my ride." And my designated driver.

The road down the mountain to town wasn't long, but it was winding and narrow. He'd promised to drive so I could enjoy a few drinks to celebrate my friend's marriage.

I set my champagne down, staring longingly at the bubbles. So much for a fun night. "I'm guessing he didn't leave alone."

"No." Crew picked up my glass, handing it over. "I think

her name was Sara? Or Samantha? He asked me if I'd give you a ride into town."

"Oh. Well, it's unnecessary. I can get a ride."

I was born and raised in Penny Ridge, and there were plenty of people here tonight that I'd known for years. Someone would let me hitch a ride.

Though most people would be spending the night at the hotel. I'd considered it too, but the idea of spending money on a hotel room when I lived so close had seemed silly, so I hadn't made a reservation.

I could probably snag a key to an empty room in employee housing. Most of the seasonal staff had already moved in to prepare for opening weekend, but there was likely one spot empty. Not that I had a change of clothes. Or a toothbrush. Or anything but a tube of lip gloss in my clutch and a wad of cash for the bar.

Damn it, River.

"How have you been?" Crew asked.

"Good." I sighed. "You don't need to entertain me. This isn't the first time River has ditched me for a hookup."

The corner of his mouth turned up and he relaxed deeper in his chair. "River told me you were working here. At the ski school, right?"

I nodded. "Yep. I've been running the program for quite a few years."

"You like it?"

"It's a good job. I love the kids and being on the mountain every day. Plus I get the summers off."

The only drawback to my job was that I didn't have enough time to snowboard myself. I loved slopestyle and dropping into a halfpipe. It was a rush, being flown to the top of a mountain by a helicopter and left at the peak with nothing but your board and the world spread beyond your feet.

But snowboarding didn't pay the bills or my mortgage. And the last thing I wanted was to turn out like Dad. I'd leave chasing that legacy to River, who was doing a hell of a job at becoming our father.

"Want to dance?" Crew asked.

"With you?"

He chuckled, shaking his head. "I can always count on you to keep my ego in check."

I fought a smile. "Someone has to make sure that gorgeous head of yours doesn't get overinflated."

"Gorgeous?"

Shit. I'd said that out loud, hadn't I? There was no use denying the slip. Or that it wasn't entirely true. "You have a mirror."

Crew shifted, leaning in closer, and a waft of his cologne filled my nose. It was spicy but fresh, like cedar and citrus. The scent was unique enough that I took another inhale before meeting his gaze.

My breath hitched.

For the first time in my life, my breath hitched for Crew Madigan.

Huh. *Weird.*

He'd been the hot guy in high school. Even after his mother had died and he'd had this haunted look in his deep brown eyes, he'd been the boy every girl had pined for. He'd had it all. The natural charisma. The devilish grin. The confidence to shun school sports. He'd been destined for greatness on the slopes.

He'd been a teenage fantasy. His name had likely been written in countless diaries. He'd been the catch of Penny Ridge High, made even more of a conquest because he'd rarely had a girlfriend.

Oh, if those local girls could see him now. Crew had only grown more attractive, filling out his towering frame.

Too bad I wasn't interested. Or that he didn't have a boring, nine-to-five desk job.

"Why do you want to dance with me?" I asked. Why, after knowing me almost my entire life, was he paying me attention tonight? "Is this some challenge to score with your best friend's sister? Or is it to avoid your family?"

He'd had a reserved seat at his family's table, right beside Mark Madigan's chair. It had been empty all night. Crew had disappeared during the meal, so had River, only returning once the assigned-seating portion of the evening was over.

"It's just a dance." He stood, holding out a hand. "I promise not to bite."

The image of his straight, white teeth nipping at my skin popped into my mind. A flutter stirred in my lower belly. My cheeks flamed. What was wrong with me tonight? I wasn't attracted to Crew, was I? No. It had to be the champagne. Or his cologne.

"Raven." His voice had a gravelly edge that only made that flutter worse.

What was happening? Why was I having this physical reaction to my brother's best friend? I hadn't reacted like this before the ceremony. Or in high school. Why now?

Before I could figure it out, Crew tugged me to the dance floor, where the DJ had just put on another slow song.

My footsteps felt wobbly. My heart thumped as Crew pulled me into his arms, his strong chest just an inch from my own.

As his hand snaked around my waist, his hand settling on the small of my back, my breath caught once more. *Damn it.* Why, out of all the people here tonight, did it have to be Crew who made my pulse quicken?

His cheek brushed against my temple, barely touching. Tingles spread across my skin.

"What is it about me that you don't like?" he murmured, his lips much too close to my ear.

Nothing. The answer to his question was nothing. I didn't dislike Crew. He was just . . . Crew. He was everything I did not need in my life.

Because I was holding out for my clumsy nerd. The man who'd worship me and never miss dinner. A man who'd never forget his daughter's birthday party because he'd been too busy skiing with a buddy at Breckenridge.

"Raven."

God, what a voice. It had gotten deeper over the years. Matured, like his body. Gone was the boy, and in his place, a man I should definitely not be attracted to. Yet I couldn't seem to step away.

"Crew," I said, feigning indifference.

"You didn't answer my question."

"What don't I like about you?" I repeated. "Oh, I don't think we have that much time."

"You're such a brat." He grinned. "I see that hasn't changed."

I smiled. "Now you sound like River."

Crew twirled us toward the center of the dance floor, the sway of his hips nearly as intoxicating as that cologne.

"It's my feet, isn't it?" he asked.

I glanced down at his polished black shoes. "What about your feet?"

"They're too big. You like guys with small feet. Who was that kid you had a crush on in high school? Freddie James?"

I scoffed. "I did not have a crush on Freddie James."

Crew smiled wider, revealing a dimple on his left cheek. Had he always had that dimple? How had I missed it?

"You did too," he teased. "Remember that time River and I walked in on you and Freddie making out?"

My cheeks flamed as I laughed. "That was the most embarrassing moment of my life. Poor Freddie."

River had chased Freddie out of our house and across three blocks until he had managed to duck into the grocery store and hide out for three hours. River had finally gotten bored and given up on his promise to pummel Freddie's face for kissing his sister.

Crew's hand at the small of my back shifted, his palm splaying wider. He pulled me close, until the whisper of space between us vanished and I was pressed against the hard plain of his chest.

"What are you doing?" I whispered.

"Dancing."

"Is this how you dance with all of your friends' sisters?"

"No." He leaned in until his cheek was pressed against mine. Then he spun us in a circle, the dance floor and the world beyond a blur.

I closed my eyes, soaking in the heat from his body. I

clung to his shoulder with one hand while he laced our fingers together in the other.

Snap out of this, Raven.

Crew was nothing but trouble. He'd be here tonight, then gone by—

Wait.

Crew had avoided Penny Ridge for years. I wasn't sure exactly when the last time he'd visited, if ever, since high school. He'd skipped dinner tonight. He'd ducked out of the ceremony early. And considering he hadn't answered my question earlier, I had a pretty good idea that he was avoiding his family—at least Mark.

Which meant there was likely little chance he'd be sticking around town. He might even be gone by sunrise.

Halley wasn't the only one who hadn't had a decent orgasm in way too long. Based on Crew's dance moves, there was no way he'd disappoint. Yeah, I'd sworn off athletes. But I'd sworn off athletes as boyfriends. Crew Madigan wasn't boyfriend material.

But he might be just perfect for a one-night stand.

We'd have a good time. Then he'd vanish.

I leaned back, taking in his face.

My eyes dropped to his mouth. Desire pooled in my core. "What do you taste like?" The words escaped before I could stop them.

"Careful, Raven," he murmured. "I just might let you find out."

The heat between us spiked. The fabric of my dress suddenly felt too thick, the material too constricting. "Why did you ask me to dance?"

"Truth? I'm avoiding my family."

At least he was honest.

"And . . ." He trailed off, spinning us in a circle.

"And what?"

His gaze dropped to my mouth. "You look beautiful tonight, Raven."

My heart skipped. "What are you saying?"

"What do you think?"

"River can never know." Oh my God, what was *I* saying? That champagne had addled my brain, but I didn't take it back. And when the corner of Crew's mouth turned up, my mouth went dry.

Crew's hand unthreaded from mine so he could reach into his pocket to retrieve a key card. He slipped it into my hand, closing my fingers around the thin plastic. Then he brushed his lips across my cheek before they trailed to the shell of my ear. "Room 312. The Vista Suite. If you're interested."

The music changed, the bass boomed, snapping me back to reality.

I blinked as Crew let me go. Then he slipped past me, walking away from the crowded dance floor.

Was I interested?

Yes.

He strode through the ballroom, in no hurry to leave. Casual. Carefree. But I knew exactly where he was heading.

The exit.

I stood taller, shaking the fog from my head. Then I returned to my seat, where my champagne was waiting. I guzzled the glass, glancing once more at Crew.

He stood inches above nearly every other man in the room.

I'd always loved tall guys. A tall, clumsy nerd with broad shoulders, a narrow waist and a thick head of dark hair was practically impossible to find in Penny Ridge. After Thayer, I'd looked. Diligently. Until the right guy came along, maybe I should settle for the wrong. Just tonight.

I set the flute on the table as Crew strode through the doors.

Go home, Raven.

What if I didn't? No one would have to know. And when Crew left, he'd take our secret too.

"If you don't follow that man out of here, I'm never talking to you again."

I whirled. Halley walked my way. "I—I don't know what you're talking about."

She rolled her eyes, closing the distance between us, then tapped the key card in my grip. "Sure you don't."

I opened my mouth to lie, but she was already gone, smirking at me as she walked to a group of people chatting beside the cake table.

My eyes went straight to the door.

Crew was gone.

I worried my bottom lip between my teeth, squeezing that key card so tight it bit into my skin.

Fuck it.

I swiped up my clutch and did my best not to rush out of the room, waving and nodding to people as I passed by. Then I slipped through the doors.

The hallway was cooler than the ballroom but my blood felt too hot, the flames from that dance lingering beneath the surface. I hurried as fast as I could in my heels, checking over my shoulder to ensure no one was watching as I made my way to the elevator.

The lobby was fairly empty. I ducked my chin, avoiding the clerk at the front desk as I hurried to the elevator. The doors swished open the moment I hit the button.

The elevator wasn't empty.

Crew stood against the far wall, his hands braced behind him on the rail. His ankles were crossed, the epitome of relaxed. And that smirk on his face . . .

I mirrored it, striding into the elevator before I turned my back on him and pressed the button for the third floor.

"Figured you'd beat me upstairs," I said over my shoulder.

"I only have one key." He pushed off the wall. "It's in your hand."

I stood like a statue, barely breathing as the heat from his chest seeped into my back.

His hand came to my hair, pulling a section off my shoulder to bare my neck. His fingers trailed down my arm, the touch so light it was like a breeze.

Every nerve ending in my body pulsed as his mouth came to my neck. His arm wrapped around my waist, hauling me against him so I could feel his arousal digging into my ass.

I ached for more but he didn't move. He hovered behind me, driving me wild with just his presence alone, until the ding of the elevator sounded and I teetered my first step onto the floor.

Crew passed me, walking with that swagger, his long strides measured, as he walked toward his room. When he reached his door, he leaned against the wall at its side, waiting for me to produce the key.

I held it up, the card between two fingers, then arched my eyebrows.

He could unlock his own damn door.

A smile stretched across that sinful mouth as he plucked it from my grip. Then he slid it into the lock, the door clicking as it opened.

I was only one step past the threshold when he spun around.

Crew moved like lightning, his hands diving into my hair as his mouth crushed mine.

I gasped.

He swallowed it and took advantage of my open lips. In a slow, delicious slide, his tongue twirled with mine.

Behind us, the door slammed closed, drowning out the sound of my moan as I clung to his arms.

Crew shuffled me through the space, his mouth never leaving mine. He sucked my bottom lip into his mouth, earning a whimper. When I nipped at his top lip, he growled, the vibration like a tendril of smoke curling around my body and driving me wild.

His fingers delved deeper into my hair, following the strands past my nape to where they swished at my waist. "Raven."

"Yes," I breathed, tearing my mouth away to shove at his suit coat.

He tugged on the zipper of my dress, one fast *zzzzip*, until it was undone and the cloth stripped from my body.

I yanked free the buttons on his shirt, wanting to feel his chest beneath my palms, except his tie was in the way. I fumbled with the knot, but before I could loosen it, Crew swatted my hands away and discarded it himself.

There was only a sliver of moonlight streaming in through his bedroom windows as he hauled me into his arms, carrying me to the mattress.

We moved in a frenzy, stripping the last of our clothes. My lace panties and matching bra. His slacks and boxer briefs. Our shoes.

The light caught the peaks and valleys of his abs. It highlighted the V that cut around his hips. Crew's cock bobbed between us, thick and heavy.

I gulped. "You're . . ."

The corner of his mouth turned up, that sexy dimple teasing me again. "Big feet, remember?"

I laughed, meeting his darkened gaze.

He shifted closer, until his hardness was pressed against my belly. Those long fingers dove into my hair once more before his mouth was on mine.

One night.

Somewhere in between the orgasm he gave me with his fingers and the one he delivered with his tongue, he found a condom. By the time we came up for air, hours—*days, months*—had passed. Time had lost all meaning and my body was spent.

"Fuck." Crew collapsed on the bed beside me, his breaths as ragged as my own. Then he shifted, tucking me into his side as he snagged a sheet to pull over our sweaty bodies. "That was . . ."

"Yeah," I panted.

That hadn't just been a decent orgasm. Crew was an experience. Halley was going to be jealous.

How was this even happening? I'd just had the best sex of my entire life with Crew. My brain was struggling to keep up with reality. The intensity, the chemistry, was mind-boggling.

His body relaxed beside mine, his breaths evening out as he fell asleep. The temptation to stay, to wake up in his arms, was overpowering. Maybe do this all over again come morning.

Crew was a thrill, and I was a woman who loved an adrenaline rush.

But there was no way this wouldn't end in a crash. In broken bones. So I slipped out from under the sheets, careful not to wake him as I gathered my dress and pulled it on before picking up my clutch and shoes.

Then I silently made my exit from the Vista Suite.

CHAPTER THREE

CREW

Pounding on the door woke me from a dead sleep. I jerked awake, shoving up on an elbow and glancing at the space beside mine, expecting to find Raven.

But the rumpled sheets were cold and empty.

The pounding on the door sounded again.

"Just a minute," I called, whipping the sheet from my naked body and dragging a hand through my hair.

Sunlight streamed through the windows, showcasing the mess on the bedroom floor. Clothes. Comforter. The flannel toss pillows with a mountain goat stitched on their faces.

What a night.

I'd expected electricity with Raven after that dance, but we'd had enough voltage to power the Las Vegas strip for a fucking week. I hadn't had sex like that in, well . . . ever. Just thinking about her made my cock twitch. Her scent clung to my skin, sweet, like cherries.

Where was she? No dress or shoes on the floor. The bathroom was dark.

"Damn." I would have liked to say goodbye.

Whoever was at the door knocked again.

"I'm coming," I grumbled and swiped up my boxer briefs, pulling them on before crossing through the sitting area and ripping open the door. "What?"

"Good morning, sunshine." Reed strolled into my room wearing jeans, a sweater and a shit-eating grin.

"Shouldn't you be on your honeymoon?"

"We're postponing it until after the season," he said, walking toward the coffee maker on the counter above the minibar.

"How does Ava feel about that?"

"It was her idea. She wants to make sure everything goes well this year."

Weston strolled through the door I'd been holding open for Reed to leave through. "Morning."

"Hi." I sighed, glancing down the hall for any other visitors. Like Dad. Thankfully, only my brothers had chosen to interrupt my morning, so I closed the door and walked into the bedroom, rifling through my bag for a T-shirt and jeans.

"Great wedding," I said as I returned to the room and pulled the plastic wrap from a disposable coffee mug.

Reed scoffed. "Because you spent so much time at the reception?"

"Sorry." I shrugged. "Ducked out a little early. Headache."

"And dinner? Your chair was noticeably empty."

"Had to get something for Sutton." I put a pod into the single-serving brewer and hit the button to get it started, then went to the couch where I'd propped up the snowboard I'd hauled in from my car last night.

"Thought you didn't bring a board?" Weston asked.

"Turns out I had one after all." Two, actually. So I'd decided to give Weston's soon-to-be stepdaughter a gift.

During dinner last night, when I'd realized they'd put my chair next to Dad's, I'd decided it was the perfect time to head to the Mercedes and get this board.

River had tagged along, and afterward, we'd opted for dinner at the hotel's restaurant rather than rejoin the reception. The woman River had left with last night had been our waitress.

"This is from GNU." I handed the board to Weston for him to inspect. "It's from their upcoming line. I haven't had a chance to use it yet, but I like their stuff. It's pretty versatile. It should be solid for a park or if she's just on a hill. I know she's into skiing, but in case she wants to give boarding a try, she'll have some gear."

Weston studied the design, the bold lime and brown graphics and the black signature I'd scribbled on the top beside Sutton's name. "This is . . . thank you. She's going to flip."

"Good." I retrieved my coffee mug, taking a scalding, bitter sip, then went to the couch, plopping down on one end.

"She'll probably want to hang it up in her room and brag to all of her friends about it." Weston set it aside carefully, then took the chair next to Reed.

"My agent just got me a new sponsorship from GNU. I've got a photo shoot with them tomorrow. I'll see if I can snag a couple youth boards."

"I thought you were sponsored by Burton," Reed said.

"I am. My agent is a wizard. She's got me on with both.

I've been using GNU for more of my free time. Heading out, spending a few hours just boarding. Burton's been my competition board for ages. I'm not changing that now."

Typically, brands required you use their boards exclusively, but Syd had made it clear: I'd use GNU for my personal time. I'd do their photo shoots and star in their marketing materials. But when it came to training and competitions, I used my Burton boards, so they'd agreed to take out the exclusivity clause in my contract.

"So what's up?" I asked, taking another sip of coffee.

Reed and Weston shared a look that made me sit a little straighter.

"We were hoping to talk with you about a few things while you were here," Reed said. "Since getting you to answer your phone is nearly as impossible as getting you home."

"Been busy," I said as a twinge of guilt pinched. Yeah, I wasn't great about returning Reed's calls. Weston's, I answered, though he didn't call often.

We'd all built our own lives. We'd lost touch. Partly because the person who'd kept us together—Mom—was gone.

"We could talk over lunch," Weston said.

"How about now? I'm heading out this morning."

Weston frowned but nodded.

"We want to toss an idea out there for you to consider," Reed said. "As you know, we've taken over the mountain from Dad. Ava and I are managing the hotel and the resort's general business functions, running logistics for the mountain, employees, et cetera. Weston is focused on heliskiing."

"I have no desire to be stuck in an office all damn day," Weston added.

"A couple years ago, Dad put together a profit-sharing plan for the mountain. We'll each inherit shares upon his death, but in the meantime, for the years we work at the resort, we'll earn shares of the corporation."

"Okay," I drawled. I didn't need or want shares of Madigan Mountain.

"The expansion has gone great," Reed said.

"I noticed a lot of changes as I was coming in yesterday." The condos. The new access road on the town side of the mountain. The new runs. The new lifts. "Looks nice. Good work."

"There's more."

I stiffened, knowing exactly where this was going.

"We want to make Madigan Mountain an elite Colorado resort." Reed leaned forward, elbows to knees. "Part of that includes a place for world-class athletes to train and ride. We'd like your help doing that. We set aside 150 acres. This summer, we hired a consultant to plan a terrain park. We've even put in a lift just for that section of the mountain."

"You're trying to compete with Woodward at Copper."

"Yes." He nodded.

"If you hired a consultant, sounds like you've got it covered." Was it a good thing or a bad thing they hadn't asked me for any input? Probably smart. I would have turned them down.

But I wasn't going to criticize their plans. I was happy they'd each found a home here. A future. Madigan Mountain would be in good hands with my brothers.

It just wasn't for me.

Reed and Weston shared another look, like this was going exactly as they'd expected.

"Construction started a month ago," Weston said. "We've been building off the base, making snow where we need more. Most of the ramps and kickers are staged. Before we finish, we'd like to have you take a look. Make sure the takeoff and landing angles are solid. That we don't have a catch in the flow."

If the obstacles were too close, it could lead to a nasty crash. Too far apart, the park would be boring.

"What about your consultant?" I asked.

"Not the same as a professional," Weston said.

"Yeah, I can do a walk-through today before I leave." The best way to test it was with an actual ride, but I wasn't sticking around until it was finished.

Reed took a long breath, then sat up straight. "We're also building a superpipe."

I blinked. "What?"

"We want to get into the competition circuit too. Host events. The pipe is a half-a-million-dollar investment because we're serious about this."

"That's good." They'd need a halfpipe to rival the major training locations. "Want me to look at it too?"

"No, we'd like you to spend some time here," Reed said. "Using what we're building."

"Ah. You want to use my name to help bring my colleagues to Penny Ridge."

"No." Weston shook his head.

"Well, yes," Reed corrected. "But that's not all. We want you to be here. Train here. Live here. And whenever you decide to retire, join us. Help run the mountain."

Easy answer. "No."

"Told you so." Weston chuckled.

Reed shot him a scowl, then faced me again. "You could at least think about it."

"Why? I won't change my mind."

"Would you consider doing an exhibition event?" Weston asked.

Was this good cop, bad cop? Reed comes in with the ask he has to know I'll decline so that when Weston offers something less, I'll feel more inclined to agree?

Bastards. It was working.

"What sort of exhibition?"

Reed shrugged. "We're still refining the details, but we're thinking sometime in January. It will be casual. A chance for people to try the park and the pipe. Treat it like a grand opening. If we could have some notable names on the lineup, including yours, that would help get some press. We'd also invite some local athletes to give it a hometown feel."

All I'd have to do was show up. Maybe spread the word beforehand. I'd ride. Take some pictures and videos. Post them on social media. It was no less than I'd done on other mountains. But this would mean another trip to Penny Ridge.

"He's about to say no again." Weston stood, picking up Sutton's board and nodding toward the door. "Let's get out of here before he does. Call me when you're ready to walk through the terrain park. Maybe we could get in the helicopter too. Take a little ride."

I sighed as they headed for the door.

Weston walked into the hallway, but before Reed followed, he paused, turning back.

"I should have been there. After Mom. I shouldn't have left like I did."

"You went to college. I get it."

"Still . . . I'm sorry." He gave me a sad smile. "I see you on TV, winning medals. This career you've built, it's incredible. Proud of you, Crew."

Reed had never come to watch a competition, not since I was a little kid. It meant a lot that he'd followed me on TV. It meant a lot that he'd voice the words. "Thank you."

"I understand if your answer stays a no. I really do. It wasn't easy for me to come back here either. But you'll always have a place here. A home. We miss you." With that, Reed joined Weston in the hallway, the door closing behind them.

Did I miss my brothers? Yeah. I guess so. I hadn't really let myself miss them. I hadn't let myself miss anyone.

Except Mom.

Would she be proud too? Or would she smack me upside the head for how much distance I'd put between myself and my family?

The answer drove me from the couch into the shower. After getting dressed, I packed up my things, tossing the disheveled bedding back onto the mattress before ramming my suit into its bag. Then I shoved my wallet in my jeans pocket, pulled on the black coat I'd been wearing yesterday and headed for the lobby to check out of the suite.

There was a woman in front of me at the counter, so I stood back, taking in the lobby. There were more people here than I could ever remember seeing as a kid. Most were probably hotel guests for the wedding, but there was energy in the air. Excitement. And the mountain hadn't even opened yet.

Pride swelled. It was good to see this place thrive. If anyone had a shot at turning it into a world-renowned resort, it was Reed. Except that was his dream, not mine.

And as for my life postretirement, that was a giant question mark.

At thirty years old, thoughts of my future crept up on me more and more these days, especially after going to events and seeing my competitors get younger and younger.

Home was Park City. I'd shunned Copper Mountain, a premier training location for professional snowboarders, choosing Utah instead of Colorado.

Not that Park City was a step down. I had access to both indoor and outdoor year-round training venues. My house had a private trail that led directly to the slopes. In the summers, it was quiet. In the winters, it was exactly where I needed to be.

Today. Tomorrow, well . . . I'd figure that out tomorrow.

In the meantime, just because I didn't live here didn't mean I couldn't be more active in my brothers' lives. I did miss them. It had taken this trip back for Reed's wedding to realize just how much. It was time to get better at answering my phone, maybe even initiating a call for a change.

The woman in front of me finished with the clerk and walked away, so I checked out of my room, insisting on paying. Then I carried my bags outside, breathing in the mountain air as I stowed my bags in my car before shooting a text to Weston.

ready when you are

His reply was instant. *Meet me at the hangar in 15*

I tucked my phone away, locked the Mercedes, then wandered toward the lodge, taking in the subtle changes. The mountain goats were everywhere. I was inspecting a sign with a goat when I heard my name.

"Crew."

Fuck. I should have left. I should have fucking left when I'd had the chance.

Dad rushed my way, dressed in a pair of jeans and a coat. His hair was covered with a beanie, his breath billowing in the cold air. "Hi."

"Hi."

"We didn't get a chance to talk yesterday. How are you?"

"Fine. Just about to head up in the helicopter with Weston."

"Oh, that's great." He smiled too widely. "It's a lot of fun. Melody loves—"

I walked past him, not giving him a chance to finish that sentence.

"Crew, wait," he called to my back.

Gah. I stopped and turned.

"I, um . . . we'd love to have you over for dinner."

"I'm leaving today."

"Oh." His expression fell. "I thought you might stay until tomorrow."

I shook my head. "Can't. I need to get back."

"Right." He hung his head, then before I could react, he closed the distance between us, pulling me into a hug. "Sure is good to see you."

Good to see me? I shifted, forcing his arms to drop.

Dad could have seen me years ago. He could have been there after Mom died, consoling me while I'd had my

44

goddamn heart ripped out. Instead, he'd become a sullen bastard who'd spent every waking minute in his office. The few hours he'd come home each evening he'd spent barking at Weston and me while drowning his own sorrows in the bottom of a liquor bottle.

He could have seen me when I'd needed him. Not now. Not when it was too late.

I opened my mouth but I wasn't sure what to say. So I clamped it shut, spun on a heel and walked away.

"Crew."

"What?" I grumbled, turning once more.

"I'm sorry, son. I'm sorry."

I studied his face, sincerity swimming in his eyes.

"I'm sorry," he said again.

I believed him. Just like I'd believed Reed. But twelve years was a hell of a long time to wait for an apology.

This time when I walked away, he didn't stop me.

By the time I made it to the hangar, I was in a bad mood and all I wanted was to drive home. But Weston was already there, prepping the helicopter. So I stood back, watching my brother do what he did best, until it was time for me to climb into the seat beside him.

"You okay?" he asked after I put on a pair of headphones with a mic.

"All good."

He narrowed his eyes, not buying it, but he didn't press. He started the helicopter and took us into the air, narrating as we flew around the mountain.

It took a while, but as we headed toward the highest peak, I finally relaxed. "I just had a run-in with Dad. I wasn't nice."

Weston's laughter filled my headset. "He deserves it."

Except Mom would have been pissed. And since her death, she'd become the angel on my shoulder, reminding me to do better.

"He knows he fucked up," Weston said. "He knows he let us down. You don't have to let it go. But just know that he regrets it. He's spent a lot of hours in therapy facing his demons."

"Therapy? Are we talking about the same Mark Madigan?"

"Melody's been a good influence."

I hummed, staring out my window at the evergreens that bordered the ski runs. What was I supposed to do with that? What was I supposed to do with Dad's apology?

"Over there is the pipe." Weston pointed through the glass to where a snowcat was currently running up and down a section of the hill, blowing snow onto one side of what would become the halfpipe.

I couldn't see a snowcat and not think of Mom.

Mom and Dad had met when she'd come to work at Madigan Mountain as a groomer. She'd loved that job and had always said that there was no better place to watch a sunrise than from the cab of a snowcat sitting on the southern slope, with a thermos of hot coffee.

"We're about two hundred hours in on construction," Weston said. "Probably have another hundred to go before it's shaped and ready to run."

"How tall are the walls going to be?"

"Twenty-two feet. Close to ninety degrees vertical."

"Seriously?" My eyes widened. Those were Olympic dimensions.

"When it's done, it's going to be incredible. See that area over there?" He pointed past the halfpipe to a section of the forest. "Depending on how this year goes, we've been talking about adding a slopestyle course."

If they had both a terrain park and a superpipe plus a slopestyle course, they'd draw competitors from around the world. They could even host major competitions. And the more fame Madigan Mountain garnered, the more people would flock.

Reed had said he wanted this to become an elite resort. Apparently, he wasn't messing around.

My interest was piqued. *Damn it.* Judging from the smirk on Weston's face, he knew it too.

"This was why you wanted to fly me up here, wasn't it?"

That smirk stretched into a grin. "Things are changing around here. Reed and Ava . . . as individuals, they're both ambitious. Put them together and they're unstoppable."

"What about you?"

"I want Callie to be happy. I want Sutton to have the childhood we did."

Before Mom died.

He didn't have to say the words. They hung between us.

I stared out at the landscape, envisioning it complete. Picturing competitions and people of all ages enjoying a terrain park.

No. No way I could get caught up in this.

So I kept my mouth shut as Weston looped us back toward the helipad.

"What time do you need to leave?" he asked after we'd landed and the blades above us had slowed.

"Sooner rather than later." I'd already stayed longer than

I'd planned. "I need to be back tomorrow for that photo shoot."

"Callie was hoping you could join us for lunch. You could give Sutton that board yourself."

"What time?" I glanced at my favorite TAG Heuer watch. It was already eleven. "Ideally, I'll be on the road by two." That would put me home well after dark, but at least I'd be home, sleeping in my own bed.

The image of Raven there, her hair spread out across my pillows, flashed in my head. I really would have liked to say goodbye. And another go at it this morning.

"Give me thirty," Weston said. "I'll text Callie and we can meet in the hotel lobby."

"Sounds good." I ducked out of the helicopter, heading to the lodge to stop inside and see what was different. To see what wasn't.

Except before I could push through the door next to the rental shop, a swish of black hair caught my eye from the base of a lift.

Raven.

I grinned as she walked down the snowy incline.

She was in a pair of black ski pants and snow boots. Her coat was a bright blue, nearly the color of her eyes. She had a clipboard in one hand, rattling off orders to a guy wearing a red coat with the mountain goat logo and INSTRUCTOR written on the arm.

I changed directions as the man nodded, taking off toward the lodge.

Raven looked up and didn't so much as smile as she walked my way.

"Hey." I jerked up my chin. "Didn't get a chance to say goodbye."

"Goodbye." She breezed past me, not so much as slowing.

What the fuck? Was she pissed or something? She was the one who'd snuck out on me last night, not the other way around.

"Raven." I turned, snagging her elbow. "What's going on?"

"Nothing." She shook her arm free. "I'm just working."

She took another step, but I held up a hand, stopping her.

"Hold up." I hadn't been a dick to her last night, had I? I'd made sure she'd come, numerous times. So what the fuck was this attitude? Was she worried about River finding out? "Am I missing something?"

"Yeah. Your flight."

"I drove."

"Then drive safe." Raven walked away, leaving me with my jaw on the ground.

Had she just blown me off? *Yes. Yes, she did.* What the hell?

I huffed, planting my hands on my hips as she disappeared through a door to the lodge marked *SKI SCHOOL*.

She fucking blew me off. This was a first for me. Usually it was the other way around.

"Huh. You know what?" I shook my head. "Fuck this place."

I didn't want to risk another encounter with Dad. I didn't need pressure from my brothers to give up my life and help them here. I didn't need attitude from a woman who was hot one minute, cold the next.

It was time for me to get the hell out of Colorado.

I pulled my phone from my coat pocket, about to call Weston and cancel this lunch, but it rang in my hand, Sydney's name flashing on the screen.

"Hey, Syd."

"Where are you?"

"Just about to leave. Don't worry. I'll be home in plenty of time for your photo shoot."

"Actually, there's been a slight change of plan."

"Okay," I drawled.

"I just got a call from the marketing exec at GNU. She's hoping that we can make a last-minute change to the shoot location."

The hair on the back of my neck rose. "What's the new location?"

"Madigan Mountain, actually. She received a call from your brother. Reed, is it? He invited them out for opening weekend and to set up a display with their newest products. Since you're already there, timing couldn't be better. We'll tie in your shoot."

"You're fucking kidding me."

"What's the problem?" Sydney snapped. "This isn't just good promo for you, but for your family's resort. How about a thank-you?"

Sydney had no idea the family dynamics she was playing into here. And since it was none of her damn business, I wouldn't be enlightening her today.

"Fine," I clipped. "When is the new shoot?"

"Saturday."

That meant another six days in Colorado. Son of a bitch.

"I've already called Marianne," Syd said. "She's heading to your house and will overnight some clothes and gear."

"Super." My tone dripped with sarcasm. Of course she'd already put my assistant to work.

"See you Saturday." With that, she ended the call.

"Fucking hell." My nostrils flared as I shoved the phone away. How could Reed do this? How could he go behind my back? I never should have told them about that sponsorship.

Like he knew I was cursing his name, Reed, the traitor, came strolling out of the lodge with Raven. Both were focused on that clipboard of hers.

Raven didn't so much as shift her gaze in my direction. Three orgasms last night—no, four. Four orgasms, and she couldn't even bother with a polite smile or eye contact.

Reed glanced up, spotting me. He nodded but didn't stop. Probably because he knew I'd have words about him calling GNU.

Weston had called Reed ambitious. But that wasn't quite right.

Merciless. That was the correct term.

And clearly, given the way he ignored me and kept on walking, Reed had been taking lessons from Raven.

CHAPTER FOUR

RAVEN

A man strode into the ski lodge, coffee mug in hand. Short, styled hair. Wide shoulders. Long legs. I did a double take, my heart lifting, only to sink when I realized it wasn't Crew.

This guy wasn't as handsome or tall. He didn't have the same swagger or sharp, chiseled jaw.

"Get him out of your head," I muttered, picking up my pace and walking outside, my snowboard in hand.

One night. That's all we'd had. I shouldn't be looking for Crew in the lodge. I shouldn't be on edge, waiting—hoping—for him to pop up. One night and he'd thrown me completely off-balance. I didn't have time to be this distracted. There was work to be done.

It was the Monday before opening weekend. The mountain officially opened on Friday. Lessons started Saturday. I had just days left to make sure each of my instructors was ready for the season. Instead, I kept seeing Crew around every corner.

This was the problem with one-night stands. I wasn't a one-night-stand sort of woman. Granted, Crew had been my first. Lesson learned.

No more one-night stands. Especially with Crew Madigan.

He was supposed to be gone. That was the whole reason I'd agreed to sex in the first place. But apparently he was staying for a week. Reed had been so excited during our meeting yesterday, bragging about how he'd just spoken to one of Crew's sponsors and they'd agreed to feature both Crew and the mountain in their marketing campaign. They'd rearranged their schedule to bring some photo shoot to Colorado instead of Utah.

Reed had called it a lucky break.

More like bad luck.

Maybe my luck would change and I'd be able to avoid him all week. A girl could hope.

Three of my employees waved from where they stood in line at the lift closest to the lodge. Each was wearing their Madigan Mountain coat, a bold red the same color as the shutters on the hotel and sporting the mountain goat logo. Two were in skis, the third on a board.

They shuffled to the loading area before a chair looped around, sweeping them up and away to take another run.

Anticipation for the opening was as prevalent in the air as the scent of pine. This week was the chance for our employees to test out runs and spend some time on the hill before we had customers and students.

I'd had a staff meeting this morning for my returning instructors. Then I'd spent three hours in orientation with my new team members before dismissing them all so they could spend the rest of the day on the mountain.

Meanwhile, I'd spent the rest of my lunch and afternoon hours polishing schedules and returning phone calls from parents with questions. Finally, when my inbox had been depleted to zero and I'd returned every voicemail message, I'd pulled on my own red coat and snagged my board.

The season would be grueling, but the perk of being able to spend time on the mountain was well worth it.

"Raven!"

I turned as my brother walked my way, his board tucked under an arm. "Hey. What are you doing?"

"Just got done taking a few runs with Crew."

"Ah." *Freaking Crew.* "How was it?"

"Good. Should be sweet once they finish setting it up." River jerked his chin to the chair. "You going up?"

"Yeah."

"Want company?"

No. "Sure."

These solo rides were my chance to take a break from work and find balance. To organize my thoughts. And since my tryst with Crew, there were many, many thoughts. Sorting them out was not something I wanted to do with my older brother nearby.

No, I didn't want company. But per the mountain's rules this week, River couldn't go up without an employee escort. Though the week prior to opening was for staff, we were allowed to bring one friend or family member per day.

I wasn't going to turn him down.

"Lead the way," he said.

Before we could head to the lift, the sound of a board

scraping against the snow filled the air. The man who'd been haunting my thoughts came to a skidding stop at my side.

"Hey." Crew didn't so much as spare me a glance as he spoke to my brother.

I hated that it irked me.

I'd blown him off yesterday. Being too close to him was dangerous and what I needed was for him to vanish like he had twelve years ago. Seeing him on ESPN would be torture enough. Yet here he was, making my pulse race.

And damn it, he looked mouthwatering. Crew was made to ride a snowboard. His black pants fit his long legs to his boots. His coat was a red not all that different from my own, but it was a pullover. In place of a zipper, the jacket laced up over his heart.

Mirrored sunglasses covered his eyes. No helmet or goggles today to hide his face or dark hair. His face was dusted with stubble, giving him a rugged edge.

My core clenched.

Why me? He needed to leave Penny Ridge. Immediately. Before I had more impulsive ideas about a repeat of Saturday night.

Ever since our night together, I'd had this constant craving, like Crew had flipped a switch. No matter how many orgasms he'd delivered, I was turned on. For days I'd been stuck in the dark, patting the walls, fumbling to find that switch to turn it off.

"You going up?" he asked River.

"Was planning on doing a run with Raven." River nudged my elbow. "If she can keep up."

I rolled my eyes.

"All right." Crew bumped his fist to River's. "See you later?"

"Yeah."

Without another word, Crew bent and unbuckled one of his boots so he could walk his board to the lift. I tracked every move, unable to tear my eyes away.

More. That word screamed in the back of my mind. He'd left me a needy mess, and the longer he stayed, the more he had to go.

It took effort to tear my eyes away.

River's narrowed gaze was waiting. *Shit.* "Don't, Raven."

"Don't what?" I headed for the lift. Crew was already five chairs ahead.

River caught up, shooting me a frown as we took a seat, letting the lift carry us up. "He's a womanizer. You need to stay away from him."

"Last time I checked, I was a big girl. I can take care of myself. And besides, I don't want anything to do with Crew. He's not my type."

"He's every woman's type," River muttered.

"Not mine." I held my chin high, keeping my eyes trained on the view in the distance as we eased past the lift's towers one by one. When I finally risked a glance at River, he was staring at my profile. "Stop. I have no intention of dating a snowboarder ever again."

It wasn't entirely a lie. I had no intention of dating Crew. Fucking him again? It was tempting. But there would be no date. No relationship.

No broken heart.

River kept his blue eyes, mirrors of my own, locked on my face, until he must have believed me and relaxed. "Yeah.

Just . . . that would be weird. He's my best friend. And he's not good enough for you."

I gave him a smile. "Thanks."

In River's eyes, no man would ever be good enough. Even my future nerdy husband would be found lacking. River had filled Dad's missing shoes early on in life, becoming my protector.

He'd chased boys away, like Freddie James, when they'd gotten too close. He'd threatened my senior prom date with an ice axe if I wasn't returned by midnight in nothing less than perfect condition. And lately, he'd been the shoulder I'd cried on when my heart had been bruised because I'd broken my own rule to avoid snowboarders and skiers.

The first skier I'd dated had been after college, when I'd moved home to work on the mountain. John and I had both been new to the staff and teaching. He'd come to Colorado from Australia. His accent had won me over and we'd had this intense, all-consuming relationship. If we hadn't been working, we'd been together. Burn hot. Burn fast.

Burn out.

He'd quit one day without warning or notice. I'd gone to his place in employee housing to find it empty. When I'd called to find out what was happening, he'd told me he was on his way to South America for a job at La Parva. He'd wanted to get down there early before their season started.

Two years later, I'd dated a guy who'd also worked here as a lift operator. He'd lasted three weeks before disappearing to Chile, leaving a note for both me and his boss. It had been so eerily similar to Dad—who'd gone to Chile for a weekend ski trip and stayed away for an entire summer—that I'd sworn never to date a fellow employee again.

I hadn't broken that rule. Except I should have broad-ened my criteria to athletes in general. Then maybe I wouldn't have gotten into that disaster with Thayer.

Crew wasn't a ski bum surfing from couch to couch. He wasn't a liar or a cheat—at least, he'd always been honest with me, now and in the past. But his dedication to the sport of snowboarding would always be top priority.

And I had my sights set on being number one.

River was right. Crew wasn't good enough, not when I was striving for a man who'd never put me in second place.

Saturday had been a temporary lapse in judgment. I blamed my moment of weakness on the lack of sex in the past year. Unfortunately, Penny Ridge was a small town and, at the moment, devoid of attractive, clumsy nerds.

"What run do you want to take?" River asked.

"Whatever you want," I said.

"Devil's Snare?"

I shrugged. "Sure."

It was his favorite run.

Crew hopped off the lift ahead of us. When our turn came, I unloaded and nodded to the operator—he was new this year and I had yet to learn his name.

I strapped my board on, following River as he led the way down the familiar path. These were trails we'd taken as kids, first learning to ski before switching to snowboards, despite our dad's objections.

River dropped over the incline, past the sign that marked Devil's Snare with two black diamonds.

I took a deep breath and eased over the edge, feeling the rush of speed as I fell into the movement. The wind whipped through my hair and the air stung my cheeks. My heart soared, adrenaline spiking in my veins.

Snowboarding was as natural as breathing. As comforting as a hug from Mom. As thrilling as sex with Crew.

The thought of him made my knees wobble. My balance faltered, just barely, but as fast as I was going, there was no way I could stop myself. My board went out from under my legs and I slammed into the snow, white billowing around me as I skidded against the hillside, coming to a flailing stop.

"Ugh." When was the last time I'd crashed? I shook my head, sighing as my brother disappeared around a bend.

River glanced back, never slowing as his laugh echoed off the trees.

He wouldn't wait for me to pick myself up. But he would be at the base, ready to give me shit when I arrived. At the moment, I just wasn't in the mood.

"Shit." I pushed myself up to a seat, placing my board downhill and balancing my arms on my knees as I took in the scenery.

The view from up here was stunning. Not as magnificent as it was on the tallest peaks, especially those only Weston's helicopter could reach. But the mountains rolled in the distance, indigo blue, capped in white, against the bright sky.

I closed my eyes, tilting my face toward the sun. Then I filled my lungs, doing what I'd wanted to do on this run in the first place.

Breathe. Think.

When I'd come to work this morning, two of my instructors had been talking about a regional competition in

January, both requesting the weekend off before they registered.

Part of me had thought about tossing my name into the ring too. Except I hadn't been training, and the last time I'd dropped into a halfpipe had been last season. There was a chance I could get into shape and put together a rotation, especially if Reed's superpipe construction finished on time.

But work was demanding. The beginning of the season was the most stressful as instructors found their rhythm. Practice time would be scarce, and I had responsibilities.

I liked knowing when my next paycheck was coming. I liked the stability of a schedule. I liked helping kids learn how to ski and snowboard and to love something that had been a staple in my life.

This wasn't such a bad life, was it? Did I need more?

Once upon a time, I'd had dreams of competing. Of traveling the world with my snowboard. But I was twenty-eight years old. Most professionals rode over one hundred days a year. I was going as often as possible, but I couldn't swing those hours. And training in the summer meant moving away to a place with a year-round facility—or a different hemisphere.

Was it too late? Was it time to find new dreams?

Snow crunched at my back, and I twisted. Crew shifted his board, slowing until he was stopped and seated at my side.

"Where's River?" I asked, glancing behind us.

"Don't know. I didn't wait for him."

"Oh," I muttered, turning my attention once more to the view.

"Want to tell me what that was about yesterday?"

"You were supposed to leave."

"Sorry to disappoint." He huffed. "Don't worry. You'll be rid of me soon enough. I'm leaving on Sunday."

Sunday. Less than a week, and I probably wouldn't see Crew again for years. That was what I wanted, right? So why did my heart sink?

Crew drew in a long breath, eyes skimming the horizon. "It's strange being back here."

"When's the last time you visited?"

"I haven't. Not since I left."

Twelve years. Wow. I couldn't imagine not coming home for twelve years. "Why'd you stay away for so long?"

"Memories." He spoke so quietly it was barely a breath on the wind.

Memories. Of his mother.

Those of us who'd spent our lives in Penny Ridge knew what had happened to Natalie Madigan. During Crew's freshman year in high school, she'd died from Creutzfeldt-Jakob disease.

My mom was a nurse at the hospital, and after Natalie had died, she'd explained the disease to me and River. It was caused by an infectious protein called a prion. They built up in the brain and caused permanent damage to nerve cells.

No one knew how Natalie had contracted it. All I really remembered was the day River had come home, telling me that Crew's mom was sick. Apparently, it had taken the doctors a while to diagnose her condition. And just a year later, she'd been gone. Mom had bought me a black dress to wear to her funeral.

"I'm sorry about your mom," I said. Condolences I hadn't given when we'd been kids.

"Thanks." He gave me a sad smile. "She would have liked seeing this. Reed, expanding the mountain. Weston, flying his helicopter."

"And you?"

"I think she would have chased me all over the world, being the loudest person in the stands, cheering me on."

"I think so too."

Natalie's death had touched us all. She'd been a staple in our community. A fixture on this mountain, always smiling and greeting us when we came to play in the snow. And the way she'd loved her sons was the gift every child should have. Always a cheerleader. Always a champion.

When she'd died, there'd been a void. In Crew's position, I might not have come home for twelve years either.

We sat together, not speaking, just staring out at the clear, afternoon sky. We let the slight breeze blow away the weight of the conversation until Crew nudged his elbow to mine, nodding to my board.

"So you run the ski school," he said.

"I do."

"Like it?"

"Yeah. The kids are cute. Sometimes the parents can be a pain in the ass, but for the most part, it's a fun job. And I can usually squeeze in a few runs every day."

"With or without a wipeout?"

I laughed. "I didn't wipe out."

"The snow in your hood would suggest otherwise."

"This is a new board," I lied, sharing a smile. "Sorry for blowing you off yesterday."

He chuckled. "No, you're not."

"Okay, no, I'm not." I stared at his profile, memorizing the straight bridge of his nose and the soft pout of his lips.

Holy hell, was he something. It kept throwing me off-balance. Crew had always been gorgeous, but now that I knew what he tasted like, exactly how he could use that incredible body, I couldn't tear my eyes away.

He was here until Sunday. What if this was a no-strings, casual, sex-only—

No. Noooo. Nope. I had rules. I had rules for a reason, and I'd already broken them on Saturday.

No athletes. No skiers. No snowboarders. Certainly not River's BFF.

Crew shoved his sunglasses into his hair, then turned and locked those brown eyes with mine. They had just as many gold flecks as they'd had at the wedding. Mixed with the smooth chocolate color were striations the color of caramel and whiskey.

That brilliant gaze dropped to my lips.

Mine dropped to his.

I wasn't sure who surged first. But before I could blink, our mouths were fused and Crew's tongue slid against my own.

God, yes. Who cared about rules when a man could kiss like this? He licked at my lower lip, then fluttered his tongue. He'd done the same on Saturday night between my legs and fuck . . . My entire body went up in flames, needing to strip him out of those clothes.

Sitting in the snow, on a mountaintop, I was on fire.

His hands came to my face, his gloves cold and soft against my skin. Except I didn't want soft. I wanted hard and fast and anything to satisfy this ache.

"Crew," I moaned, fisting his coat, holding him close.

He tore his lips away, our breaths mingling as we panted.

"You need to leave me alone," I whispered.

"Why?"

"River," I lied. He was the easiest excuse. Really, I didn't trust myself around Crew.

"River doesn't need to know everything, Raven." He let me go, shoving to his feet and holding out a hand to help me up.

My ass was frozen from sitting that long. I wanted Crew to help me warm it up.

"I'm leaving Sunday," he said. "How about we make a deal?"

"I'm listening."

"If you beat me down the hill, I'll leave you alone. But if I beat you down the hill, you come to my room tonight."

I huffed. "That hardly seems fair. You snowboard for a living."

"Yeah, you're probably right. You don't stand a chance against me."

Why did I have a feeling he wasn't talking about snow-boarding? I rolled my eyes, but as he stood there smirking, I reached up and knocked the sunglasses off his hair. Then I shoved forward and took off down the mountain.

"Cheater!" he called.

I laughed as I flew down the slope, giving it everything I had to beat him to the base. I'd just rounded the last turn that would take me to the bottom of the chairlift when a flash of red came from the corner of my eye.

Crew streaked past me, like I'd hardly been moving, coming to a sliding halt next to an empty ski rack. *Damn.*

I stopped beside him, panting and unable to contain my smile.

"Nice try, baby." He smirked.

I bent and unstrapped my boots from my board. When I was free, I took a step closer, speaking so only he could hear. "You're so sure, aren't you?"

"So sure of what?"

"That I didn't just let you win."

CHAPTER FIVE

CREW

P hoto shoots were a pain in my ass. But according to this photographer, I'd been made for the camera.

What the fuck ever.

"One more, Crew," the photographer said, positioning the camera to his eye. "Go ahead and look straight at me. Good. Tilt up your chin. A little more. And slightly to the left."

I obeyed, ready to be done with this ordeal. We'd been at it all damn day.

"Yes." *Click. Click. Click.* Whatever I was doing, he liked. He shifted slightly, his finger hitting the camera's shutter button in rapid succession. Then he dropped it, checked the display and smiled. "This is awesome."

"Is that it?" I asked.

He glanced at GNU's marketing executive, who'd flown to Colorado yesterday with Sydney. "I'm good, unless you want anything else?"

"No, I think we've got it." She shared a smile with Syd and Reed. "This was a fantastic idea."

Reed beamed as he shook the exec's hand. "Appreciate your willingness to come to Madigan Mountain. I'd love to sit down and chat more about a partnership. How about a coffee? We can go inside, warm up and visit in my office."

"Perfect," she said, leaving his side to come over to me to shake my hand. "Thanks, Crew."

"Welcome." I shifted, taking my arm off the board where I'd been leaning on it, per my photographer's pose. "Thanks again for the gear."

"Absolutely."

She hadn't just brought along the photographer, but about ten boards too, all to my specifications, and a bag full of brand apparel and merch. She waved, then turned and fell into step beside my brother as he led her toward his office in the hotel.

I left the photographer to pack up his stuff and walked over to Sydney. "Happy?"

She nodded, adjusting her black-framed glasses. "Very."

"Good." Because when Syd was happy, so was my bank account. "You need anything else?"

"From you? No." She checked her phone. "I have a meeting with your new sister-in-law to talk about a marketing campaign."

Fuck. "My brothers have already pitched me their thoughts. I'm not willing to commit to anything here yet, okay? I'm not moving to Penny Ridge. So don't agree to anything."

"It's just a discussion. Though I don't know why you're

so opposed to spending more time here." She glanced around, taking in the people sprawled in every direction. "I like this place. It's got a quaint and charming feel."

The gleam in her eyes made me nervous. "Sydney," I warned.

"Relax." She waved it off. "It's just one meeting with Ava."

"That's what I'm afraid of," I muttered.

She patted my arm. "Good job today. I'll see you for dinner. Let's meet at seven."

"How about six?" I wanted to wrap up this business so I could have as much time as possible with Raven on my last night.

"That's early." Sydney frowned.

"Tonight is the opening night parade and shindig. I don't want to miss it," I lied.

"Fine. See you then."

Tomorrow, she'd drive the seventy miles to Denver to get on a plane and head back to Miami. Her agency represented athletes and entertainers from all over the world, so now that this campaign was over, she'd be on to the next project.

I loved Syd and how hard she worked for me, but as she disappeared into the hotel, it got easier to breathe.

"Here you go." My assistant, Marianne, appeared at my side with a to-go cup of coffee.

"Thanks." I took a steaming sip, hoping the caffeine would kick in soon.

We'd been up since dawn, preparing for this shoot. Even Reed had tagged along for a few hours.

First, we'd started on top of the mountain, taking a snowmobile to a peak to catch some sunrise shots. Then we'd taken a few runs, with the photographer and his assistant following, cameras in hand, as we'd boarded down the mountain.

Once the actual lifts had opened, there'd been more people to contend with, so we'd found a few secluded places for staged shots. Then finally, after a quick lunch at the lodge, we'd come out here to do a few shoots with me beside this GNU board.

The photographer had told me that he wanted the people milling around in the background. He was going to edit the shots so that they were all a blur, while the board and I were the focal point. Whatever his plans for editing, I didn't really care. I was just glad today's work was done.

Marianne had a duffel bag on her shoulder, the seams stretching because of the stuff inside. Coats and pants and gloves and hats. I'd changed six times for this.

"How are you doing?" she asked.

I sighed, taking another sip of my coffee. "These are draining."

"Let's go sit down." She nodded toward the lodge.

"I'll carry that." I grabbed the duffel before she could object, slinging it over an arm. Then I hefted up my board and followed her across the snow, weaving in and out of people, until my board was in a rack and we were inside, picking a table next to a bank of windows.

I'd just unzipped my teal coat when three kids appeared with rosy cheeks and wide smiles.

"Are you Crew Madigan?" the tallest one asked.

"I am."

"Dude, I told you so." He elbowed his friend. "Could we get your autograph?"

"Sure." I patted my pocket but it was empty.

The kids looked around, totally unprepared for me to sign anything.

"Here." Marianne produced a silver marker. "How about you sign their helmets?"

"Yeah." The kids nodded wildly, each scrambling to unbuckle them, but I held up a hand.

"Hold still." I stepped closer, signing the helmets and then putting the cap back on the Sharpie. "Thanks, guys."

After a fist bump, they walked away, giggling, and I took off my coat and tossed it to the other side of the table by the duffel.

I slid past Marianne, sagging into the chair closest to the window, while she sat at my side, next to the aisle.

Even with a petite, five-foot-one frame, she was a hell of a buffer. We'd learned over the years that if she was on the outside and I was on the inside, if we looked like we were locked in an intimate conversation, it did a lot to divert extra attention and visitors.

"Here's your phone." She plucked it from her pocket and slid it across the table. "And your wallet."

I checked my phone, screen empty. Then put it and my wallet in the pocket of my pants. "Thanks for coming to this."

"That is what you pay me to do." She smiled. "That went pretty well. The photographer showed me some of the initial shots. They'll be great. And I took a bunch myself for Instagram. I was thinking we could do this—"

"Lalalala." I cut her off, plugging my ears.

"Oh, stop." She shook her head. "Do you want to know how many followers you have at the moment?"

"Nope." I hated social media, hence why I'd delegated it entirely to Marianne.

"You just hit two million."

I hummed and took another sip of my coffee. "Good job."

It might be my face in the photos, but the credit went to Marianne. The image was important. The image got me brand deals and sponsorships.

Beyond the windows, the base was flourishing with activity. Lines crowded at the lifts. Every night this week it had snowed. Every morning, the clouds had cleared to reveal a beautiful November day. As far as opening weekends went, this was hard to beat.

"You like it here, don't you?" Marianne asked as I stared out the glass. "I'm sure we could extend this trip if you wanted to stay."

"Nah. I need to get home." There was training to be done. Though I'd had my fair share of time on a board this week.

My days had been spent on the mountain, taking the paths of my childhood. Wrestling with memories from the past, good and bad. Most of my evenings I'd spent at Weston and Callie's old Victorian house in town. My nights had been saved for Raven.

Maybe she'd let me win on Monday during our little race. I didn't give a shit. Because having her in my bed was the real prize.

Raven was an addiction. We'd spent countless hours this week exploring each other's bodies. In the midnight hours, usually after I'd fallen asleep, she'd slip out and return home. And every morning when I woke up, I'd start counting the hours until she'd be back in my suite, naked and writhing on the sheets.

It was just a fling. But damn, we burned hot. The sex was incredible. Night after night, it only got better.

"Crew." Marianne nudged my elbow.

I followed her gaze, sitting straighter as my father walked toward our table.

Dad and I had seen each other in passing this week. He'd smile and wave. I'd keep on walking. I'd expected an ambush at Weston's place when I'd gone over for dinner, but my father had given me space. Now that I was leaving, apparently this reprieve was over.

"Hi, Crew." He was dressed in snow pants and an unzipped red parka. His feet were in ski boots. "How's it going today?"

"Fine." I gave him a sideways glance. He sounded so . . . chipper. Dad wasn't chipper. He was more of a bitter, surly beast. Who was this guy and what had he done with the real Mark Madigan?

"I'm Mark." Dad held out his hand to Marianne. "Crew's dad."

"Marianne." Her voice was flat as she returned his shake. Her dark eyes cold.

"Given that glare, I'd say you know about me." Dad sighed, then looked to me. "Heard you're taking off tomorrow."

"Yeah." I nodded. "Time to head home."

"Right. Well, I, uh . . . it sure has been wonderful having

you here. I don't suppose you'd want to head up? Do a run with your dad, for old time's sake?"

A run? Was he serious?

"I don't know if I can keep up, but I'll try." He looked at me with such pleading in his eyes, I felt my resolve weaken.

Dad had taught me to ski. He'd taught us all to ski. The last time we'd done a run together had been, well . . . a long damn time ago.

"Please?"

Marianne must have heard the vulnerability in his voice because her glare softened as she looked over and shrugged.

Damn it. "Yeah. Sure."

"Great." Dad's chipper smile returned. "I just need to get my skis. Meet me outside?"

I nodded, waiting until he was gone until I dragged a hand through my hair. "Fuck."

"It's only one run," Marianne said, standing from her chair. "Besides, it might be good for you to clear the air."

"I thought you were on my side."

She gave me a sad smile as she picked up the duffel bag. "I am."

Marianne was one of the few people who knew my family's story.

"You've been angry at him for twelve years, Crew." She tucked a lock of her curly black hair behind an ear. "Would it really hurt to hear him out?"

"Yes." Yes, it would hurt. Because for twelve years, I'd ignored the ache. I'd ignored the hole in my chest from my broken family. I'd thrown myself into snowboarding so I wouldn't have to think of Mom, Dad or Penny Ridge. "But I'll go."

She smiled, triumphant, as I stood.

I snagged my coat, pulling it on, then I tucked my phone in my pocket and took my coffee cup to the trash as she followed at my side.

"Thanks." I tossed an arm around her shoulders and pulled her into my side before dropping a kiss to the top of her head.

"No thanks needed. That's what friends are for."

"You want to come with us?" I asked.

"Nope. You're on your own for this one. But you can give me the recap at dinner."

I grumbled, glancing up just in time to catch a pair of crystal-blue eyes locked on my arm around Marianne's shoulders.

Raven's beauty was disarming and I smiled, about to walk over and kiss that pretty pink mouth. But then I remembered we were in public. So I just jerked up my chin. "Hey."

She blinked, then marched for the door.

I opened my mouth to ask what was wrong, but stopped myself.

This was part of the deal. In public, we rarely spoke. We pretended not to know what the other person sounded like when they came.

"Um, who is that?" Marianne stepped away from my side, looking up with a knowing smirk.

"No one," I said, heading for the door that Raven had just shoved through.

"You're the worst liar." Marianne laughed, following me outside. "Is she the reason you didn't want to stick around the bar for a drink last night?"

Hell. The last thing I needed was Marianne in this. I

loved her, but damn, she was nosy. She'd been dating this guy in Park City for the past year. He worked at the indoor facility where I trained, that was how they'd met. Now that she'd found love, she wanted it for everyone in her circle and had been relentless about setting me up on dates.

"She's just someone I know from the past," I told Marianne, heading to the rack where I'd leaned my board. "That's Raven. She's River's sister."

"Ah. So it's a secret."

"Do you have gloves in there?" I pointed to the duffel bag.

She plopped it on the snow, tugging the zipper to pull out gloves along with my helmet and a pair of goggles.

"Dinner is at six," I told her.

"You like her, don't you?" she asked.

Yeah, I liked Raven.

I liked that we were so explosive in bed. I liked that she was sexy and smart. I liked the way she loved this place. I liked that when we'd sat together on that mountain slope, she hadn't pushed to talk about my mom.

When people learned about Mom's disease, they'd ask question after question since it was so rare. Not Raven. She'd just acknowledged my pain and let it slide.

Yeah, I liked her. A lot.

But it didn't matter since I was leaving tomorrow. Finally, it was time to get out of Penny Ridge.

I shoved my gloves in a coat pocket, then fastened the buckle of my helmet beneath my chin, leaving the goggles on the brim.

Raven stood by the ski school area. That silky dark hair always looked pretty against her red coat. Today, she'd braided it over a shoulder. Hopefully tonight, she'd keep that braid because I wouldn't mind wrapping it around my fist.

"Oh, you really like her." Marianne giggled.

I tore my eyes away. "Shut up."

"Crew." For once, Dad came to my rescue. He strode over, his skis on a shoulder and his poles in his other hand. "Ready?"

"Yep." I popped the p, then took off for the lift, letting Dad trail behind.

When I glanced at Raven, her eyes were waiting. She was too far away for me to read her expression but she looked . . . blank.

Pretending not to know a woman intimately was a goddamn pain in the ass.

I got in line at the lift, clipping on my board as Dad stepped into his skis. Then we stood together, inching forward.

"There's nothing like the energy of opening weekend." He puffed up his chest a bit, taking in those around us.

He wasn't wrong. The energy was tangible, people excited to be back in the snow.

The lift was running max capacity to keep the lines moving fast, so as we moved forward, we faced off with the line on the opposite side of the lift.

The kid with the scan gun got to us, searching for our passes. But neither of us had one. Dad, because this was his mountain. Me, because the photographer hadn't wanted the ticket in any shots. "Where's your—oh, sorry, Mr. Madigan."

"It's fine." Dad patted his shoulder, then it was our turn to get on the lift.

We followed the chair forward just as a kid swooped in beside me, going too fast and almost crashing.

"Whoa." I grabbed his arm, keeping him from passing the load line and toppling over.

"Sorry." He huffed, his cheeks red, as he swayed, attempting to get his balance.

The chair came quickly, picking us up and swinging forward.

The kid squirmed, not quite getting his ass on the seat. He fumbled with his poles, nearly dropping them before almost whacking me in the head.

Definitely a first-timer and probably twelve or thirteen, in the throes of those awkward, clumsy years. Adding skis to the mix wasn't helping. My guess was he'd spent the morning in one of Raven's lesson groups.

Dad took a look at him and just shook his head.

"You set?" I asked.

The kid nodded so wildly his helmet rattled.

"Cool." I relaxed in my seat, taking in the view.

"If you're free tonight, we'd like to have you to the condo for dinner," Dad said. "Melody is making her famous lavender shortbread cookies."

"Sorry, can't. I've got a meeting with my agent."

Dad blew out a long breath. "When will we see you again? Or do we have to wait for the X Games and watch you on TV?"

There was a familiar bite to his tone, one I'd heard count-less times. This was the Mark Madigan I knew.

Yes, I'd stayed away from Penny Ridge, but it wasn't like he'd made much of an effort to remain connected to my life.

"The games are in Aspen. I compete every year. How many times have you made that trip?"

"How many times have I been invited?"

"Then consider this your standing invitation," I clipped.

"Wait." The kid beside me leaned forward, shoving his goggles onto his helmet. His eyes widened as he took in my face.

Fuck. I should have put my own goggles on. The last thing I needed was some teenager getting on Twitter and talking about how he'd overheard an argument between Dad and me.

"Oh my God. You're Crew Madigan!" the kid practically shouted in my ear. "You gotta take a picture with me."

He tucked his poles under an arm, again nearly hitting me in the face, then put his gloved hand to his teeth, pulling it free so he could reach into his pocket.

Except as he tugged out his phone, he fumbled it, the device slipping out of his grip. It flew forward.

And the kid stretched too far to try and save it.

"Ah!" he yelled, slipping from his seat.

I moved on instinct, grabbing his arm, catching him before he could fall. "Hold on!"

"Help! Help me!" He flailed, his legs kicking, skis clacking, as he clung to my arm, nearly pulling me off my own chair. His poles sailed to the snow, thirty feet below.

"Crew!" Dad's arm slid through mine, locking on my elbow. "Can you pull him up?"

The kid was screaming and thrashing.

Behind us were panicked gasps and people shouting. "Call ski patrol!"

"Stop the lift!" another person hollered.

"Hold still," I barked at the kid, using all my strength to keep my grip on him. Except we were still moving and he was zeroed in on the ground, terrified at the drop.

"Kid. Hey, kid!" I yelled, getting his attention. "Look at me."

He finally did, just enough to stop screaming. Tears filled his eyes.

"Stop struggling. On the count of three, I'm going to pull you up. Grab the back of the chair, okay? Ready?"

He nodded, sobbing.

"One. Two. Three." I used every ounce of strength in my body to pull, Dad's arm still locked on mine.

The kid gripped the back of the chair, managing to get his belly on the seat.

"Come on, kid." I yanked harder, enough that he was able to turn, lying sideways.

But in the move, I twisted too far. I shoved the kid enough so his ass could find the seat. And my own slipped off the edge.

"Crew!" Dad still had a grip on my arm, a hold that saved me from falling.

But there was no stopping me from sliding off the chair, nearly pulling Dad off with me.

I gasped, scrambling for anything to hold and managing to grab the metal bar beneath the seat's pad.

Shit. My heart was in my throat.

I glanced to the ground, then adjusted my grip. Thank fuck I hadn't put on my gloves yet. "I'm good, Dad. I'm hanging on. Let go."

"No." His panicked eyes were glued to mine.

"I've got the chair. You can let me go."

"You're sure?"

I nodded as he loosened his grip, sliding his arm free.

My weight shifted, my legs dangling. The chair swung as the kid bawled. I glanced down below at the drop, then up again. No way I'd be able to climb back into the chair.

Fuck my life.

This was going to hurt.

CHAPTER SIX

RAVEN

J ealousy was a nasty bitch.

My molars had been grinding together since the moment I'd spotted Crew in the lodge with his arm draped over that other woman. When he'd kissed her hair, so affectionate and intimate, I'd wanted to scream.

Of course she was stunning. Petite with curly, black hair and smooth, dark bronze skin. Were they a couple? If he'd cheated on her with me, I would shove a ski pole through that asshole's heart.

My teeth ground together harder.

"Raven!"

I turned as my brother jogged my way, his board under an arm. "Hey."

"Do you have five bucks?"

"Yes, I'm having a great day. Thanks for asking."

He rolled his eyes, then held out his hand, palm up. "Glad you're having a great day. So? Can I borrow five bucks?"

Borrow. River didn't understand the concept of borrowing money. "You mean can I give you five dollars."

"Whatever. Yes or no. I'm hungry and wanted to snag a slice of pizza from the cafeteria."

I sighed. "No."

"Then can I put it on your account?"

"Pack a lunch. Seriously." I knew for a fact that Mom had all of the fixings for peanut butter and jelly in her pantry because she made her own sandwiches for her shifts at the hospital.

"I didn't have time today. I'll remember tomorrow."

But he'd had time to pack a bag of weed. The scent of smoke and marijuana clung to his jacket. And no, he wouldn't remember to pack a lunch tomorrow. Just like he hadn't last season, or the season before.

Last year, by the time we'd closed down for spring, my account balance at the cafeteria had included hundreds and hundreds of dollars of food for my brother.

"Fine," I muttered. "Just today. But this is it, River. I mean it. I'm not funding your meals all year."

"Last time. Promise." He held out his hand for my employee card as I dug it from my pocket.

"Put it on my desk when you're done."

He ruffled my hair, something I hated, then strode off without so much as a thank-you.

No way he'd get just a slice of pizza. I pinched the bridge of my nose, knowing I was just making it worse. But I wasn't in the mood to fight with my brother today. And last year, I'd let the mooching slide because of what had happened with Thayer.

"Hey, Raven." Pete, one of my long-time instructors, walked over.

"Hi." I forced a smile. "How's it going? How was the lesson this morning?"

He groaned. "Exhausting. That was maybe the worst private I've ever had."

"What? Why?"

"That poor kid. Not a coordinated bone in his body. We went on two runs."

"That's it?" Normally for a half-day private lesson, you could fit in at least five. The larger group classes did at least four. "Was he happy? Or should I expect a phone call from an angry parent later?"

"I think he was happy." Pete shrugged. "He was going to go up himself this afternoon. Practice what we worked on. I hope he won't wipe someone out."

"Me too." So far, opening weekend had gone smoothly. We didn't need any injuries to dampen the positive energy. "You're on float rotation today, right?"

Float rotation was my overflow contingency. The instructors on float would teach a half-day private in the morning, then jump in to help with whatever afternoon classes needed an extra body. It was something I'd implemented a couple of years ago to spread the load on the harder classes and also have someone available to cover sick calls and last-minute adds.

"Yeah," he said. "Julie is up on the Easy Rider chair with a pretty big group of five-year-olds. I'm going to go check in with her and see if she needs a hand."

"Great. Thanks. See you tonight at the parade?"

He nodded. "I'll be there."

The opening ceremony for the mountain was something I looked forward to each year. For the past couple of years, I'd been the person to lead the torchlit ski run down the Lower Bowl—perks of being one of Ava's best friends.

The entire resort staff would be out tonight along with guests, customers and locals from town.

And Crew.

Would he bring that woman with him? Who was she? He'd had that photo shoot all morning. Last night, before I'd left his hotel suite, he'd told me his team and the sponsors had arrived. Maybe that was his agent? Or assistant?

Why was I letting this bother me? Crew and I weren't exclusive. We weren't anything. We were just sleeping together. Which, after seeing him kiss another woman's hair in the lodge, was now in the past. Last night had been our last rendezvous in his suite.

It was for the best to end this. Before I got attached.

"Hey, Raven." Another instructor waved as she walked by, her skis on her shoulders as she led a group of teenagers toward a lift.

Lucky kids. All I wanted was to grab my board and spend an hour on the mountain, shoving away thoughts of Crew and that woman.

Except there was no way I could get away. Not on a Saturday, and the first Saturday at that. The weekends were crazy with activity.

I needed to get to the office and check to make sure no one had come in with problems. I wanted to swing by Kid's Korner and make sure the instructors were managing the little kids who'd done a morning session and were now playing inside. They were usually the four- and five-year-olds who didn't have the energy for a whole day, so we had a daycare set up for the afternoons. And before I did anything else, I needed more coffee.

I yawned, digging my phone from my pocket to check the time. Crew had been keeping me up late each night, and I was exhausted. I turned, ready to retreat to the lodge for a latte, when the radio clipped to my pants pocket buzzed.

"Ski patrol. Emergency on Chair Nine."

My heart stopped and I yanked the radio off the clip, raising it to my ear.

"We've got a guy hanging from the chair."

"Oh my God." I spun on my heels, running toward the base of Chair Nine.

It was a triple chair that served as an arterial to the lifts midmountain that led toward the summit and more challenging terrain. It was also a chair we used a ton in lessons because it gave access to the majority of the beginner runs.

Please, don't be a student.

My boots pounded the snow as I sprinted toward the lift hut.

The guy stationed there came running through the door. The woman at the loading zone had hit the kill button, stopping the chair. And the guy scanning tickets was as wide-eyed as the skiers and boarders who'd overheard the radio message.

"How far up?" I asked the woman.

"We don't know."

Fuck.

The whir of a snowmobile cut through the air, followed by another. Two ski patrol guys zoomed in my direction. One of them, Donny, had worked here with me for years.

"Keep your radios on," I told the lift operators, then raised my hand, flagging down Donny.

He nodded, slowing long enough for me to hop on the back.

The other machine pulled a stretcher.

"Go," I yelled when I was seated.

He hit the throttle, speeding up the line of towers as my heart crawled into my throat.

This was my nightmare. Fatalities from a chairlift fall were incredibly rare. In twenty years, there'd only been a few actual deaths across the country. But even if the person survived, it could mean a severe injury.

To the person. And to the resort.

People on the lift above us had their phones out, videoing whatever was happening.

I spotted legs first, dangling with a board attached to one foot. Then I saw a flash of teal and gasped.

Crew had been wearing a teal coat.

"No," I whispered, shifting to get a closer look.

The lift was stopped. Crew's chair was ten feet from a tower. It was one of the highest points on this lift, about thirty feet in the air.

The snowmobile jerked to a stop, Donny climbing off and running forward. "Hold on!" he yelled.

"Crew!" I hollered.

He was hanging by both arms, somehow having managed to grab the bar beneath the pad of the seat. "Start the lift."

"No!" Mark was in the chair, leaning over with a hand outstretched for his son. "Get some padding. Anything to break his fall."

The ski patrol guys shared a look, then one of them ran for the tower, cutting the padding that we had around the bases in case someone crashed.

"Get the goddamn chair going!" Crew yelled. "Now!"

"Just wait, Crew." I cupped my hands to my mouth as I hollered. "We're getting something for you to land on."

"I don't need something. I need you to start the chair."

It was against protocol. Our procedure was to find anything to break the skier's fall, then rush them for the ambulance waiting at the base.

"Just hold on." Oh God. No. He'd be okay. He'd fall and it would suck, but he'd be okay.

People rushed forward, taking off their skis and boards, offering coats and help. The other ski patrol guy was running toward a section of orange boundary fence, yanking it from the poles keeping it in place.

If we could get that high enough on the tower, then we could create a landing area. A slide to at least give him some sort of cushion.

"Start the lift!" Crew shouted, adjusting his grip on the bar.

"No," Mark called.

"Shut up, Dad." He shot his dad a glare, then looked down, locking his eyes with me. "Start the lift."

"We need to stay put so when you fall, we have something beneath you."

"I'm not dropping where there's no incline. I'll break my fucking legs."

And potentially end his career.

"Crew—"

"Do it, Raven!"

My stomach twisted. "We can't."

"Goddamn it. Trust me. Please. Start. The. Fucking. Lift!"

"Ah." *Shit.* I reached for my radio, hitting the button. "Start the lift."

"Are you—"

"Start it!" My voice cracked.

The ski patrol guys both whipped my way, eyes wide.

Donny crossed his arms. "No."

"Just trust me," I yelled. Don't let this be a mistake. Don't let him fall.

The lift started, the chairs swinging as they inched forward, then gained speed.

I watched Crew's chair pass the tower, then sink into the swale between it and the next. He let go with one hand and I yelped.

But it wasn't because he couldn't keep ahold. He lifted his legs, trying to get his free boot strapped into its binding.

"What are you—" I gasped, realizing his plan. "He's going to jump."

He was going to get to a steeper incline and jump.

"What the hell do you think you're doing?" Donny jogged to his snowmobile where he'd left his radio, about to call in for them to stop the lift again.

But I ran over, taking his hand. "You have to just trust me. That's Crew Madigan. He knows this mountain better than you do. Just, please. He has something planned. And Mark is up there with him. Look."

Donny followed my finger as I pointed toward their chair.

"Come on." I hopped on the seat. "We need to follow them."

He grumbled but climbed on, turning the key to start the engine. Then we were off, racing to follow.

The other ski patrol machine wasn't far behind.

When I looked back up, Crew had managed to get the high back open and his ankle strap attached. I doubted it was tight, but it would work. Then he stretched for that bar, using both hands to hold as the chairlift creeped higher and higher.

I held tight to Donny as the snowmobile's angle changed, its track bouncing over the moguls beneath this steep section beneath the lift.

Crew looked over his shoulder, then down to the ground. He raised his legs, swinging his board back and forth as hard as possible, trying to rock the chair so that when he let go, his body had some momentum and it wasn't a straight drop.

I patted Donny's shoulder for him to stop, waiting until we'd slowed enough for me to hop off the sled. "Park over there," I ordered, pointing to the trees that lined the slope.

He obeyed, driving out of the way, and when he cut the engine, I could finally hear more of what was happening on that chair. The kid next to Mark was bawling, his shoulders shaking with sobs.

Mark was saying something to Crew, but I couldn't make out the words. He also had an arm stretched to hold the kid's shoulder.

I didn't so much as blink as Crew kept swinging. *Please let this work.* My hand came to my heart.

It happened in slow motion. Crew swung his legs once

more, and then he was falling, his arms lifted, held wide for balance.

Gasps filled the air, my own included as my stomach plummeted.

In midair, he shifted, angling his board downhill as he tucked, like this was a trick, not some freak accident. One second he was falling, the next, he landed with a whoosh, his board carrying him down the slope, just like a stunt in a terrain park.

He cut a quick turn, using it to slow his momentum, then he twisted the other direction, coming my way.

Crew stopped his board perpendicular to the slope, then he sank down to a seat, dropping onto his back as the people above us cheered.

I scrambled up the hill to meet him, doing my best not to trip and fall.

"Are you okay?" Mark yelled.

"Yeah," Crew called.

"Stay put," Mark said as the lift started again. "I'll be right there."

Crew raised an arm in the air to give a thumbs-up, but the movement made him wince. "Fuck."

I reached his side and dropped to my knees, my hands instantly roaming over his body, searching for injuries. "What's wrong?"

"My shoulder." He closed his eyes, still breathing hard. "Shit."

"What do you need?"

"Just . . . give me a minute."

"Okay." My hands kept traveling head to toe. No bones

were protruding. I knew there weren't. I'd watched him the entire time.

But anyone else and we would be loading up the stretcher.

"You're okay." My voice was shaking.

Crew opened his eyes, then lifted his good arm to cup my cheek. "I'm okay."

Snowmobiles buzzed the air as the ski patrol crew descended.

Crew shoved up onto an elbow, meeting my gaze. "I'm okay."

I swallowed hard, the adrenaline ebbing so that the fear beneath could come surging forward. "We're going to a hospital."

"I don't need to go to a hospital."

"You're going," I insisted.

He didn't argue as he shoved to his feet, grimacing as he bent in half to tighten his ankle strap and lock in the toe strap too.

"What are you doing?" He should be unbuckling.

Crew jerked his chin down the slope. "Did you want me to go to the hospital or not?"

"Yes, but—"

"Then let's go. I'm not riding on a damn stretcher." A quick pivot and he was gone, breezing past the snowmobiles that were descending on me.

My jaw dropped.

"Did that just happen?" Donny had parked beside me, asking the question in my mind.

I blinked, staring at Crew as he got smaller and smaller.

"Yeah." I let out a dry laugh. "I guess it did."

CHAPTER SEVEN

CREW

"It's either a sprain to the ligaments or a strain on the muscles," the doctor at Penny Ridge Medical Center said, stating the obvious. "We'll have to do an MRI to determine exactly what we're dealing with here."

Fucking MRIs. I didn't need one, because I already knew what it would show. My shoulder was messed up and had been for a while. Surgery loomed on the horizon, but I'd been delaying it for as long as possible.

"This isn't your first injury to this shoulder, is it?" he asked.

"Nope," I muttered while he poked and prodded at the joint. It hurt like a motherfucker, but I clenched my teeth, breathing through the pain as he finished his exam.

"We can get you in for an MRI tomorrow."

"Not necessary," I said. "As long as it's not dislocated, that's all I care about."

"I'd strongly recommend—"

I held up my good hand, cutting him off. "I'm good."

"Treatment?" Marianne asked as she stood beside my bed in the emergency room. She'd barely moved in the hour we'd been here after the drive down from the mountain.

"For the moment, ice to keep the swelling down. Ibuprofen for the pain. Wouldn't hurt for you to wear a sling. If those tendons get locked up, you're going to have a hard time moving it around. There's a chance you'll need to come in for a cortisone shot, but let's see how the next day or two progresses."

I blew out a long breath. "Anything else?"

"You need to lay off that shoulder. Even for a moderate sprain, you need six to eight weeks to let it heal."

"Got it." That timeline was one I'd heard before. But if he knew exactly what I'd done to this shoulder before, he'd probably tell me to take three to five months. That, and to get the surgery my orthopedic specialist had been pushing me to have for the past year.

The doctor nodded, then moved to leave, but paused beside the foot of the bed. "I heard about what happened. That was a brave thing you did."

I waved it off. "No big deal."

"It is to that kid and his parents." The doctor walked toward the curtain surrounding my bed. "Keep me posted."

"Will do." I nodded, waiting for him to leave before I hung my head. "Fuck."

Marianne collected both of our coats from the chair where they were folded. She draped them over her arms, then fished my car keys from a pocket. She was pissed. Mostly at me for that "stunt" I'd pulled. But I knew her well enough to know her anger was just a mask for her fear and worry.

After I'd reached the base earlier, I'd been swarmed by people. Ski patrol. My brothers. Dad had blazed down the trail to catch up. The chair incident had garnered immediate attention, and it seemed like the entire resort had come out to gawk.

In the crush, I'd lost Raven. One moment she'd been standing beside a ski patrol guy, then the next, my brothers had converged, and I'd lost her in the shuffle.

And with so many people around, I hadn't been able to search her out. So the moment Marianne had pushed her way through the crowd around me, I'd told her to lead the way to the parking lot and drive me to the hospital.

"We need to get this looked at by your orthopedic specialist in Park City," she said.

"I know." I pinched the bridge of my nose. "Goddamn it."

"It's not dislocated again," Marianne said. "That's something, at least."

Throughout my career, I'd dislocated this shoulder three times, each after an epic crash. This also wasn't my first strain or sprain. They seemed to get worse each time, and my doctor at home had said surgery was a given.

It was only a matter of time.

I'd been careful this year. So fucking careful. Until today.

Well, I'd just have to deal, wouldn't I? The season was just getting started, and I refused to sit it out. "I'm not having surgery until after the season is over."

"It's going to be hard to train if your arm isn't working, Crew. And if you push too hard, you're going to end up doing permanent damage and ending your career."

"Knock. Knock." A nurse came to my rescue, cutting our conversation short as she stepped through the curtains. Then I was greeted with a familiar face I hadn't realized until this moment I'd missed. A lot. "Hi, Crew."

"Hey, Robin." My frame relaxed as Raven's mom walked over. I lifted my good arm to pull her into a quick hug. "How are you?"

"Better than you." She smiled, then nodded at Marianne. "I'm Robin. Crew used to terrorize the neighborhood with my son."

"Not exactly terrorize," I teased. "This is Marianne, my assistant."

"Nice to meet you," Marianne said, shaking Robin's hand.

Robin nodded, then looked me up and down, holding up a sling she'd brought along. "Doc said you might need this."

"Nah. I'll be all right."

"Wear the sling, Crew."

I chuckled. "Yes, ma'am."

"You always listened better than River." She smiled, then went to work fitting the strap around my neck and carefully positioning my arm in the envelope.

Her dark hair was up in a bun. There were a few gray streaks that hadn't been there the last time I'd seen her years ago. There were more fine lines on her face. But her blue eyes were the same, full of laughter and love.

Raven looked so much like her mother it was almost uncanny. The only difference was that Robin didn't have a dusting of freckles across her nose like her daughter.

"Lots of ice," she said once the sling was in place. "Rest. And since you don't know what rest means, I'll spell it out for you. You don't go back up to that mountain and strap on a snowboard this week. Got me?"

"Got you."

She sighed, studying my face. "You're not going to rest, are you?"

Robin knew me well. "I'll take it easy."

"How long are you in town?"

"I'm heading out tomorrow."

"So soon?"

I nodded. "Yeah, I need to get back."

"Shame on you for not coming to visit me."

"What do you mean? I strained my shoulder just so I could sneak my way into your ER."

"Smartass." Robin laughed, her eyes softening. "It's so good to see you. It's been too long."

"You too."

After Mom had died, Robin had done her best to step in and fill the endless void. She'd hugged me often and harped on me to do my homework. The afternoons when I'd gone to River's place after school, Robin hadn't asked if I was staying for dinner. She'd just set a place for me at their table.

Her house had become a sanctuary when mine had become a living hell. Even Rowdy, the rare times when he'd been home, had been more supportive and patient than my own father.

Rowdy. Robin. River. Raven.

My last two years of high school, I would have killed for a different first name. Anything that started with an *R*. Just so I could escape my home and belong to theirs.

"One more hug." Robin waved me off the bed where I'd

been sitting and pulled me into her arms. "Take care of yourself."

"Stay out of trouble."

"Hey, that's my line." She let me go. "I'll get your discharge papers. Hang tight."

I bent and kissed her cheek, then waited as she left the room.

Marianne was staring at my sling, her forehead furrowed.

"Later." We'd deal with the ramifications of this injury later.

At the moment, I was holding out hope that my body would knit itself together, and in a few days, I'd be good as new. It had happened before. Granted, I'd been a younger man, but there was a chance this would go away.

We waited until Robin returned with a few printouts and post-care instructions. Then I said one last goodbye and strode out of the ER, Marianne falling into step at my side.

She dug her phone from her pocket as we walked.

The screen filled with notifications. "What's happening?"

"It's all over social media."

"Super." *Hell.* A social media shitstorm was exactly what we didn't need. This would mean interviews. No doubt Sydney would want to capitalize on this press—assuming it was good.

I shoved through the exit doors into the waiting room.

"Crew." Weston's voice slowed my steps. He, along with Dad and Reed, were all standing up from chairs beside the waiting room windows.

"Hey. You guys didn't need to come down here."

"Where else would we be?" Weston jerked his chin to the sling. "What did the doctor say?"

After my quick recap, Reed blew out a long breath. "So nothing major. That's great news."

Marianne stiffened but stayed quiet. She'd been with me long enough to know that I wasn't going to share the details about my shoulder and past injuries with anyone, including my family. That was inner-circle knowledge only.

"I'm sorry." Dad's hand rested on my good shoulder. "About the lift. And everything."

"Don't worry about it." I shook off his touch, then strode for the doors.

Except before I'd even taken one step into the parking lot, a camera clicked and a man came rushing my way. "Mr. Madigan, how are you doing? What's the status on your injury?"

A reporter. This kept getting better.

"Back off." Weston stepped between me and the reporter, but the reporter just shifted, leaning past my brother.

"Will you be able to compete this year?" he asked.

"Shoulder's all good," I lied. "Sling for a day or two, then I'll be back."

"What happened on that chairlift?"

He could watch the YouTube videos to answer that question.

"Let's go," I told Marianne, picking up the pace as I marched through the lot for my Mercedes.

"Crew, wait up." Reed jogged to my side. "If there's a reporter here, then they're probably staked out in the hotel lobby too. You know the rear employee entrance? We put in a keypad last year. I'll text you the code."

"Appreciate it."

Marianne beeped the locks on the G-Wagon so we could climb inside.

That reporter appeared right outside my window, his camera raised. *Asshole.*

"Go," I ordered.

Marianne obeyed, speeding out of the lot.

We took the winding road up the mountain in silence, her concentrating on the road and me breathing through the pain in my shoulder. The doctor hadn't given me any pain medication in the ER and my bottle of ibuprofen in the hotel was calling.

Marianne followed my instructions to the rear employee entrance, parking close to the door. There were people everywhere, milling about as the sun was beginning to set. They were likely sticking around for tonight's opening ceremony.

"You're pushing too hard," she said, breaking the silence.

Being the best required push. So yeah, I pushed.

And I wasn't going to stop, no matter how much my assistant urged me to slow down.

"See you in the morning," I said, opening my door. "What time do you want to meet?"

"Eight."

"Have a good night," I said, shoving out of the car. Then I strode for the door, keying in the code Reed had texted me.

The stairwell was quiet and empty as I climbed to the third floor. Was this how Raven had been coming into the building? Would she come up tonight?

I wished we hadn't gotten separated earlier. Maybe she was in the same boat as Marianne, pissed at my stunt. But I hadn't known what else to do. It had happened so fast and I'd just . . . reacted.

Everyone had been yelling for me to drop. The ski patrol had been trying to piece together a cushion. But I knew this mountain. I knew what happened when you fell thirty feet onto a relatively flat slope.

Bones broke.

So I'd taken the gamble that my grip could hold out until I made it farther up the lift line to where I knew the slope was steeper and the drop shorter.

My phone rang in my pocket as I reached the third floor. I opened the stairwell's door, checking that no one lingered outside my room, and when I found the hallway empty, I answered my manager's call. "Lewis."

"What the hell were you thinking?"

I sighed, digging out my key card and opening my door. "I was thinking 'better me than that kid.' "

"Who gives a shit about some kid?"

Lewis's heart was slightly smaller than Sydney's. "I'm not debating this. It's done. Let's get on with it."

"Any injuries?"

"Nothing major," I lied.

"Damn it, Crew." He huffed. "I should have been there. I told Marianne I'd fly out and be there but she said it was just a photo shoot. That you had Sydney with you. But I should have been there."

To keep me on his leash.

Lewis managed the business aspect of my career. His duties often blended with Marianne's, sometimes Sydney's, so the three of them would opt to skip out on certain activities if the other two were around. Lewis left the promotions and sponsorship events to Syd. She only came to the competitions they'd feature on ESPN while Lewis attended them all. And Marianne was with me always, mostly because Lewis had deemed her a worthy babysitter.

No doubt after he hung up on me, she'd get a call and lecture too. If he hurt her feelings or placed the blame on her shoulders, we'd be having words.

"This was my decision," I said. "It was my call. And it's not the end of the world, so can we just let this go and relax?"

"Let this go? Relax? You're going viral. Those videos of you are everywhere. Social media. Prime time. This is national news."

No. I stifled a groan. "So?"

"We have to respond."

"Then call Erin and come up with a statement." That was why I had a publicist, wasn't it? To make these statements? Erin also gave Marianne social media direction from time to time, but for the most part, Erin's job was to promote good press and downplay bad. I wasn't sure which category this would fall into yet. Good, right? I'd saved that kid from falling.

"Do we know if the kid is going to sue?" Lewis asked.

"What the hell could he possibly sue me for?" I took a seat on the suite's couch, wishing I had ignored this call.

"Any number of things."

"Well, then I guess it's good so much of it is on YouTube, considering I pulled that kid into the chair."

"And the resort? Have you heard anything from them?"

"You're worried that my family will sue me?"

"Yes."

"Unbelievable." With my phone pressed between my ear and shoulder, I bent to use my good arm to untie the laces on my boots. I kicked them off, each landing with a thud.

My clothes were too hot for inside since I was dressed to ski. I'd left my snow pants on at the hospital because all I wore beneath was a base layer that was rather snug, especially on my ass and thighs. But I was alone now, so I stood and unbuttoned my ski pants, shoving them to the floor to join my boots. My wool socks came off next.

"I'll get Erin on a statement. And we need to be proactive. I'll call your lawyer."

"Whatever. I'm done with this conversation," I said. "Make a statement. Say nothing. I don't actually give a fuck. I'll talk to you after I get home."

"Crew—"

I ended the call and sank to the couch again, tossing my phone aside. It vibrated with an incoming call.

That wasn't the first time I'd hung up on Lewis. It wasn't the first time he'd immediately called back.

On a sigh, I leaned my head against the back cushion. "Damn it."

How was the kid? Had anyone checked on him? I'd forgotten to ask Dad at the hospital.

I was about to pick up the phone when a knock came at the door, so I shoved to my feet, going over to open it for Reed.

"My manager is sure you're going to sue," I told him as he walked inside.

Reed chuckled, going to the same chair where he'd sat

last week when he'd visited my suite. "He does know that we're brothers, right?"

"Lewis doesn't trust anyone, especially siblings." I took the couch again, holding back a wince. Showing any sort of pain meant questions. And I wasn't in the mood to deliver answers. "How's the kid from the lift?"

"He's all right. Before I came to the hospital, I met with him and his parents. They're also worried we're going to sue. Maybe it's me? Am I sending out lawsuit vibes?"

I grinned. "Bet that's the last time he attempts to ski."

"Well, if he does try again, let's just hope he heads to Aspen or Vail."

"You didn't need to stop by. I'm fine. I know you've got a lot happening with the opening ceremony stuff tonight." At dinner on Thursday at Weston's place, Reed and Ava had talked for an hour about their plans for the event.

Reed leaned forward, elbows to knees. "Look, you're hurt. You won't be riding for at least a week. What if you stayed here instead of making the drive home?"

"Marianne will drive me."

"Okay, then let me put it this way. What if you stayed here just because? We've all loved having you home. You're hurt. You can ease back into things. Give us a chance to fuss over you before you're off traveling the world. Just another week. And we're about done with the halfpipe."

"Ah," I said. "The truth comes out."

He smiled. "I meant for that to be the cherry on top. Whether you look at the pipe or pretend it doesn't exist, it makes no difference to me. I'd just like you to stay a little longer."

"Why?" If it wasn't for the halfpipe, then why?

Reed shrugged. "Maybe I'm worried that when you leave, it will be another twelve years before we get you back."

Well . . . damn. I wanted to say he was wrong. That I'd be back soon. But we both knew it would probably be a lie.

"I can't." It was time for me to go home. Marianne would throw a damn fit if I wasn't in my doctor's office first thing Monday morning.

Another cherry for staying.

Staying meant another week with Raven. The biggest cherry yet.

Fitting, considering she smelled like cherries.

Wait. Was I actually considering this?

"I don't exactly have a place to stay," I said.

"Something wrong with this room?"

"I've already taken it for longer than originally planned. I'm sure you've got upcoming reservations."

"Not for this particular room."

"It's a suite." I narrowed my gaze, studying my brother's expression. The guilt. "You blocked this off for me, didn't you?"

"I want to take credit, but it was all Ava. She said she was hedging her bets. If you stayed, you'd have a place. If not, we'd rent it out."

"Seriously?" That was . . . thoughtful. Not surprising either, considering how much I liked my new sister-in-law. She hadn't even met me yet before the wedding, and still, she'd held this room. "I don't know what to say."

"A yes would work."

I reclined in the seat, staring at the ceiling. Did I want to stay? *No. Yes.* "Fine. But I'm paying for it myself."

"Deal." Reed clapped once, shoving to his feet. "I'm

leaving before you change your mind. Want me to send up some dinner?"

"No, I'll call for room service."

"Put it in early. Tonight's going to be busy." With that, he let himself out of my room.

I moved to the small table, opening the binder with the menu, quickly deciding on a burger with extra fries from the restaurant. Once that call was made, I started in on the slew of others.

First, I talked to Sydney, who'd sent me sixteen texts. She'd stayed behind instead of coming to the hospital, per Marianne's encouragement. Syd wasn't the hospital-support type. She was as unhappy as Lewis.

Next, I called Lewis again, reassuring him that my brother and the kid from the lift had no inclination to sue. It didn't improve his mood, but I suspected nothing would today.

The moment I ended the call with Lewis, Erin called to discuss the media circus and the response she was drafting. When I told her I didn't want to make a big deal out of this, she got annoyed and cut the call short. No doubt she'd ignore me and use this to drum up good PR.

Then, I called Marianne. I was sure she'd storm out of her room and to mine, smacking me in the head for even considering another week in Penny Ridge. But she calmly listed the details she'd take care of, including sending me more clothes and toiletries once she got back to Park City. She'd be hitching a ride with Sydney to Denver in the morning so that she could fly home to Utah.

My head was pounding by the time I ended the string of

calls. Night had fallen beyond the windows and the sound of music mingled with laughing, celebrating people.

I was about to duck into the bathroom for a quick shower before my food came when another knock sounded at the door. Either room service or Weston. I snagged my wallet from my snow pants pocket and strode across the room, tugging out a twenty. But when I opened the door, it wasn't a delivery or a brother.

It was Raven.

"Hi." Damn, she was a sight. It felt like days, not hours, since I'd seen her on the mountain.

"Hi."

I stepped aside, holding the door while she crossed the threshold. Then watched as she stood in the center of the room, her eyes sweeping me up and down. Arms. Chest. Stomach. Thighs.

"Doing a visual assessment?" I teased.

"Your agent really should be looking for sponsorships with thermal underwear companies."

I laughed, relaxing for the first time since I'd stepped out of my room this morning. "Thought you'd be at the opening ceremony shindig."

"I carried my torch down the Lower Bowl, then snuck out."

"Ah." Fuck, I was glad she'd come. "Want to sit?"

"Sure." She unzipped her coat, the red parka she'd had on earlier. "How are you feeling?"

"Good. Hungry. I just ordered dinner. Want me to call in another?"

"No, I'm all right."

"I lost you earlier."

"I figured you were in safe hands and there were fires to extinguish." Meaning she wasn't going to fuss over me, certainly not in public.

"Thanks for listening today. For getting the lift going."

"That was . . . crazy. But if anyone could pull that off, it was you." She went to the couch, plopping down on the edge. "Just don't do it again, okay? That scared the shit out of me."

"Me too," I admitted, joining her on the couch, unable to hide the wince as I sat. The pain was getting worse. I could feel my shoulder tightening, those tendons and ligaments locking up.

"Okay, how bad is it? The truth this time."

"It's fine. Just sore. And from experience, it will fade in a day or two."

"Experience?"

"This shoulder has been giving me some trouble for a while. Ever since I dislocated it the first time."

"When was that?"

"About four years ago. I was coming down to do a trick and misjudged the angle. Hit the edge of the pipe with my shoulder, popped it right out of joint."

"Ouch." She hissed. "What happened today?"

"Just hung for too long. Stretched it too far with too much weight."

"What did the doctor say?"

"To rest." I sighed. "My doctor in Park City says the same. Have surgery. Repair the damage. Rest. But I can't. Reed came up earlier. He convinced me to hang out here for another week. So that's how long I'll give it. That's all I can afford. I need to train."

"Do you have any competitions coming up?"

"The X Games." That was the only event that mattered at the moment. Because I'd won gold last year, I was automatically qualified for this year. But I needed to train. Which was hard as shit when your arm wasn't fully functional.

"What if you delayed?" she asked. "Took the year off."

"Not an option." I shook my head. "I'm thirty years old. I'm not just at the peak of my career, but the end. Everyone tells me I'm being dramatic. It's just a year, and in the scope of things, it's not that big of a deal to miss one, especially when we're three out from the Olympics. But—"

"But you don't want to miss a year."

"Exactly."

"Then don't stop."

I met her pretty blue eyes and saw understanding. No questioning my sanity. No offering alternatives. Just . . . acceptance.

She told me to keep pushing.

Raven couldn't have any idea what that meant to me. It wasn't something I could really put into words either. And since I couldn't articulate the feelings swirling in my chest, I leaned over.

And kissed her instead.

CHAPTER EIGHT

RAVEN

A kiss a day from Crew Madigan was good for a girl's soul.

I leaned into him, letting him sweep his tongue against mine. My body ignited, just like it did with every kiss. A rush. A thrill. It was the same jolt I felt racing down a mountain or dropping into a halfpipe.

Adrenaline junkie. Crew junkie. Same thing.

In the back of my mind, I knew this had to stop. Eventually, we had to stop. He might be staying an extra week, but he was still leaving. And though I knew it would be easier if I put an end to this now, damn it, I couldn't tear my mouth away. Instead, I just hit mute on the voice warning me that this was getting too deep. Too fast.

"Goddamn, baby," Crew murmured against my mouth.

Baby was so freaking cliché. I really shouldn't like it.

But I did.

I *so* did.

Crew shifted, trying to move closer, but as he did, he

winced. It was subtle, only for a second, but his jaw clenched.

"We should slow down," I said, leaning away.

"No." He peppered kisses against the corner of my mouth. "I don't want to slow down."

I was a heartbeat from caving when a knock came at the door.

Crew and I froze, then he growled and stood. "It's probably my dinner."

But what if it wasn't? It could be one of his brothers. Hell, it could be mine. *Shit.* I wiped my mouth dry and stood as he crossed the room, opening the door. As I peered past Crew's shoulders, my own sagged. It was a waiter from the restaurant.

"Here you go, Mr. Madigan."

"Thanks. Uh, would you mind setting it down?"

I hurried for the door, sliding past Crew. "I'll take it."

"Oh, um, hey." This guy clearly recognized me, but with any luck, he'd only assume I was a friend of Crew's.

"Hey." I lifted the tray, the scent of french fries and a cheeseburger filling my nose.

"Here you go." Crew fished out a twenty from his pocket, handing it over, then closed the door as I carried his dinner to the table.

"I'll get out of here. Let you eat and rest."

But before I could make my escape, Crew snagged my hand. "Stay. Please."

It was those brown eyes that always shattered my convictions. He stared down at me like I was more tempting, more vital, than any meal. Never in my life had a man looked at me the way that Crew did.

"Okay," I whispered.

"Hungry?"

Oh, I was hungry. But considering he'd been in the emergency room today, I doubted I'd be satisfying that particular appetite. "You should eat."

"I'll share." He winked, then nodded for me to take a chair.

So I divided his cheeseburger in half while he grabbed two waters from the fridge.

"I saw your mom today," he said as he ate a fry.

"At the hospital?"

"Yeah. She made me wear this sling."

"Sounds like Mom." I smiled. "I'm surprised she was there today. She usually doesn't work in the ER or on the weekends. Someone must have called in sick."

Mom was one of the senior nurses at the hospital, having worked there for decades. She'd taken the job after moving here with Dad. They'd met in college—well, while she'd been in college. Dad had barely finished high school.

He'd grown up in Penny Ridge, and after graduating, he'd traveled some, mostly to ski towns across the country. When he'd needed money, he'd taken jobs at ski resorts.

During Mom's senior year of nursing school at University of Colorado, while she'd been in clinical training, he'd been working at Breckenridge. Mom and a few of her girlfriends had taken a weekend ski trip and that's where they'd met.

Dad always said he'd seen Mom and it had been love at first sight. For a brief time, his obsession for her had outweighed his obsession for skiing.

Mom had fallen for his special brand of madness—that's

how she referred to Dad's lifestyle. Maddening. But the timing had worked in Dad's favor. It had been toward the end of the season, and when the resort had closed for the spring, he'd moved to Boulder to be closer to Mom.

Would they have gotten married if they'd met earlier in the year? Or would she have broken it off once she'd realized she'd always be second place to a pair of sticks he strapped to his feet?

Mom had gotten pregnant with River, so they'd married and moved to Penny Ridge to be closer to Dad's parents.

Grandma and Grandpa adored Mom so much, there were times when it seemed like she was their child, not Dad. Even after the divorce, they'd sided with her. They had her over for dinner once a week.

Mom and Dad had stayed married until I'd graduated high school and moved away to Fort Collins for school. When she'd called me to tell me she was asking him for a divorce, I'd sighed and said it was about damn time.

Mom was better off single. That way, Dad couldn't disappoint her. She had her job. She'd been overjoyed when I'd moved home after graduating with my business degree. The only anxiety in her life now was caused by my brother.

"How's your dad doing?" Crew asked.

"Good. I think." I shrugged. "I don't hear from him often, especially in the winter. He's living in Denver."

"Sorry about the divorce."

"I'm not. It's better for Mom, you know?"

He gave me a sad smile. "Yeah."

Crew and River had been best friends in high school, and Crew had been at the house more than once when we'd walked through the door and found a note that Dad had scribbled down before leaving town for some event or function or *killer snow.*

"River said he's living with your mom now. Trying to help her out since your dad is gone."

I choked on a fry.

"Whoa." Crew smacked my back as I coughed.

My eyes welled with tears as I tried to work that bite clear, then swallow it correctly this time. I guzzled some water, then caught my breath. "Sorry."

"You okay?"

I nodded. "Fine. Wrong pipe."

After another drink, I sighed. "River isn't helping Mom. He's sleeping in his old bedroom, mooching off her groceries because he hasn't had a job since this summer. And the money he does have, he spends on weed."

"Really? He said he was working construction."

"He was. Until he got fired for showing up late every single day and slacking off while he was there."

Crew's forehead furrowed. "Oh. I didn't realize."

"He was living in an apartment with another guy but he kept missing rent, so the other guy kicked him out. Mom let him move home."

"Is he trying to find another job?"

"In the winter? Doubtful."

River had enough money for a season lift ticket, gas to get him up the mountain and weed. That money came from Mom. He'd beg and guilt her into twenty bucks here and there, much like he'd convince me to let him charge lunches to my employee account.

"Is he doing any competitions where he could win some prize money?" Crew asked.

"I don't know. I sort of stopped asking."

"Why?"

I sighed, toying with a fry. "Last year and the year before, he was doing quite a few competitions. He did okay. He's good. But not good enough. Every time I brought it up, he'd get mad. He'd have an excuse about an injury or the slopestyle course was set up wrong or he couldn't get enough training time on a halfpipe because there isn't one up here."

"That'll be remedied soon enough," Crew said. "He should be able to do a lot of training here."

That wasn't the crux of the problem, something Crew probably suspected given how often he'd ridden with River, but I didn't voice my thoughts. "I hope so."

A vibration sounded from the couch before I could dive into my half of his burger. "Want me to get that for you?" I asked.

"Nope. I'm done with calls today."

"Are you getting bombarded?"

"It's a mess, but whatever. We'll deal."

The media was likely in a frenzy about what had happened on the lift today. No doubt the videos had been splashed across every social media platform. There were probably some with me in them too.

Attention I did not want. Hiding out in this room for a night, a day, a week, suddenly seemed like a really great idea.

We finished eating, Crew polishing off the fries I hadn't, and when the plate was clear, I carried the tray to the hall-way, where housekeeping would pick it up later.

"I'd better get going," I said, picking up my coat from the back of the chair. "I just wanted to check on you."

"What if you didn't?"

"Didn't what?"

He stepped closer, using his good hand to brush a lock of hair off my temple. "Leave."

"You should rest. You're hurt."

He leaned in, brushing his mouth over mine. "I'll rest. After you do all the work."

A smile tugged at my lips. Damn it, I was weak. My resolve was disintegrating like a snowflake in summer. But before the last shreds of self-control vanished, there was a question I had to ask first.

"Who was that woman you were with at the lodge earlier?"

Crew straightened, his eyebrows coming together. "Marianne? She's my assistant."

His assistant. What exactly were her duties?

Before I could ask, the confusion on his face vanished and he smirked. "Were you jealous of Marianne?"

"You seemed . . . tight. We didn't exactly define what is going on here but I have no desire to be the other woman."

Crew's smirk widened until he was holding back laughter. "I love Marianne. She's one of my best friends in the world. She's a beautiful, intelligent and wonderful person."

Wasn't he supposed to be making me feel better?

"She's also the closest thing I have to a sister."

Phew. The relief on my face must have been noticeable because Crew lifted his good hand again, this time to cup my cheek. "I really like that you were jealous. Now that attitude you threw me makes sense."

"I don't throw attitude."

He chuckled. "Sure you don't."

I rolled my eyes. "Any 'attitude' is because I don't want people to know about us. Marianne included."

Crew brought his fingers to my lips, drawing an imaginary line across them. Then he did the same to his own. "Secret's safe here, baby."

Baby. Yeah, I liked it. A lot.

Without another word, he strolled past me for the bedroom, leaving me in the living area to decide.

Stay. Or leave.

It was only for another week. One more week of sex in this hotel room. One more week of Crew. Then he'd leave and my life would return to normal.

I'd spend my evenings at home, watching Bravo or reading, instead of slipping through the rear employee entrance and taking the stairs two at a time before anyone caught me sneaking into the Vista Suite.

"Raven." Just my name. That was all it took to squash any lingering indecision.

In the bedroom, Crew was on his bed, propped up against the pillows.

My mouth went dry. Even fully clothed, there was no sexier man on the planet. Granted, those thermals didn't leave much to the imagination. Certainly not the growing bulge between his legs.

The room was mostly dark except for a muted glow coming from the windows. It cast his face in shadows, the light picking up the lines of his cheekbones and the corners of his jaw.

With my foot, I closed the door as I entered the room, not because I was worried that we'd be interrupted, but because it was like closing out the world. Crew was mine, if only for another week, and I was keeping him to myself.

He smiled, flashing that dimple, then lifted his uninjured arm, crooking a finger.

I stood beside the bed, tugging up the hem of my sweatshirt to whip it over my head and send it sailing to the floor.

Crew's Adam's apple bobbed as he took in the black, lace bralette I'd put on this morning. "This fucking shoulder."

"Does it hurt?"

"No, but it means I can't do all the things I want to do to you tonight."

I smiled, unbuttoning my pants. They fell from my hips as I shimmied out of my own thermal layer, leaving me in nothing but my panties and bra.

He sat up straight, reaching for the clip of his sling.

But my hands beat him to the clasp, undoing it and easing it off his arm. "Let me do it."

Crew's gaze stayed locked on my face as I worked up his shirt, taking it off his good arm first before dragging it over his head. Then I eased it over his bad shoulder and tossed it aside.

Those abs would be my undoing. My fingertips trailed over the washboard muscles, dropping toward that line of hair that disappeared beneath the waistband of his pants.

He took my hand, like he was about to stop me. But then he smirked and brought it to his arousal. "See what you do to me?"

My pulse jumped. My core throbbed. I tugged at the waistband of his pants, waiting for him to lift his hips so I could yank them down those bulky thighs. "I like this. You at my mercy."

"Raven, if you think I haven't been at your mercy from the beginning, then you haven't been paying attention."

My breath caught in my throat. The playfulness I'd had with him during all our nights before was gone, his tone serious.

Except we couldn't be serious.

I didn't need serious.

When he walked away, it couldn't be with my heart.

Maybe he could tell I was about to remind him that this was a casual fling because he reached out and hooked a finger in the band of my panties, tugging them as a warning. Either they came off or they'd be shredded.

"Don't you dare," I said, leaning in to take his mouth.

He let me play, dragging my tongue across his lower lip and nipping at the top. I stayed beside the bed, keeping my distance, until he let out a frustrated growl, like what he wanted was to toss me onto the bed and pin my hands above my head, except it would hurt.

I smiled against his mouth, working free the clasp on my bra. Then I shoved down my panties and straddled his thighs, letting my hands roam across the strong plain of his chest.

Crew's body was incredible. Every time we were together I found a new muscle or line to appreciate. Tonight, it was those arms. Those broad, strong arms.

The arms that had saved a kid today.

I reached for the nightstand, taking a condom from the drawer. Then I took Crew's cock in my fist, earning a groan as I sheathed his length.

I'd never put a condom on a man before. I'd never done a

lot of the things that I'd done with Crew. But there was something about him that made my inhibitions vanish.

If he wanted to fuck me in the shower, we fucked in the shower. If he wanted to take me from behind and pull my hair, I let him pull. Hard.

There were no fumbling hands. No awkward movements. We came together as lovers perfectly, his intensity matching my own.

And Crew, an athlete with a body built for thrills and sin, knew exactly what he was doing in the bedroom.

He leaned forward, searching for my mouth, those abs bunching. But I shied away, planting a hand over his heart to shove him back against the pillows and headboard.

Tonight, I was going to watch. I wanted to study his face as he came apart.

"That's how you want it?" He smirked.

"Yeah." I rocked against him, my center already soaked and ready.

"Good." Crew's deep voice filled the room. "Then take it."

I wrapped my fist around him, his cock like steel, then dragged it through my folds, positioning him at my entrance. Inch by inch, I sank down on him, my body stretching to fit his size as a rush of pleasure cascaded through my veins. It was fire. It was magic. It was so fucking right.

"Raven." Crew closed his eyes, his jaw clenching. That throat bobbed again, so I leaned in, dragging my tongue over his skin. Tasting. Breathing in that heady scent of sex and Crew.

I rocked my hips, pressing forward for some friction against my clit. "Yes."

"Ride me, baby." He leaned closer, nipping at my ear. "Fuck me. Use my cock and make yourself come."

My pussy clenched.

Then I did exactly as he'd ordered. I rode him, up and down, over and over, bringing us together until we were both panting and covered in a sheen of sweat. My orgasm was close. So close.

I closed my eyes, wanting to delay it for just a little while longer. To soak up this feeling—this toe-curling, mind-numbing feeling and the sheer intensity of this connection for another moment.

Crew had other ideas. He cupped a breast in his palm, pinching a nipple between his fingers.

I hissed, riding faster.

He jackknifed forward, claiming my mouth. Then he thrust his hips up, sending his cock deeper, and I shattered.

My back arched, my cries filling the room as I pulsed around him. His arm snaked around my waist, holding me to him as I detonated, lost to the world, only coherent enough to hear his groan and the trembling in his muscles as he succumbed to his own release.

Crew collapsed against the headboard, his chest heaving as he breathed.

I sagged against him, burrowing into his neck. "Wow."

"Fuck, Raven," he panted, bringing a hand to the back of my head. Then his lips were at my temple, dropping a kiss to my hair.

How did it always get better? We should have had one boring night by now, right? But even missionary sex had rocked my world. Part of me was grateful. The other part dreaded what was to come.

It would be easier to walk away each night if the sex was dwindling. If the addiction was beginning to fade, not brighten.

I dragged in one more breath of that spicy, fresh scent, listening to his heart beat, then I sat up and climbed off the bed. My legs were wobbly as I pulled on my panties. My base layer was tight and my skin too damp but I managed to get it on enough to hike up my snow pants.

With my bralette shoved in a pocket, I yanked on my sweater.

Crew's gaze was waiting. "You know, you could stay."

"No, I can't. I need to go feed my cat." A lie. My cat had an automatic feeder and couldn't have cared less if I was around the house. But I had yet to let myself fall asleep in this room. And I wasn't starting tonight.

Most of my rules I'd broken, but this one, I held fast.

He sighed, making no move to leave the bed.

"Are you going to be okay?" I asked.

"Yeah. I'm going to crash. Be good as new by morning."

"Need me to help you put the sling on again?"

He shook his head. "I'll manage."

Meaning he wasn't going to wear that sling at all. But I wasn't his nurse, so I bit back a comment that would have sounded too much like my mother. "Okay." I bent to give him a quick kiss, then walked for the door.

I didn't let myself look back at the bed and the tempting man lying on the sheets.

One more week. We'd have fun for one more week.

Then I'd say goodbye to Crew Madigan.

CHAPTER NINE

CREW

Nights with Raven were a favorite. But a lazy morning with her in my bed was an experience I wouldn't forget.

If I couldn't be outside with a board on my feet, there was no place I'd rather be than between the sheets with a beautiful woman. Especially this woman.

Raven was on her stomach, her arms curled around a pillow as I lay beside her, propped up on my good arm to trace lines up and down her bare spine.

It had been five days since the chairlift incident. For the first time since we'd started this fling, Raven had come to my room in the light of day.

She'd arrived this morning before breakfast bearing coffee and sandwiches from Black Diamond Coffee downtown.

The food, the coffee, was waiting in the other room, no doubt cold. I'd answered the door fresh out of the shower, wearing only a towel. Raven's gaze had raked over my bare chest, and instead of eating, we'd spent the past hour delivering each other orgasms.

"You could have just stayed last night," I said. "Would have saved you a trip to town."

"My cat would scratch your eyes out for that sort of talk."

I chuckled, my fingertips circling on her smooth skin. "What do you normally do on your days off?"

"Ride. Sometimes here. But usually I head to Woodward at Copper."

"For the pipe and park?"

"Yes. And a change of scenery. Different runs."

"And what about the summers?"

"I work."

"Where?"

"Here. Where else? Just because there isn't a ski school doesn't mean there aren't jobs to be done. I run the lifts for the mountain bike trails. I'll help around the lodge or hotel to prepare for the upcoming season. Most of the winter staff leave, so the rest of us pitch in to do whatever is necessary."

I should have known that would be her answer. My parents had been the ones to manage the summer activities. As a kid, there hadn't been many, but even then, we'd had a lift going on the weekends so people could take their mountain bikes to the top and ride down. We'd get local hikers who wanted to explore. Plus, the hotel was open year-round.

"Ava has been pushing this as a destination venue for late-spring and summer weddings," Raven said. "Last she told me, we're fully booked for this upcoming summer."

"I can't say that I'm surprised."

The more time I spent around Ava, the more I saw that ambition Weston had warned me about. But it was more than just determination. Ava said *we* when she spoke about the resort.

This was her home now. Her mountain.

Raven spoke that way too. They were each invested here. This wasn't just a job, it was family.

That was what Mom had always loved about Madigan Mountain. She'd married Dad but this place had stolen her heart.

She would have loved what it was becoming. She'd have loved the potential in the air. She'd have loved to see her sons working alongside their wives to build upon the family legacy.

My heart twisted.

I missed my mom. I'd missed her for years, but being here made me miss her just that much more.

"Are you okay?" Raven lifted off her pillow. "Is it your shoulder?"

"Yeah," I lied, swallowing the pain in my chest. "It'll be all right." My shoulder was getting better. The initial ache was gone and the stiffness was beginning to fade.

"I forgot to ask last night. What did the doctor say at your appointment yesterday?"

She'd forgotten to ask because we'd been too busy in this very bed. "Just to keep doing what I'm doing. Rest. Ice. Ibuprofen. But I think it's healing faster than the last time I tweaked it."

Not really. It felt a lot like the last injury, but I was going to pretend it was better because I needed my shoulder to be better. So here I was, pretending.

"That's a good thing."

I leaned in to drop a kiss on her sweet mouth. "You get credit. I think it's because of the sex."

"Definitely the sex." Raven licked my bottom lip.

I rolled on top of her, flicking the sheet out of the way. Then I kissed her again, savoring the slide of my tongue against hers. The way her fingertips dug into my skin as she worked her way down my shoulders to my ass.

My cock stirred, ready for another round, but I tore my lips away. "We used the last condom this morning."

"We did? Damn."

I kissed away the pout on her lips. "I'd planned to head to town this morning and get more. But someone surprised me with breakfast."

"We should probably eat that breakfast."

I hummed but didn't move. I let her feel my arousal and gave myself a minute to memorize what it felt like to have her beneath me. And then I kissed her again, breaking free before we got too carried away.

"You're a tease," she said, sliding out of bed and yanking the sheet with her to wrap around her chest.

I propped up on an elbow as her gaze wandered across my naked form. "I could call the front desk. See if the gift shop sells condoms."

"Don't you dare." She pointed at my nose. "The last thing I need is a bunch of gossip flying around the hotel and the front desk clerks trying to figure out who Crew Madigan is screwing."

I smirked, getting out of bed and reaching for the towel she'd ripped off me earlier. With it wrapped around my hips, I followed her into the living room, taking a seat at the table while she popped our sandwiches and coffees into the microwave.

"Can I ask you something?" I waited for her to sit and give me a nod. "When we were in high school, did you ever have a crush on me?"

"No."

"Really?" Most of the girls had had a crush on me.

"Does that bruise your ego, babe?"

"Yes," I admitted with a laugh. "Totally."

She laughed too, taking a bite and washing it down with her latte. "Not sorry."

"Was it because I was River's friend?" Maybe she'd seen me in some platonic way as her brother's buddy.

"No. You were just . . . Crew. Always snowboarding."

"So you hated me for my sport." I slapped a hand to my chest, feigning a wounded heart. "Ouch."

"Hate is a strong word. I just never saw you that way. And maybe, looking back, I didn't let myself crush on you. That was a time when Dad was gone more often than not, spending his life skiing instead of with his family. You were that way too."

"Fair enough."

Rowdy was a cool guy and a hell of a skier. But he had room for improvement when it came to being a father. Mine did too.

"Okay, then if not me, who did you have a crush on?"

Her face flushed. "Owen Nelson."

"What?" My jaw dropped. "The quarterback. You're fucking kidding me."

Raven giggled. "No. While the other girls were drawing your name in hearts, I was all about Owen Nelson."

"Get out." I pointed for the door, earning another laugh, so carefree and musical I'd razz her about Owen every damn day to hear it again.

Owen had been the closest thing to an archenemy. Raven hadn't been the only girl in high school to have a crush on him, no matter that he'd been an arrogant asswipe, always bragging about football and how one day he'd be playing in the NFL. He'd picked on smaller kids when no one else was looking. He'd cheated at tests because otherwise he probably wouldn't have passed.

But the guy knew how to throw a football and he hadn't exactly been ugly.

I shook my head. "I can't believe this. Football? Really?"

"Cliché, I know."

"So while I had a crush on you, you were drooling over Nelson."

Her smile dropped. "You had a crush on me?"

"Uh, yeah. You knew that."

She blinked. "No, I didn't."

"Huh. I figured that was why you always ignored me. Because you knew I had a crush on you, so you just pretended it—me—didn't exist."

"I, um, no. I didn't know." She swallowed hard, dropping her gaze. "Why?"

"Because you pretended I didn't exist."

She rolled her eyes, a gesture so adorable I'd say just about anything to earn it. "Seriously."

"Then because you were—are—beautiful."

"Thank you." Her cheeks flushed as she took a sip of her coffee.

"So did anything ever happen with Owen Nelson?"

"No. He was oblivious to my crush."

"Poor bastard."

Her eyes danced as she smiled. "I got my chance with a football player. I dated a linebacker at Colorado State. We met at a party and dated for a few weeks. Slept with him. Then he dumped me."

"Motherfucker. Who was it?" I had this instant urge to track the prick down and kick his ass. Not just for hurting her, but for touching her.

"No one important. Though I like that look on you. A little jealousy and rage. Very sexy, Madigan."

I shot her a scowl and chomped a bite of my sandwich.

"After him and a few other spectacular boyfriend failures, I decided maybe it was best for my heart if I stayed away from all athletes, regardless of the sport. I'm holding out hope to be swept off my feet by a clumsy nerd."

"A clumsy nerd. What are we talking about here? Black-framed glasses. Pressed khakis. Pocket protectors."

"Exactly." That beautiful smile widened, brighter than the pure sunlight streaming in through the windows.

Christ, she was stunning.

"What did you study?" I asked, wanting to know anything and everything about her life these past twelve years.

"Business. I figured it would be a versatile degree, and I wasn't really sure what I wanted to do after I graduated."

"What brought you home?"

"Summer. My roommates all had jobs starting, so we moved out of our house. I came home to stay with Mom for a couple of weeks before figuring out my next step. My first night back, we went to The Cheese for a burger. Your dad was there and he came over to say hello. He said he was hiring, and if I wanted a temporary gig while I was job hunting, he'd find a spot for me on the staff. That was six years ago. I've been here ever since."

"Not so temporary."

Huh. Dad was the reason she was here. I wasn't sure what to think about that, how to feel, so I focused on finishing my sandwich and draining my coffee while Raven did the same. Then I cleaned up the table and tossed out the trash.

"If you had a crush on me in high school, why didn't you ever act on it?" she asked.

"River. He would have kicked my ass."

"He still would."

I sighed, leaning against the counter. "Probably best this is a secret, then, right?"

"Probably," she whispered.

"I haven't been a great friend. I didn't realize he was struggling."

"It's not that he's struggling. He has just chosen not to grow up."

"Some might say the same about me."

She shook her head. "Doubtful."

"Regardless." I sighed. "I should have called him more." I should have called everyone more.

I'd been in such a damn rush to escape the pain trapped in Penny Ridge that I hadn't looked back. I'd driven a wedge between my brothers, my friends.

Raven gave me a sad smile. "The phone goes both ways, Crew."

"Yeah."

"You're here now."

"True." In twelve years, this was the most time I'd spent with my brothers. And River. "I did my best to forget this place. It was just too hard, you know?"

Raven stood from the chair, closing the distance between us. She rested her hands on my hips, staring up at me with those blue eyes that saw too much.

She knew about Mom. She knew that was the reason I'd left. But like always, she didn't push me to talk about it. Instead, she pressed her hand to my heart. "I get it. So does River."

I pulled her into my arms, dropping my cheek to her hair. "It's been strange being here. But not as hard as I'd thought. Part of that is because of you. So thanks."

"You're welcome." She burrowed deeper into my chest, her arms tightening around my waist.

God, it was easy with her. Confessions, feelings I'd buried ages ago, bubbled to the surface when Raven was around.

Everyone in my life was pulling me in different directions. Lewis. Marianne. Sydney. My coach, JR.

But Raven came with no expectations. No demands. Maybe the reason it was so easy to talk to her was because I could just be. She let me live in the moment and didn't push for what was to come.

So I held her tighter, not wanting to let go.

She melted, sinking into my chest, dropping her guard.

I dropped mine.

Something unlocked in my chest. Something foreign and strange. Something that I'd never felt with a woman before.

Like maybe I was exactly where I was supposed to be. Like maybe I should have made a move on Raven a long, long time ago.

The idea of letting her go, of walking away . . .

Fuck. This was casual. Temporary. There was no way I could stay in Penny Ridge. And she'd built her life here. This would come to an end, soon, and it was time I remembered this had almost run its course.

Raven felt my body stiffen because her arms unwound from my waist and she stood tall, clearing her throat. "I should probably go."

"Yeah." My voice sounded hoarse. "I promised my brothers I'd meet them at the peak lodge today for lunch."

"This, um"—she took a step away, then another, until she was out of reaching distance—"works better if we stick to what we're good at."

"Sex."

"Exactly." She nodded. "This is just sex."

That's what I'd wanted, wasn't it? We were hooking up before I headed out. Except for the first time, her reminding me of my own damn rule pissed me off. "It's great sex. Don't get me wrong. But yeah, just sex." There was an edge to my every word.

She narrowed her eyes, then swept past me for the bedroom.

I didn't trust myself to move, or I'd walk into that bedroom and show her just how much better this could be if we went beyond the sex. So I kept my feet rooted in place, listening as she pulled on her clothes.

Raven came out of the room wearing her boots, jeans and

coat. She went to the purse she'd tossed on the couch when she'd come in, digging out a hair tie. Then she smoothed away the tangled mess I'd created with my hands earlier.

With her hair in a ponytail and that purse slung over a shoulder, she walked by to leave.

"Raven." I still didn't move, but we couldn't end today like this, not when it had started so well.

She stopped, her hand stretched for the doorknob.

"Are you coming back tonight?" *Say yes.*

"Maybe."

Maybe? Oh, fuck that. I closed the distance between us in a flash, taking her face in my hands and slamming my mouth on hers.

She gasped, fighting me for a split second before she melted.

Raven always melted when I fluttered my tongue against hers.

And goddamn, I loved her taste. An addiction. This woman had become an addiction.

I slanted my mouth over hers, delving deep.

The kiss had an undercurrent of emotion, feelings we'd unlocked today. Or maybe I'd just been ignoring what had always been there.

I shoved those thoughts away and focused on one thing only. Kissing her until she was breathless. Changing her mind about tonight.

Raven was panting by the time I let her go. My cock was hard and aching behind my towel. I'd be in for a cold shower after she left. But it was worth it to stare down at her swollen lips and the pink in her cheeks.

"Are you coming back tonight?" I asked again.

She rolled her eyes.

"Yes."

CHAPTER TEN

RAVEN

"I can't stop!"

I whirled around just as a little girl zoomed my way, her arms straight out at her sides and her legs spread wide like she was trying to stop but her skis had other ideas. I shifted, bending to catch her by the waist before she could crash into the safety fence at the bottom of the bunny hill. "Whoa."

She used her mittened hand to shove her helmet higher as she looked up at me with wide eyes. "Whoa."

I laughed, making sure she was steady. "Remember to get your tips together. Pizza slice. And turn to slow down."

The girl nodded, then shuffled her skis forward to get back in line for another trip up the magic carpet—a conveyor belt that carried people to the top of the beginner's hill.

"Sorry, Raven." Kerry, a new instructor on my staff this year, came to a stop by my side. "She got away from me."

"Oh, it's fine. It happens." Even if the girl had crashed into me, it wouldn't have been the first time I'd been taken out by a six-year-old. Hazard of the job. "How's it going today?"

"Good," Kerry said. "I'm about to take them inside and get them ready for parent pickup."

"Great. See you later."

It was another busy Saturday on Madigan Mountain. It felt like minutes ago that I'd been pulling into the parking lot, a coffee in hand, ready to start the day. Then I'd blinked and the day was nearly over.

The classes had run smoothly today. Really, they'd run smoothly so far this season. Eventually, we'd have an issue. An injury. An angry parent. A lost kid. It was only a matter of time. But so far, the only drama had been Crew's chairlift heroics.

That was what the media had dubbed him.

Crew, the hero of Madigan Mountain.

To me, he was the man who'd stolen countless hours of my sleep. Not that I was complaining. Time was running out. I was soaking him in while I still could.

Last night, after I'd snuck out of his room, I'd gone home to shower and crash. Except I hadn't been able to shut off my brain. It had been that way for the past two days, ever since that moment the morning I'd brought him breakfast.

When I closed my eyes, I saw the look he'd given me that morning. I felt his arms holding me tight. I heard my own silent wish that it wouldn't end.

After tossing and turning until four, I'd finally given up and picked up my phone. I'd spent the predawn hours watching YouTube videos of Crew. Not just from last week's chairlift incident, but of his competitions and press interviews.

My favorite clip was from an event. A fellow competitor had taken a nasty crash, and the guy had been distraught, in tears as he'd hobbled away from the halfpipe.

Crew had pulled the guy aside, bending low so that the person videoing couldn't capture their conversation. I wasn't sure what he'd told that guy, but by the time Crew had given him a hug and slapped him on the back, that man's tears had vanished.

I liked that Crew had taken time to give someone hope. I liked that he'd rescued that kid on the chairlift at his own expense. I liked that he'd had a crush on me as a teenager.

But that was my problem, wasn't it?

I liked too much when it came to Crew.

Like he knew he was on my mind, he walked my way. Today's coat was a hunter green. He hadn't shaved in a few days and that thick stubble gave him a roguish edge. But he was missing something important.

"You're frowning," he said, coming to a stop in front of me.

"Why aren't you wearing your sling?"

He lowered his voice, stepping closer. "Worried about me, baby?"

Yes. "It's your body."

"Yeah. And you've got a thing for my body."

Truer words had never been spoken. I had a thing for everything Crew Madigan.

What would it have been like in high school if, instead of Owen Nelson, I'd crushed on Crew? Would we have dated? Would he have made a move, even though it would have pissed off River? Would he have still left after graduation?

"What are you thinking about?" he asked.

"Nothing," I lied. "Your sling?"

"Unnecessary." To demonstrate, he raised his arm, slowly rolling it in a circle.

I pursed my lips but let it go. "What are you doing today?"

"Meeting with Reed and Weston. We're going to take a look at the halfpipe."

My staff had been talking about the pipe at this morning's meeting. The construction team had spent weeks creating and shaping manmade snow for the feature. Even though we had plenty of natural snow around, manmade snow ensured there'd be no sticks or dirt clumps to create dangerous bumps in the walls that could trip up a rider.

That special snow was then built into a perfect U using special machines. The pipe dragon was my favorite of those machines, with its long arm of grooming blades that kept the vertical walls pristine and smooth. Maybe someday I'd learn how to operate the dragon. When my teaching days were over, I'd become a groomer.

"I heard it's finished," I said.

"Ready for testing, at least."

I narrowed my eyes. "But you're not testing it."

"Maybe I am."

"Crew," I warned.

"I'll take it easy." He held up a hand. "Promise."

"You're such a liar." I shook my head, holding back a laugh. "You don't know what that even means."

He chuckled, lifting a hand like he was going to brush a lock of hair away from my temple, something he did often behind the closed door of his suite. But then that hand dropped to his side.

We both remembered where we were standing, just outside the lodge with hundreds of people milling around.

I took a step away. So did Crew.

Just in time too. River walked up from behind Crew. "Hey, man. Ready?"

"Yeah." Crew nodded. "Just need to wait for Reed and Weston."

"'Kay." River jerked up his chin at me. "Hey. Working?"

"Yep." My brother understood the concept of work but was fuzzy on its execution. "How did your interview go yesterday?"

River shrugged. "Decided not to go."

"What?" I blinked. "You just didn't go?"

He scowled, shifting closer and lowering his voice. "I don't want to work for a landscaper, okay? Sitting behind the wheel of a truck, pushing snow around in the winter. Mowing other people's lawns in the summer. Why waste their time in an interview? Or mine?"

"Um, because you don't have a job."

"Just drop it, Raven." He glared. "Don't start on me, okay? I can't get a job right now anyway."

"Why?"

"I'm training."

"Oh." News to me. "Training for what?"

"Christ, what's with you today? Is this twenty questions or some shit?"

"Fine." I held up my hands. If River didn't want to talk about it, especially with Crew here, I wasn't going to push it.

But seriously, didn't he see the irony in his lifestyle? River was the first to criticize Dad for leeching off Mom during their marriage. Didn't he realize he was doing the exact same thing?

Dad frustrated River and me equally. When our parents had gotten divorced, he'd been relieved too. Mom finally had her chance to live her own life and stop waiting around for a man who was never going to make her his priority.

Now River was filling Dad's shoes.

"I need to get back to work," I said, but before I could walk away, Reed and Weston joined our huddle.

"Hey, guys," Reed said. "Thanks for doing this today."

"No problem." Crew dipped his chin.

"I thought for sure you'd have a board." Weston smirked. "Now I owe Reed twenty bucks."

He started to dig into his pocket, but Crew held up a hand, grinning as he glanced around, then pointed over my shoulder.

We all turned to see Crew's assistant trudging over with a helmet in one hand and a board tucked under the other.

Marianne's expression was murderous and aimed at her boss. "For the record, I think this is a stupid idea, and if you break yourself today, I'm not going to the hospital with you this time."

I think I liked Marianne.

"I'll be fine." Crew shot her a frown, then reached to take his board. It was a different board than the one he'd been using before the chairlift accident. This was a Burton board, one I suspected he used specifically for a pipe rather than freestyle on the slopes.

"Welcome back, Marianne," Reed said. "How was your trip?"

"It was good." She nodded. "Thanks for having me."

"Anytime. Raven, you should come with us." Reed jerked his chin toward the lodge. "Get your board. Test it out."

"Oh, uh—"

"Yeah, tag along," Weston said. "You're always leaving to train at Copper. Now you don't have to."

Damn it. I was going to kill Ava and Callie.

My time training at other resorts wasn't something I broadcast widely. My hope of entering a few competitions this year was something I hadn't shared with many people, including my brother. But earlier this fall, we'd had a girls' night and the wine had been flowing. Halley had been there too and my plans for this winter had slipped out.

Clearly, I should have told them not to tell their men.

"Aren't you working though?" River asked. Of course he wouldn't want me to come. This was his special invitation, and I was encroaching.

"Boss's orders," Reed said. "Grab your board. We'll take snowmobiles over. It'll be faster."

"Actually, I don't have a board with me today," I lied. There was one stashed in my office closet. But River wanted the spotlight. I was too busy and tired to tiptoe around his fragile ego.

"Then just come along to watch," Crew said. "It'll be fun."

Every gaze was on me, so I sighed and nodded. "Okay."

Weston led the way toward the helicopter hangar with the rest of us falling into step.

River kept pace with Reed, talking to him about the runs he'd been on today. Crew and Marianne walked side by side.

And I trailed behind them all, wishing I'd had a better excuse to get out of this.

Crew glanced over his shoulder, giving me a small smile. "Good?" he mouthed.

I nodded, plodding along with the group.

A row of snowmobiles waited beside the massive shop that sat adjacent to Weston's helicopter hangar. Both buildings were huge, but they'd been tucked away from the main lodge so that they didn't obstruct the view. The scent of grease and metal filled my nose. Water melted off the snowcats and dripped to the floor with soft pings.

Weston plucked four sets of keys from a rack on the wall, bringing one over. "You'd better take your own machine. In case you need to come back."

"Thanks." I headed to a black Polaris, straddling the seat. Then I waited for the others to get seated, taking the last place in line as we headed out. The rev of the engines rent the air as we made our way to the halfpipe.

I hadn't been here in weeks, not since they'd had the initial channel dug and were building snow up along the walls. When it came into view, my jaw dropped.

"Wow." My voice was lost in the buzz of the engine.

The walls had to be over twenty feet high. They'd been marked with blue lines that gave athletes a visual for landings. This was Olympic sized—something that shouldn't have surprised me, knowing Reed. He wanted to compete with Copper Mountain and Park City. So he'd built a contender.

We rolled along the sides, going to the top before parking. Everyone climbed off, marveling at the pipe.

Oh, how I wanted to ride. I should have brought a board,

whether River was here or not. But he'd pout if I outshined him today. Which was ridiculous considering Crew was here.

Did River care that Crew was a better snowboarder? Or was it just his younger sister he loathed showing him up? Regardless, it was probably better for me to simply watch. Thanksgiving was coming, and if River was sulking, it would make for an awkward holiday with Mom.

"This is sweet," Crew said, coming to stand by my side. "Nice job, guys."

"Do the honors." Reed clapped him on the shoulder, then pointed toward the lip.

A smile, breathtaking and free, spread across Crew's handsome face. God, he was something with that smile. Was it strange how much I loved his straight, white teeth? I'd never found a man's teeth attractive before, but maybe it was because I knew how those teeth felt when they nibbled at the inside of my thighs.

My cheeks flamed and I shook my head, willing thoughts of naked Crew out of my head.

He jogged up the ramp on the side of the pipe, then dropped his board to strap it on.

We all followed, watching as he clipped on his helmet and secured his goggles.

"Do me a favor and don't hurt yourself," Marianne said, holding up her phone to take some pictures. "Lewis will strangle me."

"No promises." He smirked, then he was gone in a snap, popping up the board's tail and diving over the edge as he dropped in, taking a perfect forty-five-degree angle toward the other wall.

Crew flew up the opposite side, doing any icy slash off the lip. The pipe was soft from the afternoon sun, making the snow perfect for that move. He twisted and a spray of snow shot in the air before he came flying toward our side again.

After a twist, he raced our direction again, his knees bent, ready to pop off the lip and shoot into the air. He flew, reaching down to grab his board with one hand while the other stretched in the air.

It was an easy frontside air maneuver, probably a trick he'd done a thousand times. But something swelled in my chest. Pride. Maybe relief. Definitely awe, because I was watching a champion take the first ride down his family's superpipe. *History*.

"We should have brought champagne," Reed said.

All eyes were locked on Crew as he did more of the same. Simple tricks until, toward the bottom, he tossed in a Cab 360. Then he was out, slowing to a stop at the bottom, turning to look up the pipe and at the rest of us standing in wonder.

"Now that was awesome," Weston said. "I'll go get him."

River stepped forward, ready to take his own run. He nudged his elbow against mine. "You're wishing you had brought your board, huh?"

"Yeah," I admitted.

"Too bad." He smirked, then dropped in, following the same line as Crew.

Later. I'd have my chance later.

It didn't take long for Weston to bring Crew up on a snowmobile.

"See, Marianne?" He threw an arm around her shoulders. "I didn't get hurt."

She scoffed. "Yet."

"Glad you're back," he said. "How was everything at home?"

Home.

For some reason, that word hit me like a slap.

Crew had a home. He was leaving. He was leaving *me*.

"Guess who I bumped into at the airport?" she asked. "Mia."

"Oh." He blew out a long breath. "How was she?"

"Good. She asked about you."

"That's nice." He gave her a tight smile.

Was Mia an ex? Maybe a former assistant? Did Crew only hire women whose names started with *M*?

"Why aren't you wearing your sling?" Marianne asked.

"I'm good. Stop worrying about me. I don't need the damn sling."

"Stubborn," she mumbled. "Wear the sling. At least until we get home and you can meet with Dr. Williams."

"Mari—"

"Please. Just humor me."

He sighed. "Fine."

He'd wear the sling. For her. That stung too.

"I made an appointment with you the Monday after Thanksgiving," she told him.

"I don't think—"

"You're going. I will drag your ass there myself if I have to, but you are going."

From beside me, Reed chuckled. "They argue like a married couple."

"She's my work wife," Crew teased, setting down his board and strapping it on.

"Speaking of work, I'm going to take some pictures." Marianne raised her phone, then set off down the pipe, making her way toward the bottom.

"I should do the same," Reed said, holding up a finger for Crew. "Don't go yet."

He jogged away, leaving Crew and me alone. He stretched his hand out, brushing the back of my glove. "Are you coming to my room tonight?"

"Maybe." That *maybe* normally turned into a yes when he kissed me. But he couldn't kiss me now.

"You could come earlier. We could order in dinner. Hang out."

"What about Marianne?"

He leaned closer, his lips dangerously close to my ear. "She can find her own food."

"We'll see." I inched away.

"What's wrong?"

"Nothing."

"It's just a dinner, Raven."

A dinner that would inevitably lead to sex. That wasn't just a dinner.

That was a date.

"When are you leaving?" I asked.

"In a hurry to get rid of me?"

"When?"

He hesitated, dropping those dazzling brown eyes. "Probably tomorrow."

Tomorrow. It was over. We were over.

"Will you come over tonight?"

So much of me wanted to say yes. To have one last night in the Vista Suite. But that would mean a goodbye. I wasn't sure I had the strength to say it.

Or hear it.

"I need to get back to work." I walked down the ramp, my heart pounding and my throat clogged.

Tomorrow. He was leaving tomorrow. He was going home.

My footsteps were shaky as I returned to my snowmobile, passing Reed with his camera along the way. I kept moving, eyes trained forward. But when I reached the sled, my resolve weakened.

I turned, for one last look, just in time to see Crew drop into the halfpipe.

His second ride was much like his first. Easy. Natural. Artwork.

He was meant to be a champion. He was meant for a life beyond Penny Ridge.

CHAPTER ELEVEN

CREW

"Are we leaving today?" Marianne stood in the hallway outside my room, her hands on her hips. "Because I'm not packing. Again. Just for you to change your mind. Again."

"Uh . . ." I rubbed the back of my neck. "One more day?"

She huffed and marched down the hallway, retreating toward her own room.

"Hey, I'm training. I basically have my own halfpipe."

She slowed just enough to shoot me a glare over her shoulder, then rounded the corner and disappeared toward her room.

Marianne was anxious to get home. She was anxious to get *me* home.

But I'd given her every excuse I could dream up to delay our exit.

Sunday morning, when I should have been packing my bags, I'd told her I wasn't feeling well. Not entirely a lie. My stomach had been in a knot after Raven hadn't come to the suite the night before. I'd wanted to stick around and find out why she'd been upset at the halfpipe. Why she'd stayed away.

Except when I'd gone to find her at the ski school, she'd been missing. That, or avoiding me. The same had happened yesterday morning. I hadn't gone to look for her yet today, but I would soon. I wasn't holding my breath I'd actually find her.

Where was she? Was she really going to let me leave without a goodbye? What sort of bullshit was that?

Didn't I at least deserve a farewell?

Yes. Yes, I did. So I'd stayed in Penny Ridge, delaying my whole fucking life because of a goddamn woman.

"Fuck." I was losing my shit.

It wasn't like I could even call Raven because I didn't have her number. If I asked Reed or Weston or River for it, that would reveal too much. So here I was, practically glued to the suite's windows, in hopes that I'd catch a glimpse of her silky black hair.

At least there was the halfpipe. That was the only good thing about sticking around. Like I'd told Marianne, it was mine to use exclusively this week.

Reed had decided to make a big splash of its public opening. Ava had been teasing it on social media with photos Reed had taken of me on Saturday. I had until this upcoming weekend before I had to share.

The new lift that fed the terrain park and pipe was up and running too. Reed had designated a couple of staff members to operate it for me each day, basically rolling out the red carpet.

My brothers hadn't brought it up again, but their offer lingered in the back of my mind. Could I live here? Train here? Retire here and help them run the mountain?

Wait. Why was I even thinking about this? I'd just promised Marianne we'd leave. Park City was home.

I shook my head and strode toward the closet, taking out a coat and shrugging it on.

No, I couldn't live here. Being in Penny Ridge was easier now than it had been at first, but I had a life in Utah. Friends. Favorite restaurants. A routine.

It was time to head out. Tomorrow. With or without a goodbye from Raven.

So I snagged my board and helmet, then left the room, heading to Marianne's. I knocked, texting River as I waited for her to answer.

heading out tomorrow. on the mountain today if you want to meet up for a beer

It was only nine. I doubted he was awake yet, but I wanted to see him before I left.

Marianne ripped the door open with that same frown from earlier.

"Tomorrow. I promise, we'll leave tomorrow."

"Okay." Her shoulders relaxed. "I'm ready to sleep in my own bed."

"Yeah, me too," I lied. The hotel bed was hard to beat, especially when Raven was in it. "I'm going to head up. Do a few runs."

"Want company?" Marianne was a good snowboarder, though she didn't crave it like I did. She didn't need it like oxygen.

"Do you want to come?"

"Not really. I was hoping to steal the Wagon and head downtown to explore."

"Take the day off. Do whatever you want. Shop. Hit the spa and charge it to my card."

Her eyes perked up. "You might regret that."

I chuckled. "Probably. Let's plan to meet tomorrow morning at seven."

"I'll be ready." She nodded. "Have fun. Take it easy."

"Yes, boss."

She smiled as I winked and headed for the elevator.

My shoulder was feeling remarkably good, considering how badly it had hurt after hanging from that chairlift. Maybe it was a sign that my body liked Colorado. Or maybe I'd just become numb to the pain.

Dr. Williams would no doubt list my various injuries and their long-term complications, but for now, ignorance was bliss. And besides, contrary to Marianne's beliefs, I was taking it easy. I took trips through the terrain park, testing every obstacle and the overall flow. And when I was in the pipe, I stuck to simple tricks.

This didn't even feel like training. The past few days here had been . . . fun. I loved my job. I loved competing. But there was something about doing whatever I wanted, whenever I wanted, that had recharged my batteries.

The elevator chimed before the doors slid open. The hotel was quiet as I crossed the lobby, heading for the exit. I pulled down my goggles from my helmet, shielding my eyes from the glare of the morning sun reflecting off the fresh snow.

Filling my lungs with the mountain air, I headed for

Chair Nine. There was no line yet, being too early and a weekday. Every other chair had one or two people on it and I recognized a few faces, employees enjoying a day off.

"Hey." I jerked up my chin at the lift operator as I stepped onto the loading line.

"Oh, hey, Crew." He was the guy who'd loaded me and Dad with that kid. "How's the shoulder?"

"All good."

"That was cool what you did that day, saving that kid."

"Glad it worked out."

Thankfully, the media circus had died down. According to Marianne, the videos were losing momentum, though they'd live forever on the internet. They'd likely resurface before the X Games, but for now, I was ignoring them. I hadn't watched a single clip and had no plans to change that.

By some miracle, I'd managed to convince my team not to use the accident as an opportunity for press. There'd be no talk shows. No interviews. And Lewis was ecstatic that no one had sued us.

As the chair swung toward me, I sank into the seat. "See ya 'round."

The operator raised a hand. "See ya."

I soaked in the quiet solitude on the ride up. It was rare I had alone time on a mountain. Maybe that was why I was having such a good time.

But tomorrow, it was back to reality. I'd have to say some goodbyes today. Reed and Ava. Weston, Callie and Sutton.

Dad?

We hadn't spoken much since the accident. He'd taken the hint and left me alone. I couldn't avoid him forever, but . . . *next time*. Next time I visited, I'd take Dad up on his offer for dinner. I'd get to know Melody. I'd work up the courage to return to my childhood home.

Next time.

When the chair reached the top of the lift, I made my way down a connecting run to the newest quad with heated seats that took me to the top.

The summit was breathtaking. The morning sunshine cast golden rays over the peaks in the distance. Tufts of white had settled in the nearby valleys but the sky itself was a clear, cloudless blue.

That blue was the same color as Raven's eyes. I doubted I'd be able to see a clear sky again and not think of her eyes.

Why the hell would she avoid me? What had I done?

Chances were, I wasn't going to find out.

I took a moment to appreciate the view, staring miles and miles into the distance, then picked my path, a run that had become a part of my daily routine. A warm-up that stretched all the way to the base.

Normally, I only did one warm-up before heading to the terrain park and halfpipe. But today, I opted for two, riding all the way to the base to take the long chair ride up again, enjoying the solitude of one last day on Madigan Mountain.

The powder was perfect this morning, floating up around my feet. It was deep enough that the tip of my board would disappear as I cut my path down the slope.

There weren't many tracks this early. One by one, they peeled off in different directions as I headed toward the terrain park. Except for a single swath in the snow that headed in my exact direction.

Someone must have come up early today to hit the

jumps. Maybe Reed had given the all clear to the staffers to test the halfpipe too. Hell, it could be River.

I wasn't really in the mood for company, but whatever.

This wasn't my resort.

The first obstacle in the park was a mini kicker, a good lead-in to the more challenging obstacles down the slope. I flew over it, getting a little air and letting my body warm up. Then I rode toward a rainbow rail.

The consultant Reed had hired had done a good job. The jumps and ramps were spaced well. The park would appeal to both beginners and advanced patrons.

As my board slid over the top of the rail, the scrape was music to my ears. I hit a mailbox next, then veered away from the park toward the halfpipe.

Following that single trail.

I wasn't sure who I expected to see, but it wasn't Raven.

My chest swelled, my lungs too tight to breathe.

Her hair was braided over a shoulder. She had on a gray coat that matched her helmet. Her pants were an orange red. She was sitting on the pipe's lip, her arms balanced on her knees. She'd lifted her goggles and was staring into the distance.

Damn, but she was beautiful.

And damn, how I'd missed her. It had only been three days.

At the sound of my board, she turned, looking up as I stopped beside her. "Hi."

"Hey." She sounded . . . sad.

I took up a seat beside her, taking off my goggles too. "You okay?"

"No."

"What's wrong?" If something serious was going on and I'd been pouting because she hadn't wanted a hookup, I was going to kick my own ass.

She faced me, her eyes raking over my face. "You were supposed to leave after the wedding."

"Okay," I drawled. "So?"

"So this is getting . . . muddled."

Muddled. Excellent word choice. "Would it make you feel better if I told you I was leaving tomorrow?"

She dropped her gaze, staying quiet.

I really wanted the answer to be no.

I wanted her to miss me too.

But she wouldn't. Raven had made her expectations perfectly clear. This was casual. Sex only. And we'd reached the end of our ride.

"Have you tried the pipe?" I asked, ready to change the subject.

"Not yet."

I shoved to my feet, holding out a hand to help her up. "Ladies first. Unless you don't want me to watch."

She shrugged. "No, it's okay."

"Then let's see what you've got."

Raven drew in a long breath and got herself ready, adjusting her straps and goggles before positioning on the lip. A ghost of a smile pulled at her lips, then she dropped in.

My stomach did a summersault.

It was the same feeling I got myself, that first rush of adrenaline and the few seconds when my body adjusted to the speed.

Raven flew across the pipe in a perfectly clean line, then soared up the wall to pop off the lip. She pulled her knees toward her chest, twisted her shoulders and rotated, reaching to do a method grab before she came down, landing on her toe edge.

It was a textbook backside air, and damn, it was hot.

The next trick was a frontside 360. Raven did it three more times, adding height to her vertical with each.

She took off her board when she stopped at the bottom, tucking it under her arm as she started the hike back to the top. All while I stared, my jaw slack.

I'd never had a thing for snowboarders. There were plenty of female athletes but never, not once, had I watched one of them ride and had this sort of reaction. I was hard. Rock hard.

"What?" she asked, her breathing ragged as she reached my side.

"Uh . . ." I wanted to tear her clothes off and fuck her right here in the snow, that was what. My cock ached and if I'd ever drooled over a woman, it was Raven.

"Crew." She rolled her eyes, clearly reading my expression and the direction of my thoughts.

"I can't help it. That was sexy as fuck."

Her cheeks were flushed as she smiled. Her dusting of freckles stood out beneath the sun. That braid was tempting, so I reached out and tugged the end, urging her closer as I scooted to close the gap between us. Then I towered over her, our eyes locked as I lowered my mouth, sealing my lips over hers.

She whimpered as I slid my tongue against hers in a deliberate swirl. I banded an arm around her shoulders, pinning her against my chest.

God, I'd missed her sweet taste, that hitch in her breath

when I fluttered my tongue against hers. I'd missed the way she leaned into me, like she was using my body as a pillar to keep balanced.

I devoured her, licking and sucking, until my cock wasn't just aching, it wept. It took every ounce of my restraint to pull away before I started removing clothes.

I missed you. The words were on the tip of my tongue, but I swallowed them back and eased away. "Okay, my turn."

Me, at the end of this halfpipe, with some distance between us seemed like a good move. So I fixed my board and pulled the goggles from my helmet, fitting them over my eyes. Then I was off, taking the same line and doing the same tricks as Raven, except for my last, I modified it to a frontside 540.

My muscles came alive. The haze of lust cleared slightly. When I hiked to the top, Raven already had her board on and was ready to go.

She didn't give me a chance to get close again, to kiss her again. She modified her run a bit, adding harder tricks—an air-to-fakie and an alley-oop.

I didn't so much as blink as she rode, not wanting to miss a second. And when she met me at the top, I was smiling so wide it pinched my cheeks.

"You're good."

"I know." She laughed. "Don't sound surprised."

"I just expected you to ride like River. But you're better." Her lines were cleaner. Her tricks sharper and her landings solid. Just two runs and the difference was inescapable.

Raven's expression fell.

"Is that why you didn't bring your board up on Saturday? Because you're better than he is?"

She shrugged. "You know River."

Yeah, I knew River. We'd had a few beefs in high school when he'd realized I was better. It hadn't lasted long, maybe because I hadn't given a fuck about his bruised ego. I'd just continued to do my thing and he'd gotten over it eventually.

But I could see how it would cause problems for Raven.

Their dad had been an incredible skier in his prime, traveling around the world. River had issues with Rowdy, but there'd always been admiration whenever he'd talked about Rowdy's career. River wanted to be a star too. I didn't blame him.

Except the raw talent had gone to Raven.

"You could do this professionally," I said.

"Maybe." She lifted a shoulder.

"Have you thought about it?"

"I've done a few competitions."

Something that River had never once mentioned, either because she hadn't told him she was competing or because he hadn't wanted to talk about her achievements.

"It's hard to train," she said. "With work."

"Quit."

She scoffed. "Uh, no."

Raven wouldn't take that much of a gamble. Maybe because she'd never had someone tell her it would pay off.

"You've got this now." I waved a hand toward the pipe. "So you don't have to travel to Woodward."

"True. But I'm still not quitting my job."

"I get it. It's a risk. When I left here, I wasn't sure what would happen. I worked, like you, spending my weekends operating a lift in Park just so that I could practice during the week. Got into the competition circuit. Started making money and saved it up until I could quit."

"You were eighteen, Crew. I'm twenty-eight. I have a mortgage and a car payment." She wanted the security of her paycheck. Also understandable.

At eighteen, I hadn't cared about sharing a shitty apartment with two other guys and eating cheap food for every meal. It hadn't felt like a sacrifice, but a dream.

I'd finally escaped the fog that had hovered over my head since Mom's death. Even though I hadn't had much money, I'd been free. From Penny Ridge. From Dad. Even my brothers.

It had been my chance to start fresh.

But I could appreciate why Raven wasn't going to take that leap. There were no guarantees in this sport. You could be out training and land yourself in a hospital after attempting a hard trick in a practice run.

"You love it though, don't you?" I asked.

"Yes," she whispered, so softly I barely heard the word.

"Then go for it." It was a risk. But sometimes, you had to risk it for your dream.

She gave me a sad smile, like she'd told herself the same but thought it was too late.

I raised a gloved hand, cupping her face and running my thumb across her cheekbone. There was nothing I could say to convince her. That had to be Raven's choice. "Will you do something for me?"

"Depends."

"Will you ride with me today?"

"Yes." She didn't hesitate. That faint smile was back on her lips, so I kissed it.

This was why I hadn't left Colorado yet. Not because of my family. Not my shoulder. Not this halfpipe.

Raven.

CHAPTER TWELVE

RAVEN

I collapsed on the snow at the bottom of the terrain park, my heart pounding and my body sweaty.

Crew's board slid to a stop beside mine and then he dropped too, both of us panting.

"I win."

He chuckled. "I let you win."

"Lies." I smiled, staring up at the blue sky as the cold seeped through my clothes. My body was sticky with sweat. Beneath my helmet, my hair was smashed to my head. It was the best I'd felt in, well . . . three days. Since my last night in Crew's bed.

I'd tried my hardest since Saturday to put him out of my thoughts. Except my efforts had been futile. I'd looked for him almost constantly, scanning the lift lines and base area for his brown hair and sexy smile.

On Sunday, I'd spotted him in the lodge, in line to get lunch. I'd ducked out of sight before he could spot me, then hidden in my office for the rest of the day. Yesterday, it had been my day off, so I'd stayed home, moping because he'd left Penny Ridge—or so I'd thought.

Then this morning, I'd come to the mountain to spend the day on the slopes. My plan had been to get back to normal, and on my days off, normal meant my feet were strapped to a board. But as I'd pulled into the parking lot, I'd spotted Marianne climbing into an army-green G-Wagon with Utah plates.

I'd waited, watching to see if Crew came out. My heart had been in my throat when I'd realized he'd stayed longer than expected. But she'd driven off alone. So I'd taken a lift and ridden straight to the halfpipe.

Waiting. Knowing he'd find me.

When he'd shown up earlier, I'd been torn between crying because it was so good to see him. And crying because of my epic weakness.

This was Thayer all over again.

It was going to fucking hurt.

We'd ridden hard, barely stopping. Crew challenged me in the best possible way, pushing me to try new things and hone existing techniques. And I'd pushed myself too, not wanting him to hold back on my account.

He was wild on that board. It was incredible to witness.

Today had been the best snowboarding of my life.

"That was fun," I told him. "Thanks for letting me tag along."

"Tag along?" He sat up, staring down at me. "I think that's the other way around. Do you always go that hard?"

No. Yes. "I don't get to do this every day. So when I do, I make it count."

"When's your next competition?"

"I haven't signed up for any this season yet," I said. "In February, Burton is hosting an open in Vail. I was thinking about registering."

"Do it. Burton puts on good events and you'll have solid competition. Place well and you'll get a ton of exposure and invites to the bigger events."

I shrugged. "We'll see."

"What's holding you back? Is it River?"

"No, not really." I sat up too. "River won't like it but that's his problem. Honestly, I can't really even explain why I'm hesitant. Maybe I'm afraid to fail. I've only ever competed at smaller events, and I guess I'm nervous that my lack of professional training will stand out if I'm matched up against actual professionals."

"I'm an 'actual professional' and you had no problem keeping up with me today."

"Okay, then maybe I just feel like I missed my window."

"You're twenty-eight, Raven. Not ninety."

I rolled my eyes. "Most people are late teens, early twenties."

"Most, but not all. A friend of mine didn't start until he was twenty-five. But he was like you. Grew up on a mountain. Lots of natural talent. Chances are, he'll make the next Olympic team."

That was the dream, wasn't it? So why couldn't I just go for it? "Are you going to shoot down every one of my doubts?"

"Yep."

I laughed. "I'll think about Vail."

"Good."

"What competitions are you doing this year?"

"The Winter X Games in Aspen and the FIS World Cup," he said. "I'm going to Lake Placid but only as a spectator. And I've got a couple exhibitions to visit too."

"Are you doing the exhibition here?" Did I want him to say yes? Or no?

"I don't think I'll make that one."

That was a good thing, right? That meant distance with Crew. So why did my heart sink? "Are you nervous? For your events?" I asked, not wanting to answer my own questions.

"Not at the moment. I love to ride. I love to win. There is no pressure that anyone could put on me that isn't heavier than the pressure I put on myself."

I knew exactly how he felt. Except the pressure I put on myself wasn't to win at a competition, it was to not become my father. To not abandon everything chasing an unlikely fantasy.

My heart, like Crew's, wanted to win. I wanted to know I was the best. But in my head, the practical Raven kept reminding me that my boots belonged on the ground, not a podium.

"Come on." Crew shoved to his feet, holding out a hand. "One more run for the day."

"Okay." I let him help me up, then followed him to the new lift for the terrain park.

"Want to make a deal?" he asked after we'd loaded onto a chair.

"Depends on the deal."

He checked over his shoulder to see that we were out of sight of the lift operators. Then he scooted closer, sliding his hand around my shoulders as his mouth bent close to mine.

"Another race. You have to work in three tricks. A stalefish grab. A frontside 720. And then hit the halfpipe for a McTwist."

"Is that supposed to scare me?" A map of the terrain park popped into my head as I began plotting out exactly where I'd do the first two before coming to the halfpipe for the last. "What do I get when I win?"

He brushed his mouth to mine, sending shivers down my spine. "Bragging rights. And an orgasm."

My temperature spiked. There'd been a dull ache between my legs all day. Riding with Crew had been hours of foreplay. The promise of what he could deliver with that skilled body made that throb intensify into a solid pulse. "And if you win?"

"No bragging rights. But I'll give you two orgasms."

A win-win. I nipped his lower lip. "Deal."

There was no use fighting the inevitable. I'd stayed away from his room on Saturday. But I'd be headed there tonight.

He grinned, kissing me again, before putting a few inches between us to fit his goggles over his eyes, preparing for victory.

"Crew?" I waited until he faced me. "Don't let me win."

"Never." His serious tone matched mine, almost like he could read my thoughts. Like he knew why I needed him to give it his all.

I wanted bragging rights. I wanted to earn them.

I wanted to know if there was a chance, even a small chance, that I might be good enough to keep up.

We reached the top of the lift, both of us waving to the operator as we unloaded. Then we rounded the corner and slowed, keeping pace with each other as we started down the trail.

"Ready?" he asked.

I put on my own goggles, making sure they were exactly right, then drew in a long inhale as my adrenaline surged. Oh, I wanted to win. "Ready."

"On three." Crew bent his knees, rolling his bad shoulder. "Three. Two. One."

Go.

———

"GOOD JOB, BABY."

"Thanks." I was smiling so wide it hurt as I unbuckled my board.

I hadn't beat Crew down the mountain. But he hadn't won by a landslide.

"I want my two orgasms," I said, breathless.

Crew swallowed hard, taking off his own board, and then stalked toward the hotel.

I bit my lip, glancing around to make sure no one was watching. But the mountain was quiet. Most of the skiers and boarders today were those, like Crew and me, who didn't spend their time lingering at the base. The few people walking around weren't paying us any attention. The only exceptions were the operators at Chair Nine. They watched Crew, rapt.

So I held back, waiting until he was a safe distance away. If any of the staffers had seen us board down together, they'd think we'd just been on a ride, not that we were heading to his bed.

When I started for the hotel, I did my best to appear like Crew and I were simply going in the same direction.

He disappeared into the hotel, letting the door swing closed behind him.

I trembled with every step, the anticipation thrumming through my veins, more turned on than I'd ever been in my life.

Everything about Crew was sexy, but after watching him ride, I was soaked.

Oh, please, I hoped he'd bought more condoms.

When I entered the lobby, I expected to see Crew on his way to the elevators or staircase. Except he was passing by the gift shop, walking toward the hallway that would lead toward the offices.

The clerk in the gift shop tracked every one of his steps, wearing a sultry smile on her face. But he didn't pay her any attention as he headed down the hallway. To anyone, it would look like he was going to find Reed or Ava.

Where was he going? That wasn't the way toward his room.

I followed, careful not to rush my steps. The gift store clerk—she was new on staff and I hadn't caught her name yet—didn't spare me a glance.

With a quick check over my shoulder to ensure no one was paying any attention, I walked the length of the hall just as Crew opened a door and slipped inside.

I hadn't been in that room before, but clearly, Crew knew where he was going. He'd grown up here, probably running around these very hallways as a kid.

He left the door open just enough for me to sneak inside. And the moment I crossed the threshold into a supply closet, he yanked my board out of my hand, propping it against a shelf before he pushed the door closed and flipped the lock.

"What are we doing in—"

He silenced my question by slamming his mouth on mine, sweeping in and tangling our tongues together.

A whimper escaped my throat. I leaned into him, savoring the feel of his tongue and those soft, firm lips.

"I couldn't wait," he breathed. "Fuck, I want you, Raven."

"Yes," I moaned as he stripped off my coat, his fingers frantically tugging at the zipper.

He took off his helmet, and with a quick snap, mine was gone too, each dropping to land on the floor by our feet.

I managed to shove his coat from his shoulders. It landed with a muffled plop. Then I unfastened my pants as he dug into his pocket, fishing out a condom.

Oh, thank God.

I was about to bend and untie my boots when Crew put his hands on my hips and spun me for the wall. I gasped as he shoved down my pants and the thermals beneath, including my panties.

He used one hand to grip my chin, twisting my face so he could lick my bottom lip. He pinned me against the wall with that strong body, using his other hand to fist his cock and drag it through my wet folds. "I'm going to fuck this pretty pussy hard, baby. Since you left me alone the past three nights."

"Crew." I tilted my hips, needing him to stop playing and get serious.

"Did you miss my cock?"

I gulped. "Yes."

"Good." With a single thrust, he buried himself deep.

I arched into his chest, melting as my body stretched to fit around his.

"Fuck, Raven." He latched his mouth on to my neck, sucking hard at my pulse as he pulled out only to thrust in again.

"Oh, God." I was pulsing already, my hands braced on the wall so I could meet Crew's strokes.

He set a punishing rhythm, in and out, over and over. His cock hit that spot inside that made me shake. His hand around my waist dipped lower, his middle finger finding my clit. He circled it once, twice, and I cried out.

"Shh." He drove deep, then paused. "Give me your mouth."

I twisted, leaning back. Then his mouth covered mine, swallowing my gasps and moans as his finger continued to torment and his hips pistoned fast. With his tongue stroking mine, there was no way for me to warn him that I was about to come, so I shattered, crying down his throat as my orgasm exploded.

Crew groaned, the gravelly rumble drawing out my release, until I was utterly spent and collapsed forward, forcing our mouths apart so I could breathe.

The sounds of skin slapping, my ragged breathing and his labored breaths filled the tiny space. Then Crew wrapped his arms around me, holding me tight as he thrust to the root, rocking against me as he shuddered through his own orgasm.

The two of us collapsed against the wall, each shaking and sweaty.

"Fuck, that was hot," I whispered.

"It smells like sex in here now."

I giggled, quickly slapping a hand over my mouth.

"Do you still think a football player or a boring nerd is better than me?"

"Yes," I teased. There was no one better than Crew, but his ego didn't need my help.

He shook his head, chuckling. Then spanked me.

The crack of his palm on my bare ass earned a yelp.

His cock twitched inside me, hardening for another round. But instead of acting on it, he slipped out, quickly taking care of the condom in a paper towel from the supply rack while I bent and pulled up my panties.

I was just tugging up my thermals when the door opened.

The locked door.

"Ah!" I jumped, my hand going to my chest.

"Shit." Crew whirled away, hiding his dick, but in turn, flashing his ass to his stepmother.

"Oh my. Uh . . . sorry?" Melody shielded her eyes, raising her hand with the door key dangling from a finger. She pulled in her lips to hide a smile but a little laugh still escaped. "Hi, Raven."

"Um, hi, Melody." My face flamed. This wasn't happening. Oh God, this wasn't happening.

"I'll just come back later." She laughed again, then turned, walking out the door. Except before she left us, she leaned back in. "Good work, you two."

"Wait." I paused until she turned. "This—Crew and me —is not exactly something we need broadcast."

"Gotcha." She zipped her lips closed, then turned an

imaginary lock before handing me the invisible key for safe-keeping as she winked.

Now it was my turn to laugh as she closed the door, leaving us alone.

"What the hell was that?" Crew tugged up his boxers. "Did she just say 'good work'?"

"You don't know Melody, do you?"

"No." Sadness flashed across his face, but it was gone just as quickly as it had appeared. Crew pulled up his thermals and snow pants as I did the same. Then he bent to swipe up both of our coats, handing mine over. "Come to my room."

"Maybe."

"I'm not asking this time, Raven."

No, he wasn't.

The practical thing for me to do was go home. Say goodbye and end this on a high note. We'd had a blast together on the mountain today, then this romp in the supply closet.

He shuffled closer, his fingers diving into my hair. "I promised two orgasms."

I really should go home. But we both knew I wouldn't.

"So you did."

Crew kissed me, slowly, beautifully, until I was aching for more. He nodded for me to leave the supply closet first.

I kept my chin ducked, my board tucked under one arm with my helmet in the other, and hoped I wouldn't bump into anyone who might notice the flush of my cheeks and the scent of Crew on my skin.

Instead of going to the elevator, I walked outside, taking a detour to my car to drop off my gear. Then I went to the rear employee entrance, using the same staircase I always did to sneak to the third floor.

The last climb.

My footsteps lingered on the top stair. I doubted I'd ever see this corner of the hotel and not think of Crew. On a sigh, I pushed through the door, going straight for his room. I raised my arm to knock but the door opened and there he was, his hand outstretched to tug me inside.

Crew didn't just deliver that second orgasm. He worshiped me, for hours. He consumed every shred of my energy until the stars were shining beyond the windows and I was draped across his body, sated and limp.

"What are you thinking?" he murmured, his hand in my hair. Somewhere between the second and third orgasm, he'd pulled out my braid.

"I should go home."

"You should stay."

I closed my eyes and yawned. "I'll leave in a minute."

Except I drifted off to sleep, waking as sunbeams began lighting the room.

Crew didn't so much as stir as I lifted off his chest, carefully unwrapping myself from his arms.

The clock on the nightstand showed it was a quarter to seven.

So much for my rule of not spending the night. When it came to Crew, I'd broken a lot of rules.

I slipped out of bed, rushing to collect my clothes. With them clutched to my chest, I took one last look at Crew.

Maybe another woman would have woken him up. Would have said goodbye. But I couldn't bring myself to say it. So I studied his handsome face, handsomer than ever as he slept. His mouth was parted slightly, his dark eyelashes perfect crescents above his cheeks.

I soaked in every feature, then eased out of the bedroom, quickly dressing before I crept down the stairs and to my car, parked alone with icy windows in the employee parking lot.

Time to get back to reality.

Time to let him go.

So while my windshield defrosted, I stood outside, my breath billowing, and stared at the hotel's third floor.

"Bye, Crew."

CHAPTER THIRTEEN

CREW

Six weeks later ...

"Crew, are you listening to me?" Marianne asked.

I tore my eyes away from the plane's window. "Yeah."

She closed her eyes, drawing in a long breath. A telltale sign she was losing patience.

"Sorry," I said. No, I hadn't been listening. Not really.

Marianne set her phone on the table between us, sagging into the plush leather seat.

Lewis had taken up his preferred space in the back of the plane, where he could be alone to catch up on emails and phone calls while drinking cup after cup of black coffee. He had his earbuds in, his fingers flying over the keyboard on his laptop.

We'd chartered a private jet for this trip. It was the best way to fly, but no matter how comfortable the chairs and polite the flight crew, I wouldn't relax until the wheels touched down. That was always the case with flying. I didn't mind being in the air as long as I was wearing a snowboard.

"What's with you?" she asked.

"You know I don't like flying."

"It's not the airplane. You've been off for weeks. Is it your shoulder?"

"The shoulder's fine." Not according to Dr. Williams, but at the moment, the ache was manageable and my range of motion was back to normal. It was enough I could compete, and even though there was always a twinge when I raised it out to my side, it wasn't excruciating.

"I'm sorry about Mia," she said.

"It's fine." I waved it off. "Not your fault."

We'd spent the past three days in Lake Placid for the Winter World University Games. The ten-day event was still going, but we'd left early, having concluded our business. Both Lewis and Sydney had been at the event. They'd lined up meetings with sponsors and media outlets, and up until last night, everything had gone smoothly.

I'd sat for a magazine interview and gone out to dinner with a team from Burton. The GNU execs had been there too, each gushing over the material they'd gotten in November in Colorado. Yesterday, I'd spent the day watching the competition, and afterward, I'd met with some friends for a drink at the hotel bar.

It should have been a fun night, except not fifteen minutes into the evening, Mia had arrived.

The two of us had dated a few years ago. She was a reporter, working for a blog, and after an interview, we'd gone out to dinner, had a few drinks and wound up in my bed.

We'd stayed together for about six months, and during that time, she'd become friends with Marianne.

They'd stayed friends, even after I'd called it off. Mia had wanted a serious commitment, a ring and a wedding date. But the only commitment I was willing to make at this point was to the sport of snowboarding. The pressure she'd put on me when I hadn't been ready to propose had killed any feelings I'd had for her.

Or maybe I'd known deep down she hadn't been the one.

Maybe I hadn't realized it until I'd met a woman with black hair and a nose full of freckles.

Whatever the reason for our breakup, for Marianne's sake, I'd never talked badly about Mia. That could be why she'd always held out hope Mia and I would get back together.

After last night, I'd made it clear I had no intention of speaking to Mia ever again.

She'd shown up at the bar, at the event for work. At first, we'd just caught up. Exchanged pleasantries and belated holiday wishes. But then she'd shifted into reporter mode, and surrounded by people, when an escape attempt would have been awkward, she'd hammered me with questions about my mother and how her death had influenced my career. About my father's history with alcohol abuse. About the dynamic with my brothers.

Mia had taken information from our private relationship and broadcast it openly.

Why was any of that shit newsworthy? Had she asked to hurt me? To humiliate me in front of friends and colleagues? Instead of answering her litany of questions, I'd stormed out of the bar, leaving behind a group of stunned faces and Marianne.

I'd let her deal with Mia.

"Crew." Given the look on Marianne's face, she knew I wasn't fine.

"It's okay," I lied. "I'm just tired. Mia caught me off guard."

"It wasn't right. For her to do that to you."

"Why?" That question had been pinging around my head. "Why would she do that?"

I'd shut down, but Mia had been the person who'd looked like a fool.

Marianne's expression was clouded with guilt. "It's my fault. I met her for lunch yesterday. We were just talking. Gossiping. She asked about you, like she always does. She asked me if you'd consider trying again and I was honest. I told her no. I think it hurt her. I think she's been waiting, holding out hope."

"I never gave her any, Marianne."

She dropped her gaze to her lap. "I think I did."

I pinched the bridge of my nose. "Let's just . . . forget it. Let's just go home."

Home to an empty house and a lonely bed.

"I'm sorry, Crew."

"Like I said, not your fault." I sighed, ready for a new topic. "I have no desire to get back on this plane in two days."

On Tuesday morning, we were scheduled to fly to Jackson Hole. It was a trip we'd planned for months to look at some property. Lewis was concerned that my investment portfolio lacked diversity and he'd gotten a tip on an upcoming property development.

Wyoming was nice. I liked Montana better. And if I was being honest with myself, where I really wanted to be at the moment was Colorado.

"I don't want to buy a condo in Jackson," I admitted, keeping my voice low so Lewis couldn't hear.

Marianne glanced down the aisle, checking on him too, then leaned forward. "Why?"

"What am I going to do in Wyoming?"

"Take vacations?"

I scoffed. "Because I take so many vacations."

"You don't have to buy anything. But would it hurt to look?"

No, it wouldn't hurt. And Lewis wasn't wrong.

At the moment, the only property I owned was my place in Park. I had a pile of cash invested in the stock market but it would be good to follow Lewis's advice. He worried about the worst possible outcomes and if he didn't have chronic ulcers by the time he hit sixty, it would be a miracle. But his worrying was in my best interest. He agonized over potential lawsuits so I didn't have to. The same was true with my investments.

"What if we didn't go to Wyoming?" I asked. "What if we went to Colorado instead?"

"Um, okay. Where in Colorado?"

I swallowed hard. "Penny Ridge."

Her eyes narrowed as she studied my face. "You spent years avoiding everything about Penny Ridge. Then you went back and I couldn't get you to leave."

"Maybe I stayed away for too long."

Maybe I hadn't realized just how lonely my life had become.

I'd spent Thanksgiving at home alone, eating a delivered meal while binge-watching the latest Netflix hit. The weeks of December had been spent training. Hard. I'd taken one day off for Christmas, then it had been back to work until this trip.

The last time I remembered celebrating a holiday had been with Mom. But she'd died around Christmas, and since, I'd preferred to block out the anniversary of her death by doing anything to keep my mind distracted.

This year had been no exception. But it had been noticeably lonely. Miserable, actually. Especially Christmas. So much so that I'd almost caved and called River to beg for Raven's number, just to hear her voice.

To talk.

Things that I'd bottled up for years, things that I hadn't confided in anyone, including Mia much to her frustration, had come bubbling out of my mouth with Raven.

Confiding in her—my truths, my fears—had been effortless.

What happened when snowboarding wasn't the major component of my life? Where would I go?

Park City was nice but I was alone. If I stayed, I'd become the has-been athlete who didn't have a life to move on to after retirement.

My brothers were making something of Madigan Mountain. Even in Lake Placid, there'd been a few murmurings. Mostly because of my last name, but they were getting attention. Reed had pulled out all the stops to put our family's mountain on the radar.

And as it happened, they had property developments too.

I twisted in my chair, leaning into the aisle. "Lewis."

He kept typing.

"Lewis." I raised my voice but he was still tuning out the

world, so I pointed to Marianne's notebook. "Give me a piece of paper."

She ripped a page from the spiral binding.

I crumpled it into a ball, then fired it at Lewis's forehead.

"Hey." He scowled as it hit him and bounced to the floor. Then he plucked out his earbuds. "You're a pain in my ass."

"Hey, I hollered for you twice."

"I'm busy. What do you want?"

"What if we don't go to Wyoming?"

He blinked. "What? No. I've been setting this up for a month. We've talked about this, Crew. You need to find something to invest in. A few long-term assets."

"I agree. How about property in Colorado?"

"Like Vail or Aspen? I mean . . . they won't come cheap. But it's not a bad idea. Let me talk to a few people, and I'll line up some showings for us after the X Games. We'll still go to Jackson because I want you to see—"

"Lewis."

His nostrils flared, like they always did when I interrupted him in planning mode.

"I'm thinking Madigan Mountain."

"Seriously?" He looked to Marianne. "You've avoided Penny Ridge for over a decade. One trip home and now you want to buy property there?"

I looked between him and Marianne. "You two share a brain, I swear."

Marianne laughed. "I'm not sure if I should be terrified or say thank you."

"Thank you," Lewis answered. "Okay, back to Colorado. Are you sure about this, Crew?"

No. No, not really.

"What do I do when I retire?" I asked.

"You're years from retirement," Lewis said.

"Am I?"

His eyes bugged out. "What are you saying?"

"Nothing." I dragged a hand through my hair. "I just . . ."

I was lonely. I was anxious. I was jealous.

I envied my brothers for building a future.

And damn it, I couldn't get Raven off my mind.

Never in my life had a woman consumed so much of my headspace. No woman had ever competed with snowboarding.

Just the idea of seeing her again made my heart race.

Maybe she'd tell me to fuck off. Maybe I'd see her and whatever feelings I'd dreamed up in my head would vanish. Maybe she'd already met someone else. That idea set my molars grinding.

There was only one way to find out.

"We have to be in Aspen in two weeks, right? What if we went to Colorado instead of Wyoming? The trip to Aspen would be shorter."

"Where are you going to train?" Lewis asked. "You need more than just a halfpipe. You need a decent gym. You need your coach."

And JR was in Park City.

I turned to Marianne, silently pleading with her to solve this problem.

She frowned but nodded. "I'll make some calls."

"Thank you." I turned. "Lewis?"

"I repeat, you're a pain in my ass. You were supposed to get some training time in Wyoming and then straight back to Park. These last-minute schedule changes are not what you should be focusing on before a major competition. We need your head in the game."

He wasn't wrong. But this wasn't about my head. This was about my heart. Something was missing. It had been missing for six weeks.

And that something just might be Raven Darcy.

This trip wasn't about real estate. It was about her.

If the feelings from November were gone, then I'd walk away. Maybe I'd buy a place in Penny Ridge. Maybe I'd let Lewis sell me on a property in Jackson. But at least I could move on.

On the flip side, if the connection between us was still as strong, well . . . that changed everything, didn't it?

"I guess I'd better make some calls. Find a realtor." Lewis grumbled something under his breath I couldn't hear. "Where are we going to stay?"

Marianne opened her mouth, but I held up a finger. "Let me take care of that."

I dug my phone from my pocket and pulled up Reed's name. He answered on the third ring. "Hi. Everything okay?"

"Uh, yeah. Why?"

"Normally I call you. Sometimes you even answer."

I grinned. "I called you at Christmas."

"Ha!" He laughed. "No, you called me back."

"Oh." I guess that was true. Even after the last visit, I needed to work harder to reach out. But if I had a place in Penny Ridge, maybe that would be easier.

"What's up?" he asked.

"Any chance you have three rooms open at the hotel?"

"You're funny," he said dryly.

"Employee housing?"

"The jokes keep on coming."

I waited, letting him think it over. *Come on, Reed.*

"When are you coming?"

"Uh, tonight?" Hopefully the pilots could swing a change in the flight plan.

"Tonight. You're killing me here." Reed paused. "Yeah. Okay. We'll make something work. But I'm going to need a favor."

"Name it."

"Remember that exhibition I told you about?"

CHAPTER FOURTEEN

RAVEN

January in Penny Ridge was magical.

Mom preferred June, when the weather was warm and the grass was green, but January in my hometown had always been my favorite. Partly because of the influx of new faces.

Downtown bustled with tourists, those who were spending their Monday exploring the local shops instead of on the ski slopes.

I meandered the sidewalk with them, falling into the same relaxed pace as our visitors, sipping the latte I'd just bought.

For the first time in weeks, I felt like myself again. Or . . . almost. I hadn't scanned the crowd at the coffee shop for Crew. That was a first. Progress.

Ever since he'd left, I'd found myself searching for him. At the hotel. In the lift lines. On the mountain. But he was gone. And it was time for me to move on.

The cold winter air filled my lungs. The sun warmed my

face. I smiled as a couple passed by, each wearing a Madigan Mountain hat.

I'd be heading up later this morning. River had asked me to ride with him today—probably because he knew I'd spring for lunch—so we were meeting at eleven. That was, if he dragged his ass out of bed in time.

My internal clock had woken me at seven, and after some cleaning around the house, I'd decided to walk the three blocks for a coffee.

Downtown had changed since my youth. My favorite childhood shops and restaurants were weaved in with new businesses and new neighbors.

Two Scoops had the same pastel sign in the shape of an ice cream cone as they had for decades. The Cheese still made the best burgers around. But Penny Ridge Realty had freshened up their building last summer, giving it a fresh coat of paint and modern signage. The public library had moved to a bigger building on the outskirts of town and in its place was a wine bar.

There were those around town who resented the growth. They feared we'd become the next Aspen or Vail, catering too much to the wealthy tourists and not providing for our local community.

Personally, I was glad to see the mountain expand and, with it, bring in opportunities. Residents. Halley and I had gone to dinner last night and she'd told me about the guy she'd just met. A lawyer who'd moved away from Denver for a slower pace. They'd gone on three dates already, and given the blinding smile on her face, I had a feeling this guy might just last.

She'd tried to talk me into a double date with her

boyfriend's brother, but the thought of any other man touching me but Crew . . . I grimaced.

That would fade eventually, right? Someday I'd find someone who was better suited for my life. Someone who wouldn't be traveling around the world and making the highlight reel on SportsCenter.

My phone vibrated in my pocket. When I pulled it out, Dad's picture appeared on the screen. We hadn't talked in months, not since he'd left in October for Europe. "Hi, Dad. Everything okay?"

"Hey, kiddo. Yeah, it's great. Why?"

"It's January." I couldn't remember a time when he'd called me in the peak of ski season.

"Huh?"

"Never mind." Dad had no clue that he was absent. He lived in his own world and the rest of us were merely objects in his orbit. "What's up? How's Europe?"

"Not bad. But I've had a change of plans. I was supposed to be staying with a friend for the next couple of weeks but, uh, that sort of fell through."

"Oh, okay." I had a hunch that this *friend* was actually a girlfriend. Since the divorce, Dad hadn't been shy about dating. He'd plaster his Instagram with pictures of his latest attachment. Mom hadn't said it aloud, but I think she wondered if he'd been faithful to her during their marriage.

I sure as hell wasn't going to ask. I had enough problems with my father; tacking on *cheater* to his repertoire would only make me resent him more.

"I'm heading your way next week," he said. "I've been trying to get ahold of your mother, but she won't call me back."

"She's been busy with work."

"Too busy to return a phone call? I was hoping I could stay at her place."

"And that's probably why she hasn't called you back." The words flew from my mouth before I had a chance to think them through. *Shit.*

"What's that supposed to mean?"

"Nothing," I muttered. "Forget it."

"You always pick her side." Dad was an incredible skier but his true talent was taking us on guilt trips.

Yes. I always chose Mom. Because he made the decision too easy.

"I just want to see you, Raven. Spend some time together. What do you say? Mind if I crash with you for a week? I'm not staying long."

I stopped, kicking myself for walking straight into this trap.

No, I didn't want Dad to stay with me. The last time he'd come home to crash had been three years ago and a week had turned into two. We'd been at each other's throats by the end of it because he was the worst house guest. He hadn't picked up after himself or once offered to make a meal. He'd kept strange hours, spending all day on the mountain and then coming home for late nights with friends. I'd been an afterthought, a maid and a chef, and I doubted this trip would be any different.

"Um . . . no." Why was that so hard to say? I cleared my throat, standing taller. "Not this time, Dad. Sorry."

The phone went silent for a few long moments. "Oh. Sure. No problem. I can stay with your grandparents."

"I'm sure they'd love to see you," I lied. Their relationship with Dad was just as strained as his with Mom. Hell, they might tell him no too. Maybe they already had.

Dad had burned most of his bridges in Penny Ridge.

"I just miss you," he said.

Maybe part of that was true. Or maybe none of it was. Maybe if he'd made more of an effort these past years to stay in touch, I'd believe him. "Let me know when you get to town. We could spend the day on the mountain together. A lot has changed since last season."

"Yep." Without a goodbye or an *I love you*, he hung up.

I stared at the phone for a moment before putting it away. Then I took a sip of my coffee, wishing I hadn't answered that call.

My mother was a smart, smart woman.

And damn it, I felt guilty. I hadn't seen Dad in months. Maybe I should call him back. Let him stay.

No, Raven.

In the past six weeks, I'd thought a lot about myself. My strengths. My weaknesses. I had Crew to thank for that. His leaving had made me take pause.

Because he'd left.

They all left.

Crew. Dad. Thayer and a line of men before. I'd never broken up with a man. Not once. I'd always been dumped.

And damn it, I was tired of being dumped. I was tired of being left behind.

No, I wasn't going to change my mind and let Dad crash at my house. So I shoved my doubts aside and unstuck my feet, ready to trudge home and pick up River.

Except the moment I glanced up, I froze.

Crew.

He stood on the corner of the block, his eyes locked on me.

I blinked. Was this real? Or had I dreamed him up?

He started walking, closing the distance between us with that sexy swagger. The corner of his mouth turned up. "Hey."

"H-hi." I blinked again, and sure enough, he was still there. "You're back?"

"I'm condo shopping."

"In Penny Ridge." I pointed to the ground as my heart began to gallop.

"Yeah." Crew smiled and my heart leapt. It freaking leapt.

Of course on my first normal-ish day, he'd come back just to torment me. But why was he looking for condos? Was he moving here? Did I want him to move here? *Yes.*

"How long are you staying?" I asked.

"I don't know. Not long."

Not long. Wasn't that exactly how Dad had described his trip?

I hated that I'd missed Crew. I hated that I'd thought about him every day since he'd left. I hated that I couldn't look at him and not . . . feel.

Crew stepped closer. "Want to come over tonight for dinner?"

No. Just say no.

"I'm staying at the hotel. Reed got me into the same suite. We could order room service."

No.

It was there, on the tip of my tongue, but then Crew

lifted a hand to push the hair away from my temple. A barely there touch that pulverized my resolve. "Okay."

This was Dad's fault. I'd given him the *no* I should have saved for Crew.

"God, it's good to see you." His eyes raked over my face.

I still wasn't sure if he was actually real. Or if I'd just conjured him from thin air because I'd missed him.

He looked incredible. No surprise. Crew always looked incredible. The gold flecks in his eyes caught the morning sun. His dark hair was styled and begging my fingers for a tousle. And that coat would look so much better on the floor of his hotel room.

"Crew!" a man across the street hollered, breaking the moment.

Crew's jaw ticked as he stood tall, leaning away.

A man stood outside the real estate office, waving him over.

"That's Lewis," he said. "My manager."

"Ah. Right. The condo shopping. Good timing. Real estate values are on the rise." Thankfully, I'd bought my house years ago before the mountain expansion and the market had spiked.

"I gotta go," he said. "Tonight?"

This was the same pattern all over again. I knew exactly what would happen when I went to his room. I knew he'd leave again. But did I say no? Did I change my answer? Nope. I whispered, "Tonight."

THE HIKE up the hotel's staircase to the third floor felt a lot like a walk of shame. Invisible grime coated my skin. I walked to Crew's suite, raising my hand to knock, but hesitated.

This wasn't what I wanted. Not anymore.

So I dropped my hand and took a step away from the door.

I'd spent the day on the mountain alone. Once River had found out Crew was in town, he'd ditched me to ride with Crew instead.

The day alone had given me a chance to think. To feebly attempt reconstruction on the walls around my heart, an effort to preempt the sting when Crew left town.

It was inescapable. He'd leave. And I'd be here, looking for him again.

Not this time. Just because he'd invited me here tonight didn't mean I had to sleep with him. We could be . . . friends.

I rolled my eyes.

Crew and I hadn't been friends *before* we'd started this fling. Afterward? Unlikely.

I was about to turn and force myself down the stairs, to retreat home, but the door opened and there he was.

"Hey, baby."

Oh, hell. I'd missed him calling me baby. Would it be strange if I told him to keep calling me baby even if we weren't sleeping together?

Crew reached out and snagged my wrist, tugging me inside before I could protest. Then as the door closed behind us, he framed my face with his hands and sealed his mouth over mine.

One sweep of his tongue and I melted.

Having friends was overrated.

I lifted to my toes, needing more, but he broke the kiss, leaning away to study my face like he had earlier on the sidewalk. "What?"

"Nothing," he murmured, then let me go. "I ordered dinner."

"Okay." Well, I was here. I might as well eat. So I followed him into the living space and took off my coat, draping it over the back of a chair at the table. "How was condo shopping?"

"Good. Have you been in them before?"

"Yes." We'd had a girls' night there once. Melody had heard about our regular margarita nights, and after she and Mark had moved into their condo, she'd asked to host a night with Ava, Callie, Halley and me. "They're beautiful."

"I bought two."

My mouth parted. "Two?"

He nodded. "One for me. Another as an investment that I'll use as a vacation rental."

Those condos were currently listed for one million dollars, minimum. I doubted Crew had bought the lowest-end finish package either. Not that there was much low-end about those condos. They were the definition of luxury, with expensive custom finishes and ski-in, ski-out access to the mountain.

"How's the season going?" he asked, opening the fridge to take out two waters.

"Good." I took a seat on the couch. "Busy. We're at capacity in the ski school, so weekends are hectic."

Crew sat right beside me, not leaving more than an inch between us.

That spicy cologne, citrus and cedar, filled my nose and I almost moaned.

"How's training going? Still thinking about the Burton in February?"

"I registered." I shrugged. "We'll see what happens. I've got no expectations. But I've been trying to fit in as much time as possible at the halfpipe."

It was open to the public now, but I'd found that if I went in the early mornings, I could squeeze in an hour or two by myself.

"How's your shoulder?" I asked.

"Shoulder is okay. Still sore at times but I'm not broadcasting it."

"You don't want people to make a big deal out of it."

"Exactly." He gave me a small smile. "I was worried this would be awkward."

It wasn't. Not really. In a way, we just picked up where we'd left off.

And that was the problem. I didn't want to go back.

So I inched away, earning a frown. "How is training going? Ready for the X Games?"

"Pretty much. I've got a couple more weeks to get my routine nailed. But I'm not doing anything new, so I'm sure it will all come together. I'm actually going to train here for a while. I was hoping you'd come with me tomorrow. Spend a day riding before my coach shows up. What do you say?"

"Sure." That was the easiest question he'd asked so far.

Compartmentalizing this with Crew was easier when we were on the mountain. Out there, it was just us and the snow.

He leaned in closer until our noses were almost touching. Then he dropped his forehead to mine, his entire body relaxing as he closed his eyes.

I held my breath, my heart racing. I should pull away, put space between us. But I couldn't move.

Crew opened his mouth, then closed it. Opened it again, then closed it again, like he was at a loss for words. Or maybe he knew what he wanted to say but wasn't sure how.

"Raven, I—"

A knock came at the door.

I jumped, startled and snapped out of the moment.

Crew grumbled and stood from the couch. "That's dinner."

I breathed, standing as my head spun. What was happening? What were we doing? What was I doing?

Falling into the same old pattern. Again. *Damn it.*

He was like a magnet. When he was in the room, I couldn't fight the pull. And somehow, he'd become my confidant. I hadn't told anyone I'd registered for the Burton open. No one, not even my friends.

As he walked to the door, I ducked into the bathroom to wash my hands, needing just a moment of separation.

When I came out, Crew had put two plates, each covered with a silver dome, on the table. "I hope pasta is okay. It was the special, and when I called down to the restaurant, the guy said it was really good."

"Pasta is great," I said, just as another knock came at the door.

"He probably forgot something."

I hovered back, still not wanting to be seen. Small-town gossip was bad. But mountain gossip was like a rumor mill on steroids. If anyone saw me in this room, it would be all over the resort by dawn.

Crew opened the door and his back instantly stiffened. "Uh, hey. River."

Shit. Shit. Shit.

I tiptoed backward, step by step, disappearing into the bedroom. Then I whirled, careful to keep silent as I slipped into the bathroom, easing the door closed except for a crack. I flicked off the lights, hovering in the darkness as I listened to Crew and my brother.

"Hey," River said. "Just ran into your hot assistant and she said you were lying low for dinner tonight. Thought I'd keep you company."

What? No. "Go away," I mouthed.

"Oh, I was just about to eat."

The sound of footsteps echoed from the other room, then came the clank of a metal dome being lifted off a plate.

"Did you order enough?" River teased.

"I was hungry," Crew said.

"So am I."

A chair scraped, followed by the unzipping of a jacket.

Oh, shoot. My coat. What if River spotted it?

"Let me, um, just get this shit out of the way." Clothes rustled, then came a *plop* on the couch, probably my coat being tossed with his.

"Great day today, wasn't it?" River asked with his mouth full of food.

My food.

"Yeah," Crew muttered.

"What are you planning to do for the X Games?"

I sighed, easing away from the door. Then I bent and

quietly took off my boots, leaving them against the vanity before padding to the wall next to the shower and soaking tub. I took one of the thickly woven bathrobes off a hook and folded it into a messy square to use as my cushion as I sat on the floor.

Fuck.

How ridiculous was this? My brother was out there eating the dinner intended for me. River was talking to Crew about his plans for Aspen, asking questions that I'd wanted to ask. They talked about Thanksgiving and Christmas. They talked about plans for the rest of the winter and where Crew would be traveling over the season.

Meanwhile, I was hiding with a growling stomach.

Twenty-eight years old and hiding like a teenager. Why? Why was I such a fool? But I didn't want River involved. He'd insert himself, maybe get pissed at Crew.

What was the point of that drama when Crew and I were fleeting? We'd be done the day he disappeared from Penny Ridge again.

So I stayed quiet, I stayed hidden, waiting as they talked for an hour because my brother had come to his friend's hotel room to keep him company.

"I think I'm going to head to bed soon." Crew yawned. "I'm beat. And my coach shows up from Park tomorrow, so he'll be kicking my ass."

Finally. My butt had fallen asleep ages ago.

River chuckled. "Thanks for dinner."

"Yeah. See ya later."

I stood as the door closed, then put the robe back on its hook. My legs were stiff as I bent to retrieve my boots.

Crew pushed open the bathroom door as I was stepping

into the first. "Fuck, I'm sorry. I tried to get rid of him but he just kept talking."

Their conversation had been lopsided, with River carrying the bulk of the weight and completely missing Crew's one-word answers as a hint he'd worn out his welcome.

"It's not your fault." I pulled on my other boot. "I asked you to keep this a secret."

"We don't have to. We could just tell River—everyone."

"Tell them what?" It was the same question that had been rolling around my brain while I'd hidden in the dark. What exactly would we tell everyone? "This is just sex, Crew. If we tell people, then this gets messy. It's better to keep the secret."

Crew dropped his gaze to the floor, his jaw ticking.

Tell me I'm wrong. Tell me you'll stay.

He stayed quiet.

"I'm going home." I walked toward him, rising on my toes to plant a kiss on his cheek. "Bye, Crew."

He let me leave the room without another word.

Obviously, I'd left this room before. Mostly, while he'd been asleep in the bed. But this exit was different. It wasn't about logistics—going home to sleep for a few hours before I woke to shower and get ready for work.

This time, it felt like . . . a statement.

It was strange, being the person to leave, not the person being left.

It was awful.

CHAPTER FIFTEEN

CREW

"How are you feeling?" JR unclipped his helmet.

"Good." Exhausted. Mostly because I hadn't slept much after Raven had left my room last night. But also because Coach had worked my ass off today, both in the hotel's gym and on the pipe. And I'd let him, in an effort to distract myself from replaying our conversation on loop.

"Today was a good day," JR said. "Get some rest tonight."

"Will do." I nodded. "Thanks again for coming out here."

"You bet. I like it here." He turned away from the ski racks, staring up the mountain toward the summit. "Are you thinking about making this a permanent spot?"

"No." Not after last night.

Raven had said goodbye. What the fuck did that mean? Bye? I'd just gotten here. I hadn't had a chance to even talk to her about us. Whatever *us* was.

Over. If she'd meant that goodbye, then *us* was over.

Maybe River showing up had saved me from making a

damn idiot of myself. From confessing my feelings and being slapped in the face at the realization that this was entirely one-sided.

Except it wasn't one-sided. It couldn't be. No way I'd read her wrong. There was something between us. There were feelings here. Weren't there?

If I could just find her, talk to her . . .

I glanced around the base, scanning the fences and signs that marked the different meeting areas for ski lessons. There weren't many kids today, being a Tuesday. And Raven was nowhere in sight. I hadn't seen her this morning when I'd met JR either.

"I'm heading in for a shower," he said. "Tomorrow morning?"

"I'll be ready."

He jerked up his chin and carried his board inside.

I did one last look, searching for dark hair and sapphire eyes. "Damn."

This was familiar. This was Raven avoiding me.

I'd come to Penny Ridge to see if this thing with Raven was real. I guess I had my answer.

"Crew." Weston held up an arm, snagging my attention as he walked my way.

"Hey." I smacked him on the back as he pulled me in for a hug.

"Heard you were back. I didn't expect it to be so soon."

"You can thank Lewis." I chuckled, letting him go. "He spent a pile of my money yesterday on a couple of condos."

"Then you've made Ava's week." Weston laughed. "How long are you sticking around?"

"Until Aspen. Reed pulled whatever strings he had to

pull and got me and my crew places to stay." Both Marianne and I were in the hotel. Lewis and JR were in employee housing.

"You could always stay with us," he said. "Callie and Sutton would love it."

"Thanks." They had a nice place, but I wouldn't intrude. Plus I'd wanted privacy for Raven. Though that didn't matter now either, did it?

"Did you hear about dinner?" Weston asked.

"No. What dinner?"

"Oh." He grimaced. "I figured Reed would have told you."

"Yesterday was crazy. Lewis and I spent most of it looking at condos and sitting at the realtor's office, putting the offer details together."

It felt unnecessary to use the realtor, considering I was buying the condos from the family business. But Reed had hired them to sell the condos because it freed up his and Ava's time to focus on other aspects of the company.

"What about dinner?" I asked. "I just saw Reed in the lodge after lunch."

"And he probably didn't mention it because he thinks it will be harder for you to say no to me."

I smirked. "It's not."

"Reed and Ava are having everyone over for dinner tonight. They'd like you to come too since you're here."

"No." See? Easy.

"Crew—"

"I'm not going to that house."

He sighed. "It's not easy to go there the first time. I didn't want to either until Callie pushed me to face it. But I'm glad I went. It's helped me deal with the past."

"So this is you pushing me?"

"If you hate it, you can always leave." Weston gave me a sad smile. "Please?"

Well, shit. It actually was hard to say no to Weston. Especially when he said please.

It reminded me of the conversation we'd had my junior year in high school.

After Mom's death, I'd cared less and less about grades. I'd been on the verge of dropping out, ditching as often as possible, just to spend time snowboarding. Competing. Because if I was on the mountain, the pain was manageable. Adrenaline chased away the grief.

The principal at the school had called home, getting Weston, not Dad, because Dad hadn't been home much. She'd told him that I was one unexcused absence away from flunking out.

So Weston had made me a deal. If I went to school, he'd help me get to competitions. I'd had my driver's license, so I hadn't exactly needed a ride, but being under eighteen, I'd needed someone to sign my liability waivers. Most of the events required a guardian or parent close by in case shit went sideways.

I sure as fuck couldn't have counted on Dad to come to the events. Or bother to come home. Or when he was home, be sober enough to pick up a pen.

Weston had done his best. He hadn't stepped in as a parent, he'd just been the brother I'd needed. And the day I'd graduated, we'd both been free.

He'd flown one way.

I'd gone another.

I owed him a lot. When he said please, I obeyed.

"Fine," I grumbled. "I'll go to dinner."

Weston's frame relaxed. "Thanks. I need to go meet Callie. She was taking pictures today. We'll head home. Pick up Sutton from school. Get cleaned up. Then we'll come to the lobby. We can all walk over together."

"Sounds good." At least I wouldn't have to walk to the house alone. "Text me when you're ready."

He clapped me on the shoulder, something he'd started doing after Mom, like he knew I needed a hug but wasn't going to make a big deal out of it. Then he left me to find Callie.

I rubbed a hand over my jaw, the stubble scraping my palm. After a long day, I needed a shower. But instead of taking off my gear and heading inside, I grabbed my board and strode for the closest chair.

When Weston texted me that they were almost at the lobby, I'd just finished my final run, so I raced inside, bolting up the stairs. I took the fastest shower of my life and changed into a pair of jeans and my favorite hoodie that I'd snagged at the Olympics. Then I rushed downstairs, tying my tennis shoes in the elevator, to meet my family.

"Sorry I'm late," I said.

Weston waved it off.

Callie gave me a hug. "We're not late."

She was an angel for lying.

"Hey, Sutton." I held up my hand for a fist bump.

"Hey." She smiled, her eyes widening at the logo on my sweatshirt. "Did you get that at the actual Olympics?"

"Yep."

"Whoa."

I chuckled, thankful this kid and her mother had found their way into Weston's life.

Weston took Callie's hand, holding out the other for Sutton, then the three of them led the way out of the hotel and into the night, down the familiar path that led home.

Home.

A blast into the past. From the outside, it looked the same. The A-frame's roof was covered in snow. The tall, peaked windows glowed gold from the lights inside.

My stomach churned as my foot hit the landing outside the door. My feet were heavy, my legs not wanting to work as Weston knocked, then pushed inside. But I couldn't bring myself to follow. It was like my body was revolting against this visit.

Weston glanced over his shoulder, giving me a nod of encouragement. So I swallowed hard and trudged through the door after him, drawing in a long breath.

It smelled different, like cinnamon and wood polish. Mom had always preferred vanilla. The shelf where she'd kept her pottery was brimming with art pieces, but these weren't Mom's. They had to be Ava's creations.

The living room furniture and décor were new. Reed had upgraded the appliances in the kitchen, and the walls had been painted a fresh white.

Different. Was that worse? Or better?

"Hey." Reed strode across the house to greet us, shaking Weston's hand and hugging Callie and Sutton. Then he came to me, hand extended. "Thanks for coming over."

"Yeah." My throat felt like it had been rubbed with sandpaper.

Dad emerged from the back of the house with Melody following close behind. Each wore a wide, white smile.

"Everybody's here. All right." He clapped. "It's party time."

Dad walked straight for Sutton, holding out a hand for a high five. But it wasn't just a high five. It morphed into a secret handshake that ended in a wink. "How was school today? Beat up any boys?"

She giggled and shrugged off her coat. "Nope."

"Aw, rats."

It wasn't the first time I'd seen this chipper version of Mark Madigan, but it still threw me entirely. Who was this guy and where had my father gone? The gruff, abrasive man who'd grunted more than spoken. This version of Dad was too . . .

"Jolly." Reed nudged my elbow, finishing my thought. "Weird, right?"

"Very."

Reed had sent a text years ago, after he'd come home, warning both Weston and me that Dad was jolly. Like aliens had swept in and planted a happy person in Dad's body.

"Who needs a drink?" Ava asked as she pulled containers from the fridge.

"Me." My hand shot in the air. The only way I was surviving this night was with a beer in my hand.

"I'll help," Dad said, dancing to the kitchen. He slid past Ava to retrieve a tumbler from a cupboard that he filled with ice.

I expected him to go for a bottle of whiskey next, but instead, he filled that glass with water.

He sipped it, giving an exaggerated, "Ah." Then

smacked his lips together. "There's nothing quite like a cold Blue Dolphin."

Melody giggled, her bright green eyes dancing as she stared at Dad.

"Dad quit drinking," Reed said, lowering his voice. "It's been good. There was a little hiccup along the way but he's sober."

"Huh." Aliens. Dad had definitely had an encounter with aliens. I gave Melody a sideways glance, searching the top of her head for antennae.

"How was Lake Placid, Crew?" Melody asked, walking over as I hung my coat up on the hook beside Weston's and Callie's.

"Uh, good." How did she know I'd gone to Lake Placid?

"I follow you on Instagram," she said, clearly reading my mind.

"Ah." Marianne must have posted some photos. "It was good."

"That's great." She smiled wider.

I waited, expecting her to make a comment about the last time I'd seen her: in a supply closet with a bare ass after I'd fucked Raven. Except she just stood by my side, smiling as we watched everyone bustling around the kitchen, getting drinks and chatting.

A family dinner.

Except the woman at my side wasn't the woman who belonged in this house.

In high school, after school when I'd come home, I'd have to remind myself that Mom was gone. I'd walk through the door every single day expecting to hear her voice. Expecting her to ask me about my day and how much homework I had to do.

Every single day, I'd had to tell myself she was dead and not coming back.

It had been that way until the day I'd left Penny Ridge.

Except tonight, when I'd walked through the door, I hadn't expected to see her. To hear her. It was like losing her all over again.

"I, uh . . ." I took one step away from Melody, then another. Then another. Until I was at the door, about to escape. I was seconds away from ducking out when Weston appeared at my side.

He put his hand on my shoulder and, with the other, handed me a beer. "Let's get some food."

Weston practically steered me toward the kitchen, thrusting a plate into my free hand.

"I was lazy and had dinner catered," Ava said. "The caterer we used for the wedding is such a sweetheart and she asked if we could be the taste testers for some new menu items."

"I love taste testing." Dad rubbed his hands together, then picked up a plate, handing it to his wife.

"Thanks, honey." Melody let him kiss her cheek, then led the way through the buffet before we all went to the table.

Conversation was seamless, though I listened more than spoke. There was a bit of gossip. A bit of shop talk. Callie and Ava dropped Raven's name a few times, talking about their girls' nights. Then the discussion turned to Weston and Callie's upcoming wedding. By the time Ava brought out a box of cookies she'd ordered for dessert, my head was pounding.

There hadn't been a single mention of Mom. Not one. We were sitting in her house, yet she wasn't even a ghost in the conversation.

Maybe I'd missed those dinners. Maybe I'd been traveling the world, competing, while my brothers had sat at this table and mourned our mother.

Or maybe everyone had moved on with their lives and she'd been erased.

"Want another beer?" Reed asked me.

"No, thanks. I actually think I'd better get going. Training tomorrow."

"Right. How was the pipe today?"

"Good." I stood from my chair and carried my empty plate to the sink. Then headed for the door, finally making the escape I should have earlier.

"Crew, wait up." Weston's chair scraped on the floor as he stood. "We'll walk out with you. We need to get home since it's a school night."

"Can we stay a little longer?" Sutton begged Callie.

"You have math."

Sutton groaned but stood, clearing her plate as Callie followed.

Everyone from the table stood, coming to the door to say goodnight as we pulled on our coats. The moment I'd said my farewell, I walked outside, not bothering to wait.

It took three long inhales of the mountain air before the weight came off my chest, but I still couldn't completely fill my lungs.

"Good night." Weston pulled the door closed behind him, then took Callie's hand.

I stared at the hotel as we walked, the lights still on in my corner room. It was the last place I felt like going at the moment. "Hey, do you think I could catch a ride into town?" I asked.

"Sure," Weston said. "Where to?"

I dragged a hand through my hair and turned to Callie. "Could you drop me at Raven's place?"

It wasn't like I could drive myself, because I wasn't sure where she lived. I really needed to get her number too.

Callie's jaw dropped, but she recovered quickly. "Of course."

Fuck. I was going to pay for that. There'd be questions. Lots of questions. And Raven would be fielding those questions, given the look that Callie shared with Weston.

Whatever. Tonight, I was selfishly seeking her out. I was in desperate need for just a little bit of steady.

That was Raven.

Somehow, in only weeks and after even more apart, she'd become my steady.

I climbed in the back of Weston's truck with Sutton, silently staring out the window as he drove us to town. He took a few familiar side streets, almost like he was going to Robin's place, but before he reached Raven's mom's house, he turned two blocks away, parking in front of a cottage.

"Thanks. This is, uh . . . not public knowledge. Got it?"

Weston nodded. So did Callie.

"See you guys later." I hopped out, closing the door quickly and striding up the sidewalk. Then I hit the doorbell, holding my breath as I waited.

Maybe she'd send me home. Maybe I'd get another goodbye.

Raven answered the door wearing a pair of blue flannel pajamas with a winter penguin print. Her dark hair was in a knot, her face clean and beautiful, the freckles across her nose on full display.

The tightness in my chest vanished. One look at her and I could breathe. "Hi."

"Hi." She glanced past me as Weston pulled away from the curb. Then she frowned.

"I didn't know where you lived." I shrugged. "Sorry." Not sorry.

"What are you doing here?"

"You weren't at work today or on the mountain."

She dropped her gaze to her bare feet. "I stayed home."

"Hiding from me?"

"Maybe," she whispered, then shifted to the side, waving me into the house.

I closed the door as I stepped into the entryway, then toed off my shoes. Presumptuous, maybe. But I hoped she'd let me stay. Hell, I'd sleep on the couch.

She was too close not to touch, so I snagged Raven's arm and hauled her close. Then I framed her face with my hands and kissed her lips, holding it. Waiting.

Three. Two. One.

She sagged into my chest, melting as she parted her lips.

I swept inside, fluttering my tongue against hers, earning a moan.

Her hands went to my coat, dragging the zipper free. Then they slipped under my hoodie, her palms hot against my bare skin.

I bent, cupping her ass as I hoisted her up, hauling her to the closest wall. I kept my mouth fused to hers, licking and sucking, nipping with enough bite to make her gasp, as we frantically stripped each other naked, our clothes puddled on the floor.

"Crew." Raven wrapped her legs around my hips, letting me pin her back to the wall.

There was no hesitation as I thrust inside, sliding deep. "Yes, baby."

"Oh, God." Her head lolled to the side, her nipples hard against my chest.

This. This was why I'd come to Penny Ridge. "Damn, but I missed you."

Her eyes flew open, locking with my own. Our breaths mingled, our heartbeats thundering. "What are we doing?" she whispered.

I pulled out and slammed inside, her inner walls squeezing my aching cock.

This wasn't a casual hookup. Not anymore. This went way beyond sex.

There'd be no goodbye, not this time.

What were we doing?

"I don't know," I lied. Deep down, I knew. "But I can't stay away from you."

And at this point, I wasn't even going to try.

CHAPTER SIXTEEN

RAVEN

I t was surreal to have Crew in my bed. He fit so naturally it was like the pillow he rested on had been waiting for his head.

"I like your place." He drew circles up and down my calf as he glanced around my room. The lights were on because after he'd fucked me in the entryway, we'd shuffled to my bed for round two.

Crew was propped up against the headboard, the white sheet low on his waist, like he knew I wanted to stare at those washboard abs.

I was leaning against the footboard, our legs tangled in the middle of the bed as we faced each other.

"This bed is sweet." He ran a hand along the headboard's cobalt-blue velvet tufts.

"It was an impulse buy. But I've never regretted it."

I wasn't sure exactly how an interior decorator would classify my style. It wasn't shabby chic or eclectic. It wasn't modern or traditional. It was this odd mix of pieces I'd found and fallen in love with. So they'd stayed and, somehow, mixed together. It worked.

Around the room I'd hung my collection of vintage ski resort prints, mostly from places I'd been but some from places I wanted to go, like Austria and France. The walls were white in my room—the bed itself gave the space plenty of character—but every room in the rest of the house was a different shade. Hunter green. Mustard yellow. The guest bathroom was coral.

"What will you tell Callie?" he asked.

I lifted a shoulder. "The truth." She was one of my best friends. I'd kept this a secret long enough. From Ava too.

Maybe I should have been pissed, since I'd told him just last night that this needed to stay a secret. But I wasn't mad. Eventually, I would have told Callie, Ava and Halley anyway.

"Sorry." He squeezed my foot.

"It's okay. I just need to figure out how to tell River." And *what* to tell River.

"Want me to do it?"

"What would you say?"

He thought about it for a moment until the corner of his mouth turned up. "That I like his sister's bed."

"Smooth." I kicked at him, rolling my eyes. "No, I need to be the one to tell him."

"He's not going to care, baby."

"Yes, he will. Not just because you crossed some imaginary line where you slept with his sister. But because you're his." River wouldn't want to share Crew, and if I knew my brother, he'd see this as a betrayal. That I'd stolen his friend.

"You're overthinking this." Crew sat up straight, leaning closer.

"Probably. I just . . . it would be easier if I knew what we were doing." I summoned my courage, more nervous at this moment than I had been in years, and asked the question I'd asked in the entryway. "What are we doing?"

We weren't dating. We weren't casual, at least, not for me. Though I'd tried my hardest to classify it as just sex last night.

"Last night you said just sex," he said.

"Yes, I said that."

"Did you mean it?"

"No," I whispered.

Relief flashed across his face. "What do you want?"

"All or nothing." With Crew, it had to be all or nothing. And *nothing* loomed on the horizon.

Crew dropped his gaze to the bedding. Either because he wasn't sure which of those two choices to pick. Or because he did and he knew I wouldn't like the answer.

After Aspen, he'd return to his life. Maybe he'd make a few trips to Penny Ridge to stay in his new condo, but this was a vacation destination, nothing more. I couldn't keep my life on pause, waiting for him to come back.

I wasn't letting anyone leave me again.

This time, it would be on my terms.

All or nothing.

"I don't think I can live here," he said. "I went to dinner at Reed's place tonight. It was . . . hard."

So after dinner, he'd come here. Did that make me his refuge? Or his escape? "What happened?"

"It's Mom's house. There have been some changes, but it's still her house. And no one talked about her. Not once. I can't tell if it's because I just missed those conversations being gone for so long. Or if they've forgotten her. It feels like they've forgotten her."

Not Crew. He'd held her close for years and years. I suspected he always would.

"You know how Mom died," he said.

I nodded. "Yes."

"We went so long not knowing what was wrong with her. The doctors. The tests. The trips Dad would take her on to Denver. They'd come home frustrated. And the longer it went on, the more Mom would doubt herself."

"What do you mean?"

"I'd overhear conversations where she'd basically convince herself it was imaginary. But Dad was the one to push. To keep looking for an answer. Keep driving her to the hospital. And then . . . then they got an answer."

It hadn't been an answer anyone had wanted.

"I'm sorry, Crew."

"Me too," he whispered. "I'm glad we had that last year with her. We had time, even though it was hard knowing it was terminal. Mom was miserable, we could all see it, but she never stopped smiling. She did her best for us, especially me, until the end."

I sat up, stretching to take his hand and lace our fingers together. There weren't a lot of words to say, nothing to take away that pain, but I could be here. I could hold his hand while he talked.

"Dad was supposed to be there. After she died, he was

supposed to step up." Crew gritted his teeth. "Instead, he disappeared. He spent every waking minute in his office. He'd come home late, long after dinner was over, never asking if I'd eaten or if I was doing okay. Hell, he never even checked to see if there was food in the fridge. If not for Weston sticking around . . . I don't know what would have happened."

"Wait. What?"

"He just checked out," Crew said. "He drank a lot. When he was home, he was an asshole, barking at us for not cleaning up the kitchen. When I broke my hand in high school, he didn't care that I was hurt. He was just pissed that he'd had to leave work and come to the hospital. He was angry that I'd made him set foot in the place where Mom had died."

My jaw dropped. "I had no idea."

Everyone around Penny Ridge had known there was a rift between Mark and his sons, but no one really knew the cause. Most thought that after Natalie had died, they'd all just drifted apart. But this? Crew had only been fourteen when his mother had passed. For Mark to abandon him wasn't just wrong, it was cruel.

And all this time, I'd looked at Mark as a mentor. The man who'd given me a career after college.

"Raven." Crew wiggled his fingers, enough for me to realize I'd started to squeeze. Hard. "You don't have to be angry at Dad on my behalf."

"Well, I am."

His eyes softened. "He apologized to me when I got here in November. It was weird. I wasn't really sure what to say. He hasn't done much to reach out to me since I left. Not that

I'd answer when he'd call. I came here expecting to find the grumpy bastard he'd been. But he's different. I'm not sure what to make of it. And honestly, I wish he weren't so . . . happy. I sound like an asshole, but it's true."

Not an asshole. Just a guy laying it all out there. For me.

Crew fidgeted with my fingers. "It feels like he forgot Mom. He's got Melody. He's chipper. Mom died and it wrecked me. Dad should have been there and he wasn't. So to come home, to see him living this new life, pisses me off. And deep down, I don't want him to be miserable. Hell, I like Melody. I just . . . I don't know how to feel. It was all easier to ignore before."

"Then why'd you come back again?"

His eyes locked with mine. *For you.*

I wouldn't ask him to stay here if it caused him this much pain. There was no missing the anguish and conflict in his voice. But could I leave? Could I give up my career, my home, my family, my *life* to follow this man around the world?

What happened when it ended? What happened when I became my mother, waiting at home for Crew to return, only to finally realize, years too late, that I'd never been the love of his life?

I wasn't the only one in this bed with Daddy issues.

"I'm angry at Mark," I said. "But for your sake, maybe you should be telling him this, not me. I don't think he's forgotten your mom. I don't think anyone could forget her. But I think your dad, and your brothers, have found peace."

"Yeah," he muttered, dragging in a long inhale. On the exhale, he changed the subject. "I don't think Melody told anyone about us. Callie was pretty shocked when I asked them to bring me here."

"Oh, I'm sure Melody kept it quiet. She zipped her lips and gave me the key, remember?"

"No, I missed that. I was too busy trying to keep her from seeing my cock."

I giggled. "I like Melody."

"She seems cool. She's nothing like my mother."

"Is that a good thing?"

He thought about it for a moment. "Yeah. It is."

I relaxed, leaning into the footboard again as Crew traced circles on my ankles. The clock on my nightstand showed it was well after midnight and normally I crashed around ten.

When I yawned, he stretched forward to capture my hand, tugging me to the pillows. Then he tucked me beneath the covers before getting up to shut off the lights.

"I'm boarding tomorrow," he said, curling my back into his chest. "My coach is here. Are you working?"

"No." I'd taken today and tomorrow off to practice for the Burton open.

"Come riding with us."

"Are you sure your coach won't mind?"

"He'll love it. Especially if you don't care if he gives you some pointers."

Seriously? That would be a dream. "Okay." I smiled, snuggling deeper.

"I'm spending the night."

"I sort of figured that out since you're naked in my bed and you don't have a ride."

He buried his nose in my hair. "Do you care?"

"No," I lied. The truth was, when it came to Crew, I cared too much.

And it was probably going to get my heart broken.

But instead of worrying about it, I let him hold me until I fell asleep.

CHAPTER SEVENTEEN

RAVEN

JR Thomas was giving me pointers. *The* JR Thomas—one of the most well-known snowboarding coaches in the world—was coaching *me*.

River would be green with envy if he knew I was here today, learning from Crew's coach.

"I need you to pinch me," I told Crew as we waited on the lip of the halfpipe. "This can't be real."

Crew chuckled, glancing around to make sure no one was watching. Then he leaned close, his lips brushing across my jaw before he gave it a nip. "I'll pinch you later."

A rush of heat bloomed in my core. "Don't distract me."

He grinned. "Wouldn't dream of it."

"Do you want to go next?"

"You go. I like to watch."

Even that sounded like a sexual promise. Knowing Crew, it probably was.

He'd woken me up this morning with his fingers stroking

my pussy, and after an orgasm, I'd been tempted to skip riding today and keep him trapped in my bed.

But JR had come all the way to Madigan Mountain, and the X Games were approaching. So after we'd showered together, Crew and I had headed to the lodge. He'd gone to his hotel room to get his gear while I'd gone up on a run solo. Then I'd come to the halfpipe and waited.

When Crew had introduced me to JR, by some miracle, I'd kept the fangirling to a minimum.

"You're up." Crew nudged his elbow with mine.

I shifted toward the lip, pulling my goggles over my eyes, scanning the area just to make sure someone hadn't dropped in before me.

The halfpipe was open to the public now and a few guys were out this morning, getting in some rides. The afternoons would be even busier, so Crew and JR were here early to capitalize on their training hours.

Don't crash. Don't crash. Don't crash.

"You're not going to crash." Crew laughed and shook his head.

"You weren't supposed to hear that," I muttered, my cheeks flaming.

"Go." He jerked his chin at the pipe. "Show off for me. All or nothing, right?"

All or nothing.

I wasn't sure how I'd recover if we became nothing. But today, I didn't want to think about the future. I didn't want to look past this week. So I took a deep breath and dropped in, letting my heart soar as I did the three tricks I'd been working on this morning. When I came out at the bottom, my blood was pumping and pulse racing.

It was almost as exhilarating as sex with Crew.

"Nice." JR held out a hand for a fist bump. "You nailed the alley-oop rodeo. How'd that feel rotating your shoulders differently?"

"Much better." I smiled, breathing hard. The trick was a backside 180 while doing a backflip on the frontside wall. I'd worked my ass off for years trying to get it just right. It was the stunt I landed only half of the time.

JR's tips had been simple, changing my approach and how I angled my body. But they'd made all the difference in the world.

Thayer had tried to coach me when we'd been together. I hadn't realized it at the time, having never been coached before, but there'd been such arrogance in his instruction. A frustration when his tips hadn't worked and I'd done it my own way.

I fought a smile, thinking about what he'd say if he could see me now, standing with JR Thomas. "Thank you."

"Of course. You're doing awesome. That would be a great sequence for a competition."

JR Thomas had just told me I was doing awesome. It was a fight not to let my jaw hit the snow.

"Crew said you're doing the Burton open?"

"Oh, uh, yes?" It came out like a question. Why, I wasn't sure. I'd registered. I'd taken the weekend off work, making sure I had people here to cover for me.

If I thought about it too much, I'd turn my body inside out with anxiety. So I tried not to think about it. I didn't talk about it either.

Even though Halley, Ava and Callie had all been urging me sign up for months, Crew was the reason I'd taken the plunge. His support was different than that from my friends.

He was an athlete. He knew what it took to compete at that level. He knew how miserable it was to lose.

I'd never had anyone in the sport encourage me like Crew. Not my father. Certainly not my brother. Not Thayer. Not even my mother, really.

Mom didn't spend a lot of time on the ski hill, mostly because Dad had brought us up here as kids. This had been his arena, not hers. And in a way, I think she resented this mountain at times.

So I downplayed my dreams. I clutched them to my chest, hiding them from the world.

Until Crew.

I cast my eyes up the pipe, finding him on the lip. He lifted one arm in the air, signaling he was about to drop in, then he flew.

If my heart had been in my throat during my own run, it was beating out of my chest as I watched him do flip after flip. He made it look easy. He was flawless. Hypnotic.

My heart was in my throat as he did one last trick, a double cork 1440 that he'd been working on today. He nailed it. The others watching along the pipe cheered.

"Wow," I whispered, forgetting JR at my side.

"Of all the athletes I've coached, Crew is the best. It comes to him naturally. He leaves it on the pipe, every time. No hesitation. No reservation. I'm not sure what drives him. Hell, I'm not sure that he even knows. But it's incredible to watch, isn't it?"

"Yes, it is."

What drove Crew? The man loved to win. Even in the

bedroom, he reveled in earning my orgasms. But beyond his talent, his love for victory, I think loneliness drove Crew.

He'd fled Penny Ridge. I hadn't realized until last night when he'd told me about Mark just how awful high school must have been. All I remembered was how he'd been at our house all the time. How he and River would come up here every chance, even if that meant ditching school.

Crew had used snowboarding to fill the holes. To escape.

I wish I'd known. Not that I would have known how to handle it. I'd been too young and too naïve to be the person Crew had needed at that time. Still, I wish I'd known.

Crew came to a sliding stop in front of us, his breath billowing as he panted. "Still not quite right."

Not quite right?

"Looked good from here," JR said, voicing my thoughts. "What feels wrong?"

"I don't know." Crew rubbed his jaw with a glove. "It feels . . . stiff."

"Is it your knee?" JR asked.

His knee? What was wrong with his knee?

Crew sighed, giving his coach a single nod.

"We pushed hard yesterday," JR said. "Let's back off it today. Why don't you spend some time on the mountain, easy runs. Don't push. Give your legs a workout but don't go to the extreme. Then tomorrow morning, we'll meet in the hotel's gym."

"Okay. You want to go up?"

JR looked to me, then back at Crew. "Why don't you two go together? I'll ride with you tomorrow."

As much as I wanted to spend every moment with JR, soaking up each kernel of advice, a day on the mountain, alone with Crew, was far too appealing. So I kept my mouth shut, hoping that Crew didn't object.

"Sounds good." He held out a hand to shake with JR. "See you tomorrow."

"Nice to meet you, Raven. Good luck at the open." With a wave, JR walked away, leaving Crew and me at the base of the halfpipe.

"If you need to train or take it easy—"

"You heard the man." Crew grinned and unstrapped one boot from his board. "You're stuck with me today."

Yes. I did a mental fist pump, then unstrapped my own boot before following Crew to the lift. I waited until we were halfway up the slope before turning to him. "What happened to your knee? I thought it was your shoulder that was hurt."

"Yeah." He frowned. "My shoulder. Then I tweaked my knee. I'm just struggling this year. Everything feels . . ."

"Stiff?" I stole his word from earlier.

"Stiff. Mechanical. I don't know exactly how to describe it." Crew cast his gaze over the terrain park, watching as a guy slid across a rail. "The best days I've had all year are the days I ride with you."

"Why does that sound like a bad thing?" It stung to hear the disappointment in his voice. My best days had been riding with him too.

"It's not a bad thing." Crew gave me a sad smile. "If there was ever a compliment I could give you, it would be how much I love chasing you down this mountain. But competing, riding at the big events, training for them, there's never been a higher high. This year, something's missing."

And if I'd been the best days, in Crew's life, that meant

trouble. "You haven't even competed yet. How do you know something is missing?"

"Trust me, I asked myself that same question. But I feel it. There's a hole. I've never once thought about retiring. Not once. There has always been a next season."

My eyes widened. "You want to retire?"

"Yes. No." His shoulders slumped. "I feel like this year, it's not about boarding. I'm doing it because I have something to prove."

"What could you possibly have to prove?" He'd won at every level.

"That I still have it," he whispered. "And I'm scared. Because what if I don't."

My gloved hand reached for his. "You do."

"It feels like my body is betraying me. First the shoulder. Now my knee."

"How did you hurt your knee?"

He shifted, turning slightly to face me, but he didn't let go of my hand. "I was out riding last month. On Christmas Day. After Mom, holidays—especially Christmas—got weird."

Natalie had died right around Christmas.

"Even in high school, Weston and I would split up," he said. "Do our own thing."

Probably because Mark hadn't organized an actual holiday. That man was getting my fiercest glare the next time we crossed paths.

"After I left town, I just always spent them alone."

"For twelve years?" I asked, my heart aching.

He shrugged. "It's always a good day to spend riding. It's quiet. This year, I was going too hard. Crashed on a stupid stunt and fucked up my knee. Twisted it the wrong way. It's manageable. I wore a brace for a few weeks. But yesterday I pushed hard. Too hard. Now it's just one more injury that will heal but only if I rest. One more future surgery if I don't back off."

"I'm sorry." For his shoulder. For his knee. Mostly, I was sorry that he'd been alone.

He let my hand go, glancing to the top of the chair. This lift wasn't long enough. There was more to say. But instead, we reached the top and unloaded, following a trail away from the terrain park toward another chair that would take us to the summit.

Crew seemed locked in his own head as we rode the next chair, so I gave him a reprieve from my questions. I stared out at the mountains, watching the clouds dance along the distant, snowy peaks.

He paused only for a moment to strap in when we unloaded, then he was off, leading the way through the runs toward the boundary lines of the mountain.

We were on the original runs of the resort, not the new areas from the expansion. I hadn't ventured this way much lately, mostly sticking to the newer areas. But I'd forgotten just how much I loved it here. How much this area reminded me of my childhood, the days when River and I were finally good enough to come to the top with Dad.

I'd expected Crew to veer down a black diamond, but instead, he rode toward a clearing in the trees. Then he stopped and sat down on the snow, his eyes on the valley spread below.

Penny Ridge was small in the distance. The highway carved a winding line in the trees.

"When I was a kid, Dad used to bring us up here on our first run of the season," Crew said. "Like a first day of school picture, except it was a first day on the mountain. He'd line us all up in this exact spot. Reed, Weston and me, always in the same order. He'd have his Nikon strapped around his neck, tucked in his coat to take a picture. It was Mom's request. She had the pictures framed in her office at the house. I'm not sure what happened to them."

"They're in your dad's office," I said. "After he and Melody moved out of the house, he hung them in his office."

"Seriously?" Crew's face whipped to mine, and when I nodded, he sighed, turning to the view. "Huh."

Mark hadn't done right by his sons, but he loved them.

Crew didn't move as he stared into the sky, the sun climbing higher and higher. A wind picked up, blowing in clouds and more snow. A chill seeped through my layers, but I didn't move.

I gave Crew the time he needed to hopefully heal his heart.

"It's an escape," he finally spoke. "Competing. I left here and threw my life into this." He pointed toward his board.

And now he was staring at the horizon, searching for his next escape. Was that me? Was I his latest distraction to keep himself from facing the past?

"Brr." He shivered. "Let's get out of here."

"Okay." I stood, brushing off the snow from my pants.

"Raven." He stood too, grabbing my hand to stop me before I could disappear. His expression was the same one he'd had the other night in the hotel before River had interrupted us. His eyes were too solemn. His expression too . . . serious.

I'd asked him for all or nothing and he hadn't answered me.

"Don't. Don't say whatever it is you're going to say. Not yet." *Not today.*

He swallowed hard and nodded. "Then we'll just ride."

I led the way down the mountain, working our way back toward the expanded runs. There was too much history on the original part of the mountain for us both, but especially for Crew. So we spent the rest of the day exploring the expansion.

Conversation was limited. The chair rides quiet. In a way, it was almost like I was riding alone. But neither of us offered to give the other space. So we stayed together until my stomach growled, ready for a late lunch.

"I'm going to head home," I told him when we reached the base. I took a step, ready to duck out, when he caught my hand.

"Don't go. Please, Raven. Stay with me."

"Crew, this has been an intense week and it's only Wednesday."

"I know." The corner of his mouth turned up, that dimple flashing. "But I promised to pinch you."

Oh, damn him. Why did he have to be funny too? I giggled as his smile widened.

"Meet you in there." Before I could argue, he picked up his board and strode toward the hotel.

I tipped my head back to the sky. "Why am I so weak?"

The white clouds above had no answer, so I loosened a long breath and trudged toward the hotel, glancing around to make sure I didn't see any familiar faces.

As always, a few people watched Crew. No one paid me any attention.

I tugged off my gloves as I walked, shoving them into my coat. I pushed up my goggles and unbuckled my helmet, taking it off and shaking out my hair. Then I opened the hotel lobby's door, avoiding eye contact with the front desk receptionist as I strode for the elevator.

The doors were open, and when I stepped inside, Crew was waiting.

He stretched past me to hit the button for the third floor, and the moment we were in motion, his mouth was on mine.

My helmet landed by my boots. His dropped next. A whimper escaped my mouth as his tongue swept against mine in a languid swirl.

He tore his lips away, trailing them down my neck. "I need you out of these clothes."

"Yes." I clung to his arms as he kissed my pulse, then licked the same spot. My hands drifted to the zipper on his coat, tugging it free. I was about to palm his arousal when the elevator chimed, the movement stopped and the doors opened.

Crew pulled away, reaching for our boards propped against the back wall.

I bent, picking up our helmets.

Then I looked up—and met a pair of blue eyes locked on my neck, on the spot where Crew's mouth had just been.

River.

CHAPTER EIGHTEEN

CREW

"River." My voice was calm despite my racing heart.

Fury rolled off River's frame, creating this wall Raven and I had to break through as we stepped off the elevator.

"It's nothing," she blurted.

I grimaced.

She cringed. "It's not nothing. It's . . . sex?"

Seriously? A question? Apparently I needed to make intentions clear. Later. After we calmed down River, whose hands were fisted at his sides. "Sex?"

I propped our boards against the wall beside the elevator. "It's not just sex."

"Oh my God." Raven pressed her fingers to her temples. "Stop saying sex."

I almost laughed. Almost. Except River moved straight into my space, his chest bumping mine.

"What the fuck, Crew?"

"Whoa." I stepped back, holding up my hands as the scent of weed hit my nose. "Are you high?"

"Fuck off." River shoved my shoulders.

Raven gasped. "River."

There was a fight brewing in River's eyes, so I stayed quiet, hoping he'd leave and let the shock wear off. Then we could talk about it like adults.

"She's my sister," he spat. "You're my best friend. How could you do this? That's a fucking line you never should have crossed."

"I care about her," I said. He was acting like I was a damn monster. "Would you chill?"

River's answer was another shove.

"River, stop this." Raven stepped between us, our helmets dropping as she placed her hands on his chest and pushed hard enough to create some distance.

I took her shoulders, easing her to my side because if River exploded and went off the rails, I didn't want her in the middle.

"Are you stoned?" she asked, cocking her head. She must have gotten a whiff of weed too. "It's one in the afternoon."

River scowled. "You're not my babysitter, Raven. Jesus. Let's focus on the fact that you're screwing my best friend."

"No." I cut a line in the air with my hand. "We'll talk about this later. Or not, since it's none of your goddamn business."

"None of my business?" River's voice rose to nearly a shout.

Behind him, a couple came walking down the hallway toward the elevator. They paused as he yelled.

Super. Now we were causing a scene.

"Sorry," I told the couple as they turned, taking the door for the stairwell. Then I raked a hand through my hair. The last thing I needed was someone to snap a photo of this. Or worse, a video. "Let's take this to my room."

"Fuck you," River spat. "How long?"

Neither Raven nor I answered.

"How. Long?" he barked.

I swallowed hard. "It started in November."

"Unbelievable." He scoffed. "Way to keep a secret from your best friend. And here I am, up here to see if you wanted to ride together so you didn't have to be alone on this mountain of all places, and I find you sucking face with my sister. You're dead to me."

"River," Raven hissed. "Stop making such a big deal out of this. What is wrong with you?"

"Me?" He pointed to his chest. "What's wrong with *me*? What the hell is wrong with *you*? You're his fuck buddy, Raven. You don't think he's hooking up with women when he's not here? You think he didn't find someone else when he left here in November?"

Her entire body flinched. Her eyes went wide. Like she hadn't even considered our time apart, but now he'd planted that seed.

It wasn't true. I hadn't so much as looked at another woman since we'd started this in November. But before I could explain, River kept on spewing poison.

"Didn't you learn anything from Thayer?" River scoffed.

Thayer. Who the fuck was Thayer? Not Thayer Mills. Oh God, don't let it be Thayer Mills. I fucking hated that guy. The idea of him and Raven coated my vision in red.

"Thayer?" My voice was as sharp as a knife.

Raven swallowed hard, her face paling.

"You thought Thayer was bad." River scoffed. "But you just went from one player to another. And Crew makes Thayer look like a saint."

"We're not talking about this," Raven said, but he ignored her.

"Yes, we are. I got arrested defending you." River threw his hands out wide. "Fucking arrested, Raven. And here you are, spreading your legs again. Acting like a whore."

Raven's entire body jerked like he'd slapped her.

Fuck no.

I seized River's coat and rammed him into the wall. "Don't fucking talk to her like that."

"Fuck you," River screamed in my face, pushing and shoving to get free.

But I kept him pinned, using the strength I'd been honing for years.

"Let me go!"

Fine. I'd let him go. I hauled him off the wall, then shoved him backward. Hard. He stumbled, almost falling to the floor, but regained his balance and stood.

"Get out. Now," I seethed.

River looked to Raven, like he was about to say something else, but I pointed down the hallway.

He sneered, then marched toward the stairwell. When he passed a trash can, he kicked it over. It clattered and fell while he disappeared through the exit.

"Fuck." I blew out a long breath, turning to Raven. "Sorry."

She stood frozen, reeling.

Whore.

One word that ended the longest friendship in my life.

"Raven." I moved into her space, framing her face in my hands and forcing her to look at me. When her gaze met mine, her eyes flooded. "Baby."

"Is it true? Were you with other women?"

"No."

She didn't believe me. I could see the doubt swimming in those blue irises.

"There has been no one. I swear."

"I have to go." She tore out of my hold, walking straight for the toppled garbage can.

"Raven, wait."

She set the can upright, picking up the few items of trash that had fallen out, then jogged for the stairwell.

After the door slammed behind her, the silence in the hallway was deafening.

Should I chase her? Or let her go? Was she trying to catch River? Maybe she had something to say to her brother. Maybe she wanted to talk to him alone.

Fuck that. I was about to follow when the elevator chimed and out stepped my dad.

Oh, hell. I should have stayed in Raven's bed this morning.

"Hey." He smiled, too wide. "I was hoping to catch you."

"Now's not a great time, Dad."

"Oh." His smile dropped. "Uh, okay."

I snagged my board, about to grab Raven's, when Dad picked it up first, then bent to retrieve her helmet.

"I'll help."

"Great," I muttered, picking up my own helmet and walking for my suite.

The moment we were inside, I set my gear aside and took Raven's. Then I waved for the door. "I need—"

"Great to see you at dinner last night."

I sighed. We were doing this, weren't we? Now?

Meanwhile, Raven was probably outside already, heading for her car. By the time I caught up, she'd probably already be on her way home.

I'd give her that space. I'd let the shock fade. Then I'd chase her down.

Damn it. So I sighed and tore off my coat, tossing it over the arm of the couch. This conversation with Dad was twelve years in the making, maybe more. And I still wasn't prepared.

Dad took one of the chairs, leaning forward. "I, uh . . . how's the halfpipe? Reed mentioned you're training here until Aspen."

"That's right." I slumped to the edge of the couch, glancing at the door.

She'd been close to tears.

Five minutes. I was giving her a five-minute head start, then I was out of here.

"How's it going?" Dad asked.

I shrugged. "Good."

"And your shoulder?"

"Fine."

He nodded, opening his mouth, then closing it. After my one-word answers, Dad seemed to have run out of questions.

Silence stretched between us, the seconds going by slower and slower with every tick of the wall's clock. Until I couldn't take it anymore. I couldn't stand that goddamn apologetic look, the hopelessness, on his face.

"I don't know if I can ever forgive you for what you did after Mom."

He gulped. "I doubt I'll ever forgive myself."

"I needed you. More than Weston or Reed. I was fourteen and needed a parent. You left me."

"I did." The pain in his voice was unmistakable. "I'm sorry. I'm sorry, Crew."

"It feels like everyone has forgotten her." A lump formed in my throat.

"I didn't." He pressed his hand to his heart. "She's always been right here. And in you. More than anyone, I see her in you. She wasn't wild like you. But she loved like you. Fiercely. Until the end."

Was that why he'd buried himself in work after she'd died? Why he'd barely looked at me those miserable years? Because he saw Mom?

I closed my eyes, hanging my head. Maybe when I'd come here in November, I'd planned to punish him. That was why I hadn't sat with him at Reed and Ava's wedding. Why I'd turned my back on him. But the anger, the resentment I'd held close all these years just wasn't here today.

Maybe I was too tired, too focused on Raven to be pissed at Dad. Maybe my frustration had vanished at some point after my trip here in November. Or maybe I'd finally talked about the past. I'd shared that burden with Raven, and today, it wasn't as heavy.

Hell, she'd been angry enough for us both last night. I loved her for that rage.

I loved her period.

Oh, fuck. I loved her. And I really needed to find her.

"Dad, I need to go." I shot off the couch.

He nodded once, then stood too. "Yeah. I'll get out of here. You're busy."

"Dad." I stopped him before he could leave. "I don't want anyone to forget Mom."

"No one has. We talk about her. More now than before. Melody asks questions. She wants to know what your mother was like."

Yeah, I needed to get to know his new wife. "Remember that spot where we used to take our first-day-of-the-season picture? I went there today."

His eyes softened. "I go there every time I ski."

"You do?"

"Every time. I haven't been the best father, but that doesn't mean I don't love my sons." With that, he walked for the door.

"Dad?"

"Yeah?" He glanced over his shoulder, his eyes glassy.

"Thanks for coming up."

"Mind if I come watch you train one of these days?"

"Not at all."

He nodded, then opened the door, but shied back. "Oh, uh. Hi, Raven."

My heart leapt out of my chest as I sprinted for her.

"Hi," she clipped, sliding past Dad. Even through all that bullshit with River, she was still pissed at Dad.

Yep. I loved her.

My whole life was about to change, wasn't it?

Dad held the door open for her, then slipped out of the room.

"I was just about to come find you," I said, pulling her into my arms. She burrowed her face in my coat. "I'm sorry."

236

"Why are you apologizing? River is my brother."

"He's my friend." He *was* my friend.

Raven stepped out of my arms, walking toward the windows. "He called me a whore."

"I should have punched him."

She huffed. "*I* should have punched him."

"He went too far."

She nodded. "I know. I'll talk to him about it later. I just . . . ouch."

It took every ounce of willpower not to cross the room and hold her. It took even more not to hunt down River and beat the shit out of him for hurting her. But Raven looked like she needed space. That was why she'd left.

Day by day, I was figuring this woman out. Maybe by the time we were old and gray, I'd know her better than I knew myself.

"What he said. About me and other women. There hasn't been anyone."

She turned away from the glass, locking her eyes with mine. "I believe you."

"Good." I moved to the couch, sitting on the arm. "Who's Thayer?" I asked, even though I suspected the answer.

"Thayer Mills."

My lip curled.

"My sentiments exactly." She rolled her eyes. "We dated for a while last year. Or I thought we were dating. I didn't realize until we were over that our relationship was one-sided."

Was that why she'd always kept me at a distance? Because of that prick Thayer? She'd joked about finding a nerdy guy but maybe it hadn't been a joke.

"Do you know him?" she asked.

"Unfortunately."

Thayer had made a name for himself in the sport over the past decade. Mostly he did slopestyle competitions but our paths crossed at the larger events. He was an arrogant bastard who treated younger athletes like shit, and his reputation with women was even worse.

"We met at Breckenridge. We started seeing each other. He'd come here on his free weekends. I'd go to his place at Copper."

Thayer had a whole pack of asshole friends who lived around him at Copper. Another reason I was glad I'd chosen Park City.

"Let's skip to the end," I said. The last thing I needed were any visuals of Raven with that shithead.

"It was getting serious. Again, so I thought. He hadn't asked me to move, but I'd started looking for places around Copper, just so I could see him more. Then one day, he stopped returning my calls and texts. We went from talking daily to nothing. That was how he ended it. He just ignored me."

Fool. Thayer Mills was an epic fool. But his loss was my gain.

"I felt like my mother." She cringed. "That sounds awful. I love my mom and admire her. But when it comes to Dad, I just . . . I never wanted that."

This was the reason she'd been so hesitant at the beginning. Why she'd wanted to keep us a secret. Raven was worried I'd treat her like Rowdy treated Robin. Or like Thayer had treated her.

"Shortly after Thayer ghosted me, River and I went to

Eldora. It was just a quick day trip on a random Tuesday. We were in line at the lift. I heard a familiar laugh and turned around to see Thayer with another woman."

"Prick."

"That's what I said. River took it a step further. He got into it with Thayer and ended up punching him. The cops were called and River got arrested. It was a mess."

"He never told me any of that." Not that I'd been around much to hear the story.

"We were both embarrassed." She closed her eyes, almost like she wanted to hide from this story. "So neither of us talked about it."

"Understandable." I crossed the room, hooking my finger under her chin to tilt up her face, waiting until she opened her eyes and looked at me. "I'm not Thayer Mills."

"Every snowboarder I've dated has broken my heart."

"Don't lump me in with assholes from your past. That's not fair."

"I know." She sighed. "But there's still a chance you'll break my heart."

No way in hell.

"Am I an escape?" she whispered.

"What do you mean?"

"You said snowboarding was your escape. After your mom died."

I'd told her I'd used competing as an escape. And that my career might be over sooner rather than later. So now she was worried that I was trading my previous escape for another.

I pulled her into my arms, burying my nose in her hair. "Yes, you're an escape. You're also an addiction. A refuge. An adventure. This—us—is not me escaping a reality I don't

239

want to face. This is me coming to you because it's the only place I want to be."

She clung to me, holding tight.

Raven had asked for all or nothing. The only reason I hadn't answered her last night was because I wasn't sure I could give her the all she wanted.

"I don't know if I can live here again," I confessed.

But we'd figure this out, right? Once I got my bearings. I was flying down an uncharted path. For the first time in my life, I was in love. Would that scare her as much as it scared me?

Like she could hear my thoughts, she stiffened. Then she started to squirm, trying to wiggle free.

"Stop." I kissed her hair.

"I should go."

"Go where? This is where you're supposed to be."

It took a moment, but she finally relaxed. "What are we doing, Crew?"

Like last night, I still didn't have an answer.

So I carried her to the bed and hoped that, by morning, I'd figure it out.

CHAPTER NINETEEN

RAVEN

I knocked and opened the door to Mom's house. "Hello?"

"Come on in!" she called from the kitchen.

I toed off my shoes, then wandered through the living room toward the back of the house, finding her in the breakfast nook with a steaming cup of coffee. "Hey, Mom."

"Hi. How's my girl?"

"Okay." I bent and gave her a hug before going to the coffee pot to fill my own mug. "Is River up?"

She laughed.

That meant no.

I took a seat beside her. "Not working today?"

"No, I'm off today, but working over the weekend. Another shift in the ER. I figured you'd be on the mountain already."

"Soon." I needed to head up in the next thirty minutes to get started on work for the day.

She sipped from her cup, leaning back in her chair and

arching her eyebrows. That meant she knew why I'd texted that I was on my way over.

"River told you about Crew."

"Yes."

"And?"

She sighed. "I don't want you to end up like me."

This was the first time she'd ever voiced my own fears.

I didn't want to end up like her either. I loved my mother. I admired her. But I'd been in the front row seat as Dad had disappointed her over and over and over again. For every event he'd missed, every milestone he'd skipped, Mom hadn't just felt her own pain. She'd carried ours too.

I'd witnessed Mom grow distant through the final years of their marriage. I'd overheard countless fights she'd had with him over the phone.

If that was my future, I'd pass.

Except how could I pass on Crew?

"I care about him," I said.

She reached across the table, putting her hand on my forearm. "For what it's worth, I think Crew has a good heart. I don't think he'll intentionally break yours."

"Do you think Dad intentionally hurt you?"

"In the end? Maybe. I think he loved me, or the idea of me. I loved him too, but eventually, that love wasn't enough. I caused him pain when I told him I wanted a divorce. He did some things to repay that."

"He did? Like what?"

"You have enough of your own problems with your father. I'm not going to share mine. Besides, we're talking about you today. And Crew."

"I don't think Crew is like Dad. But I don't know if I can trust my own judgment."

I'd fallen for Thayer Mills and he'd discarded me like a crumpled candy wrapper.

"I think you underestimate yourself," Mom said. "Or maybe you underestimate Crew."

"He lives in Utah."

"Utah is not on the other side of the world."

"But it's not home."

She gave me a sad smile. "I watched Crew run out of here so fast when he was eighteen he practically set the pavement on fire. But I always figured he'd find his way home. Now that Reed and Weston are home, maybe he'll surprise you."

Is that what I wanted? Crew to move here, live here?

Yes. But not if that meant he'd be gone constantly.

"I don't want to live in second place."

Mom shook her head. "I'll never forgive your father for making you feel like you weren't a priority."

"It's not your fault."

"No, it isn't. But I still hurt for you. That's my job as your mother."

Maybe none of this mattered. Maybe after Crew left for the X Games, it would be over. He'd go to Utah. I'd be here. And eventually, I'd get the nothing I was expecting.

Maybe we'd been doomed from the start. Maybe heartbreak was inevitable.

I took another sip of my coffee as my insides churned.

Regardless of what happened with Crew, I was here this morning to have a discussion with my brother. So I took a deep breath and left my mug behind while I made my way to River's bedroom, knocking before peeking inside.

"Hey." He was awake but still in bed, yawning as he stretched his arms above his head. For a moment, he must have forgotten about yesterday because he grinned. Then it fell flat as he shot me a scowl.

I shoved the door all the way open and flipped on the light, standing in the threshold with my arms crossed. "You owe me an apology."

"Raven—"

"Now, River. You owe me an apology, now."

"Later, okay? I'm tired."

"Now."

He grumbled, whipping the covers from his legs and tossing them over the side of the bed before he stalked to the closet to pull on a pair of sweats and a hoodie.

I tapped my foot on the carpet.

"Jesus, you're a lot," he muttered.

"You called me a whore." A day later and that word still stung.

River flinched. "I didn't mean it."

"You still said it."

"Crew's a player. I'm just looking out for you."

"By hurting my feelings?"

"You don't know what he's really like, Raven. I've been his best friend for years. I've been with him when he fucked a different girl every night."

"Stop." I held up a hand. The idea of Crew and other women made my skin crawl.

I believed him when he'd told me he hadn't been with

anyone else. We hadn't been exclusive, and I wouldn't have been angry if he'd moved on. But it would have hurt.

Thankfully, there'd been only truth in those striking brown eyes. That was something, wasn't it? That we'd clung to one another, even though we'd been apart?

"Fine. Don't listen to me." River ripped opened his dresser for a pair of socks, slamming it closed. "Don't come to me when you get hurt again. I'm only going to defend you so many times, Raven. You keep making the same mistakes."

"Me? How about you hold down a job for more than a week and then we can talk about who is continually repeating the same mistakes?"

"What the fuck?" he yelled. "Who elected you my keeper?"

"Why did I expect this conversation to go differently?" I shook my head. Why had I expected River to be kind and take credit for his own mistake?

Without another word, I walked out of his room.

Mom hovered in the hallway, her arms crossed and her eyes unfocused as she stared at an invisible spot on the floor. She worried her bottom lip between her teeth, something I'd seen her do a million times, whenever she had bad news to give us. Usually when Dad wasn't going to be home like promised.

But I'd seen that look more and more these past few months, ever since River had moved in.

We both knew this couldn't continue.

"There's a new doctor at the hospital," she said. "We started dating a month ago."

My mouth fell open. "You're dating?"

I'd been urging her for years to move on after Dad, but

she'd never met a guy. If the dating pool in Penny Ridge was shallow for women my age, it was only a puddle for Mom's generation. But there were a few single men, divorcés, who'd asked her out. She'd always said no.

"He's sweet. He's smart and dependable. We were out the other night and I thought, what the hell? I wanted to invite him here. To finally do whatever I wanted, just for me."

Except River was living here.

"You'd better get to work." Mom tore her eyes from the floor and forced a smile. "And I need to talk to River."

I walked down the hallway, stopping to give her a hug. I held on for a moment, knowing she might need the extra minute for what she was about to do. Knowing that my brother would probably need a hug too.

Except he'd have to get one from someone else.

Because he still hadn't apologized for calling me a whore.

———

"RAVEN."

I spun around at Crew's voice. He strode my way. "Hi."

"Hey." He grinned, walked straight into my space and dropped his lips to mine.

The turmoil in my heart vanished. The unease in my belly calmed. For just a moment, when his mouth was on mine, everything else disappeared.

Until a guy walking by did a catcall.

Crew chuckled, breaking apart.

"So much for keeping this behind closed doors," I muttered.

He tugged on the end of my braid. "Secret's out, baby."

Yes, it was. "If I end up on your Instagram, we're going to have words."

"I'll be sure to tell Marianne to tag you on the next post."

"Har har," I deadpanned.

He dropped his forehead to mine. "Hi."

"Hi." It had been hours since I'd climbed out of his bed. It still seemed like too long.

"How'd it go with River?"

I groaned.

"Damn. Sorry."

"Me too." I pressed my cheek to his heart, feeling his lips on my beanie. "Okay, I'd better get to work. How was your workout with JR this morning?"

While I'd gone home to shower and change, then stop by Mom's, he'd met JR in the hotel's gym.

"An ass kicking, as always. But my knee is feeling better, so we're going to meet after lunch to do some runs. Think you can get away to come along?"

"I can't." I stood tall. "We're swamped today. We've got the local preschool bringing up a group of four-year-olds for a special half-day lesson this morning. Then this afternoon, we're booked with private lessons, and three of my instructors are out with the flu."

It happened every year. The staff who lived in employee housing spent a lot of time together, and whenever one of them got sick, it spread like wildfire. Last year, a nasty cold had gone through the staff and it had gotten so bad that Reed and Ava both had needed to come out and run a chairlift.

After hours on her feet, watching chairs go around in circles, Ava had learned her lesson. This year, she'd hired a few extra employees to cover when the inevitable cold or flu ran through her employees. And all three of them lived in town, away from staff housing.

But I didn't have extra manpower on hand. So when we had instructors call in sick, the person who covered was me.

"I'll be drowning in kids. Normally this preschool group gets two instructors. Today, it's just me."

Crew shrugged. "I'll help."

"What?"

He grinned. "Once upon a time, I knew how to ski. And I'm sure I can teach the little boarders. Might as well pay it forward."

"What about training?"

"I'll go up with JR this afternoon."

It was maybe the sweetest offer I'd had in months. "I appreciate that you'd help, but I can handle it. Besides, you're not an employee."

He dug his phone from his pocket, hitting a contact before pressing it to his ear. "Hey. I'm going to help Raven teach ski school today. Do I need to be an employee?" He smirked as he listened to whoever was on the other end of the call, probably Reed. "We're at the base. Just outside the lodge." He hung up. "Reed's coming down with paperwork."

"Of course he is."

And sure enough, just minutes later, Reed came out of the lodge with a folder in one hand and a red staff coat in the other.

"Sign everything in here and I'll take it to HR," Reed said, handing Crew the folder. But before he handed over the pen, he held it back. "This comes with conditions."

"Of course it does." Crew laughed. "What do you want?"

"The exhibition on Saturday."

"I already agreed to do it. Even though Lewis threatened to have my balls. Now what?"

"I want a few plugs for the mountain on your social media accounts. And before you say you'll check with Lewis and Marianne, I already did." Reed turned, staring at the door, just as a lanky man with short gray hair and a thick beard came walking out of the hotel, his mouth set in a thin line.

"Of course you did." Crew shook his head. "Morning, Lewis."

"Good morning." The man took a long breath, his face relaxing. It was hard not to relax with the mountain air in your lungs.

"Lewis Finnegan, meet Raven Darcy."

Lewis shook my hand. "So you're the reason I'm in Colorado."

"Uh . . ."

"Just smile and nod whenever Lewis speaks," Crew said. "That's what I do."

"You're a pain in my ass," Lewis muttered. "Nice to meet you, Raven."

"You too."

"Lewis and I had a breakfast meeting this morning," Reed said. "Talked about how we can leverage the exhibition for us both."

"So you're just going to go straight to my team when you want something from now on, aren't you?" Crew asked Reed.

"Pretty much."

I fought a smile.

Lewis held up a finger and pointed it at Crew's nose. "Do not get hurt before Aspen next weekend."

"That's the tenth time you've warned me. I'll take it easy," Crew promised. "But I'm changing my conditions too. I'll only do the exhibition if Raven does it too."

"Great idea," Reed said.

"Wait. What?" I held up a hand. "I can't do the exhibition."

"Why not?" Crew asked. "It's not a competition. It's just for fun. Show off a little."

"There will be no showing off," Lewis muttered as he pulled his phone from his pocket. "For Crew. Raven, you're free to show off."

"See?" Crew smiled, then opened the employee paperwork Reed had brought. He started signing each page, skipping the sections that were actually supposed to be filled in with details like name and address.

"That's not how you fill out paperwork," I said.

"Lewis will do the rest for me, won't you, Lewis?"

"Marianne's on her way down." Lewis's fingers flew over his phone's screen as he spoke. "We have a meeting in fifteen minutes. She'll take care of it."

So Crew kept on signing until he'd reached the last page, tucked it all back in the folder and handed it to Lewis. Then he took off his coat, handing it to Lewis too before pulling on the red coat Reed had brought down.

"We'll let you get to work." Reed nodded for Lewis to follow him. "Coffee?"

"Please."

I waited until they were gone, then faced Crew. "I can't do the exhibition."

"Why not?"

"Because I'm not ready."

He shook his head, stepping close. "If JR Thomas thinks you're ready, you're ready. And you're doing the Burton open. Think of this as practice. What are you worried about?"

"That I'll make a fool of myself."

He brushed his thumb across my cheek. "My first competition after leaving here, I was nervous. Weston had come to almost all of my events before that and it was strange knowing I didn't have anyone waiting for me at the bottom."

"What happened?"

"I crashed. Hard. Screwed up my first trick on my first run, looked like an amateur. The video is on YouTube. You can hear the announcers and the crowd all gasp."

"Then what?"

"I nailed it on my second attempt. Won the whole thing."

My frame slumped. "I never have people waiting for me at the bottom." It was easier that way, to hide from the world.

"You do now. And you won't make a fool of yourself, Raven."

"I might."

"Then I'll be waiting at the bottom to laugh at you."

I smacked him in the gut.

"Oof." He laughed.

"Lewis is right. You are a pain in the ass."

"Does that mean you'll do the exhibition?"

God, I wanted to. I was so tired of holding back, worrying that I was too busy or too inexperienced. "Yes."

"Then we'll do it together. But first, let's teach some kids how to shred." He dropped a kiss to my mouth, then looked over my head.

The sound of little voices echoed from behind me. The preschool teachers were leading the kids our direction.

So we spent the next hour getting the kids their equipment from the rental shop, then leading them to the beginner's area. It was chaos, pure and utter chaos, attempting to keep them on their feet and off their butts.

But this was why I'd started teaching. Because no matter how many times they crashed, no matter how long it took them to do a single trip up and down the small slope, there wasn't a face without a smile.

"Yes, Holden!" Crew threw his hands in the air, his eyes aimed down the hill where one of his kids had made it from the top to the bottom without a crash.

Holden had his arms raised too, attempting to jump up and down in his celebration. He toppled over, still giggling as he landed in the snow.

Crew turned to another kid, a girl dressed in a puffy pink coat and matching pants with a rainbow tutu around her waist. He gave her a fist bump, then watched as she boarded about ten feet before face-planting.

He swept down after her, picking her up and dusting the snow out of her goggles. Then he set her in the right direction, and they did it all over again.

It was adorable. And if I hadn't been in love with Crew Madigan before today, I would have fallen for him on the bunny hill.

CHAPTER TWENTY

CREW

Raven was curled into my side when I woke up. It was only six thirty in the morning, but there was no point in trying to go back to sleep, not when my alarm was set to go off at seven.

So I slid out of bed, careful not to wake her, then padded to my suitcase in the corner to snag a pair of boxer briefs and sweats.

She was out cold, probably because I'd kept her up late last night. I'd worn her out thoroughly so she wouldn't protest spending the night. It had worked. The moment I'd tucked her against my chest, she'd crashed.

I eased the door closed to the bedroom before heading to the coffee machine, yawning as it brewed my cup. When it was done, I wandered to the windows that overlooked the mountain.

It was still too dark to see the peak, but the area around the hotel was lit from the building's lights. When was the last time I'd watched a sunrise? It had to have been in Japan on a trip two, no, three years ago. The time change had screwed with my internal clock, so I'd been awake to watch the sun light the Hida Range.

Japan was beautiful, but it didn't hold a candle to the Rocky Mountains.

I was on my second cup of coffee when twilight illuminated the resort. The white runs held a golden hue. The evergreens were dusted with fresh snow. The trails had been pristinely groomed by last night's crew.

It was primed and ready for today's exhibition.

For the first time in a long time, I was excited for an event. And that excitement had nothing to do with me. It was all for Raven.

My run could be a total clusterfuck of countless mistakes. I didn't care. As long as she had a smile on her face by the time this day was over, I'd call it a win.

Her nerves had been obvious last night. It was another part of the reason I'd exhausted her, so she could shut down and rest. She'd been fine on Thursday teaching those kids. Hell, I'd been better than fine. It had been a blast to watch those preschoolers learn, their energy contagious.

But later that afternoon, after I'd trained with JR and Raven had taught her private lesson, I'd found her in her office, staring off into space. Yesterday, she'd been busy teaching and I'd been busy training, but when she'd come to the room last night for dinner, she'd barely touched her food.

She had nothing to be nervous about. There wasn't a doubt in my mind that she'd crush it today.

I drained the final dregs of my coffee, watching through the window as a few people emerged, the staff getting ready for the day. This time of day had always been Mom's favorite. Mine too. First thing in the morning, before the crowds arrived, when it felt like your own slice of paradise.

If only she could see Madigan Mountain now. She'd be so damn proud.

Hell, I was proud.

This trip to Penny Ridge had been . . . surprising. So had the last.

Twelve years of distance. Twelve years of bitterness. Twelve years of avoidance.

Now, I wasn't sure how I'd leave.

Could I live here again? I'd told Raven I wasn't sure of it, but maybe . . .

Yes. It was worth a shot, especially if it meant keeping Raven.

"Damn." I chuckled to myself.

My brothers were going to be so smug when I told them I was moving home. I could already see Reed's smirk. Weston would give me that clap on the shoulder—the proud, fatherly clap when I made a good decision. And Dad, well . . . we had a lot of work to do to repair our relationship but there was hope on the horizon.

I unglued my feet and returned to the coffee maker, brewing a hot cup for Raven and adding two creamers, one sugar. Then I slipped into the bedroom, setting the coffee on the nightstand. I peeled off my clothes and slid into bed, my hands roaming her bare skin.

She hummed, her eyelids heavy. Then she smiled, that sweet, dreamy smile I'd just discovered on Thursday. Her morning smile, one I'd be happy to see for the rest of my life.

"Morning." I kissed the corner of her mouth, then pulled her on top of my chest, my fingertips trailing down her spine.

A flare of lust darkened those blue eyes as her hair draped around us.

I leaned up, taking her mouth for a deeper kiss. My body responded instantly to her taste and the slide of her tongue against mine. With a quick flip, I had her on her back, my hips settling into the cradle of hers.

She arched for me, spreading wider.

I lined up at her entrance and thrust home. This woman was home. No matter where we lived. "You feel so good, baby."

"Crew." Her pussy fluttered around me, her hips lifting, urging me to move.

But I stayed rooted, pressing deep, until I had my body under control. Then I pulled out to slam inside, reaching between us for her clit.

It was never enough. Every time, I craved her more and more.

Tonight, I'd worship. Tonight, we'd celebrate the exhibition. But this morning was to take off the edge, so I fucked her hard and fast, working us both up until she clawed at my shoulders, and I felt the build in the base of my spine.

Thrust after thrust, I lost myself in her body until she came on a cry, and I poured inside of her, holding her until the haze from my orgasm cleared and my heart stopped pounding.

I kissed her neck, drawing in her sweet cherry scent, then slid out and carried her to the shower so we could get ready for the day.

"Do you need to go home before the exhibition?" I asked as we stood at the bathroom's twin sinks. My jaw and chin were covered in shaving cream because there'd be cameras around today and Lewis didn't like it when I looked "scruffy" in photos.

"No, I brought my gear." She stared at me through the mirror, her hair damp and her face pale.

"Don't be nervous." I turned her toward me, dropping my forehead to hers. "Just have fun. Pretend it's you and me."

She leaned away, the worry in her eyes making it hard to breathe. "It's not the exhibition."

"It's not?" Then what was bothering her?

"It's nothing. Never mind." She waved it off, leaving the bathroom to go get dressed.

I was about to follow but stopped myself. She didn't want to talk about it now, so I wouldn't push. And we needed to get ready. So I finished shaving, then got dressed while Raven blow-dried her hair.

With our gear on, I carried our boards out of the room to the elevator.

Raven loosened a breath on the ride down, shaking her hands. "Okay, now I'm nervous."

I leaned over and kissed her hair. "You'll do great."

"Just you and me."

I nodded. "Just you and me."

She smiled as the doors opened, and the noise from the lobby swallowed us up as we weaved through the crush.

The hotel was booked for the weekend. Guests filled the space, all decked out in snow gear. Most had a coffee in hand as they visited, preparing to head outside for the day.

"Crew!" Marianne hollered, rushing over. "Hi. Hey, Raven."

"Morning," Raven said.

Marianne gave her a smile, but when she looked at me, she was wearing her game face. "Okay, so we are doing a quick introduction to a few sponsors who've come for the event. We've arranged a breakfast for you in a conference room. Reed is going to do a ribbon cutting around ten. Then the pipe will be open for practice runs. The exhibition itself doesn't start until one. Lewis will be joining us later but he asked me to remind you—"

"Don't get hurt."

"Exactly." She touched her nose. "And a warning. When I was getting coffee this morning, I overheard a few people in line behind me. One mentioned she was a reporter."

"Great," I muttered.

"Expect to be stopped."

"Fine," I grumbled, then took Raven's hand.

"I can get my own breakfast," she said. "Let you do your thing."

"No way. Today, you're stuck with me." I squeezed her hand tighter, then nodded for Marianne to lead the way to breakfast.

If we were meeting with sponsors, I wanted Raven along. I wanted them to get to know her name, her face. Because if my gut was correct, she'd be making an impression today. With any luck, she might even finish the exhibition with a few sponsorship opportunities of her own.

I understood her need to work, her desire for financial stability. But if she saw a possibility for boarding to become a career, maybe she'd be more inclined to give up the ski school and take this risk.

We shuffled through the crowd, following Marianne to a conference room with a small buffet. Raven and I both shrugged off our coats and loaded up plates. We'd just sat down when three people walked into the room, one I recognized as an executive from GNU.

"Hello," I said, standing to shake hands. Then I motioned to Raven. "Let me introduce you to Raven Darcy."

Conversation at breakfast was easy. A few other sponsors joined us, and every few minutes, I steered the conversation toward Raven, enough so they'd remember her name but not too much to make it awkward.

"Crew?" Marianne pointed to her watch.

"We'd better head out." I stood first, pulling back Raven's chair. Then after another round of handshakes, we collected our stuff and headed outside.

"You good?" I asked Raven.

"Nope." Her voice shook.

I chuckled. "Just you and me."

"Just you and me," she whispered.

"And JR." I pointed toward a ski rack where my coach was standing, texting on his phone.

He looked up, spotted us and walked over, hand extended. "Morning."

"Morning." I shook his hand, then put my arm around Raven's shoulders. "She's nervous."

"Nah. Nothing to be nervous about. Let's talk about your plan."

I smiled, letting her go so JR could take over. He was a master on the hill, but what I loved most about JR was how he had this ability to focus my mind. If I was feeling off, if I wasn't into a competition, he'd start talking me through it. In a matter of minutes, I'd be ready and raring to go.

"Excuse me. Crew?" A woman in a white coat came up,

her lips painted red. She gave me a sultry smile and a finger wave. Then she pulled a notepad and pen from her pocket.

Fucking great. The reporter.

"Hi, I'm Amanda from *Snowboard Colorado*. We're a growing blog. Do you have a few minutes?"

"Uh." I glanced over my shoulder to where the ribbon cutting was about to happen. "Just one minute. Then I need to get going."

"Are you excited for the X Games?"

"I am." I nodded. "It'll be great to compete again."

"And the Olympics? Are you planning on competing at the next Winter Games?"

"That I don't know. I haven't made any decisions that far in advance yet. We'll see when it gets a little closer."

Her pen scribbled down a few notes. "When you were here last, you had an incident on a chairlift. Then you were taken to the hospital. How are you feeling?"

"Good as new." I forced a smile, giving her the rehearsed answers I gave most reporters. Then I hooked a thumb over my shoulders. "Nice talking to you, Amanda. Thanks."

She opened her mouth, probably to ask something else, but I was already gone, turning and nodding for Raven and JR to follow.

"I hate dealing with reporters," I said, my voice low.

"Why?" Raven asked.

"They're nosy."

"That's sort of in the job description."

"Yeah, I know. Still just gets under my skin. Everyone is already talking about the Olympics and they're three years away."

"Do you not want to go again?"

"Of course I want to go. It's the Olympics. But I don't know how I'm going to feel in three years. I don't want to go and end my career on a low point." A confession I hadn't told anyone before. But with all things, it seemed like my truths came easy when given to Raven.

She took my hand in hers, holding tight.

We'd figure out the Olympics later. Together. As far as I was concerned, she'd be with me when it was time to make that decision.

All or nothing.

Reed was standing on a small podium with Ava when we joined the cluster of spectators at the base. He leaned in to talk into the microphone. "Good morning. Welcome to Madigan Mountain. My name is Reed Madigan, and today, we're here to celebrate Colorado's newest superpipe and terrain park."

He spoke for a few minutes, keeping it brief. Then he gave the scissors to Ava, letting her do the honors to cut the red ribbon they'd strung between two stakes.

Cameras were out. People clapped. I savored the surge of anticipation and put my helmet on my head. "Now the fun stuff."

Raven, JR and I made our way to the terrain park's chair, where there was already a line of people waiting to head up. There was a group already in the pipe too.

"I'll wait at the bottom," JR said. "Lewis wanted me to remind you—"

"Don't get hurt."

"And no showing off." JR smiled. "I told him you weren't going to listen."

"Nope." I laughed. I'd be careful, but there was no way I wasn't going to show off, just a little.

Raven rolled her eyes, then we got in line to head up.

The ride to the top was quiet. We did a brief warm-up through the terrain park, then went straight for the halfpipe.

It was the busiest it had been all year. Enough so that three or four athletes were going at the same time, giving the person ahead of them enough space in case of a crash, but tight enough to keep the line flowing.

So we got in line, inching forward until it was Raven's turn.

"You're up." I swatted her ass. "Have fun."

She swallowed hard and drew in a long breath, got into position at the lip. One glance, one shaky smile aimed my way, then she flew over the lip.

The guy beside me said my name. I ignored him, my eyes locked on Raven as she did her first trick, then swept back to the opposite side of the pipe.

I didn't give a shit if we slowed down the line. It was my turn and I didn't move, tuning out the grumbles behind me as I kept my attention entirely on Raven.

She went easy with tricks, mostly 180s and 360s. She was just working her nerves free and loosening her muscles, but her warm-up was flawless. For the next round, she'd amp it up.

By the time she made it to the bottom, my heart was in my throat, but damn, she was something.

"Dude, it's your turn."

I put on my goggles and dropped in, keeping the tricks simple for my warm-up too. And when I met Raven at the bottom, she was locked in conversation with JR about what he wanted her to try next. He didn't so much as speak to me before sending us back to the top on the lift.

Raven and I breezed through the terrain park again, skipping the obstacles, to get back in line on the pipe.

"Thank you," she said.

"For what?"

She gave me a sad smile. "For staying."

I had a feeling she wasn't talking about the exhibition.

Tomorrow we'd have a serious conversation. Maybe tonight after celebrating. But at the moment, she needed to focus on the exhibition.

"You're up. See you at the bottom."

"Okay." She nodded, then away she went, this time nailing a series of harder tricks.

I fist-pumped when she landed the alley-oop she'd been working on. "Yes."

"Raven's doing the exhibition?" came a snarky voice from farther back in line.

River stood three people down, so I let those between us cut in front of me, waiting until he was close.

Not exactly the place for this confrontation, but if he ruined today for Raven, I'd kick his ass.

"What the fuck is your problem?"

He scoffed. "Besides you fucking my sister?"

The way he said it, with that bullshit sneer, made my teeth clench. Yep. Definitely should have punched him at the hotel earlier this week.

"Don't screw this up for Raven today. Understood?" I shot him a warning glare.

"She's too good for you. Just ask her. She'll tell you how she's better than everyone."

"Is that what this is about?" My hands fisted at my sides. "You're pissed because she's better than you?"

"Whatever," he muttered, lifting off his goggles to readjust them. The breeze shifted, blowing off River. He smelled like weed, and with his goggles off, he couldn't hide the glassy sheen to his eyes.

"What the— Are you high?"

Plenty of people smoked when they were out enjoying a day of riding. It hadn't ever appealed to me, I liked my head clear, but I didn't judge.

Except I knew River too well. He was unfocused and clumsy when he was high. And the exhibition rules clearly prohibited being under the influence. If anyone found out, he'd get his ass banned from the resort.

"You can't do this if you're stoned."

"I'm not." He put his goggles on and raised his chin.

"Don't lie, River."

"Are you gonna go?" He swung his hand to the pipe, inching too close to the lip.

My arm shot out, keeping him from going over.

"Let go." He pushed my arm away.

"Fine." This asshole. He'd be pissed as hell if I ratted him out. But if he got hurt, if he broke his damn neck . . .

Shit. I dropped in, dreading what was going to happen when I reached the bottom, but I blocked it all out, focusing on my first trick, then moving to the second, a frontside 1080. I'd need to get a good pop off the lip to get the height to spin enough times. Speed was critical, so I flew, my knees bent, my shoulders angled and my gaze locked on the wall. But a flash came from the corner of my eye, neon orange, the color of River's coat.

I pulled my focus for a split second, glancing away from the wall, just in time to see him fly in front of me, cutting me off and forcing me to jerk. That bastard hadn't waited, hadn't given me enough time.

My body jerked, cutting my board to try and angle differently. But I was going too damn fast, and the wall was already upon me.

Fuck.

Lewis was going to be pissed.

CHAPTER TWENTY-ONE

RAVEN

I t happened in slow motion.

Standing beside JR, still feeling the rush of my ride, I watched as Crew dropped into the halfpipe. His first trick had been flawless, no surprise. But as he'd landed, River, in that neon-orange coat I'd bought him for his birthday two years ago, careened off the lip.

It had almost looked like a mistake. Like he'd gotten too close and lost his balance, enough that he'd had no choice but to drop.

He hadn't gone to the other side like he should have. He'd taken a sharp carve at the bottom, like he was just going to run it straight, but then he saw Crew flying his way, so he tried to beat him.

Except Crew had given everyone ahead of him in line a wide berth. When you flew three times as high, when you rode twice as fast, it didn't take long to catch up.

People didn't realize just how incredible he was on that board. How drastically they paled in comparison.

But as talented as he was, having my brother cut right in front of him, their boards missing a collision by inches, there'd been no way to recover.

Up, up, up and over the lip. His arms had been wide, desperately trying to contort his body to turn in time. But the angle was off. The margin of error on a superpipe was small, at best.

"Oh, fuck." JR tore off as Crew started to come down, racing up the pipe.

Everyone around us gasped, a girl yelped.

And I stood frozen, watching as Crew's torso slammed into the wall, his body crumpling. He slid down the pipe's side, lying limp when he finally stopped.

Move. Please move.

I picked up my foot to take a step, but remembered my board. So I bent, fumbling with the straps as I wrenched my boots free. My first step was wobbly, so was my second, like the world had tilted sideways.

"Ski patrol," I said, my voice hoarse and too quiet. "Call ski patrol!"

The people around me sprang into action, someone in blue running for the base of the chair, arms waving for attention.

And I bolted, following the same line as JR, straight up the pipe.

River streaked past me, his board sideways as he slid to a stop. I ignored him, my legs pumping toward the small group of people clustered around Crew.

Why wasn't he moving? He was on his stomach, his face in the snow.

Two other boarders had stopped beside Crew, resting on

their knees. JR scrambled the last few feet before dropping to Crew's side, bending close.

"Oh God." I pushed harder, my legs full of lead, until finally, I reached his side. "Crew. Oh my God, Crew."

"Ribs," he choked out.

I turned over my shoulder, searching. A snowmobile buzzed in the distance. "The stretcher is coming. Let's get your board off."

JR and I both moved to his feet, each carefully unstrapping a boot. Then when it was off, Crew pushed with one arm, trying to roll to his back. His face contorted in pain, his arms clutched his ribs, his breathing labored. "I. Can't."

"Let me help." I shuffled on my knees, trying to help him turn.

"Call—"

"Don't try to talk," I said, carefully taking off his goggles.

His eyes were squeezed shut.

"He might have punctured a lung." The color had drained from JR's face. "We need to get him to the hospital."

I turned again, my heart racing as the snowmobile with the stretcher finally appeared. "Hurry!"

The ski patrol guy at the handlebars couldn't hear me, but I yelled anyway.

"He's almost here." I put my hand over Crew's. "Just hold on. It'll be okay."

Please, let him be okay.

The snowmobile stopped beside us, forcing JR and me to move. Another ski patrol sled came next, both guys rushing to Crew.

"Raven." River stood by my side. His hair was sticking up at odd angles, his helmet and goggles discarded somewhere, probably with his board. "Fuck. I was standing too close and dropped in too soon. I tried to get out of the way but he was going too fast—"

"Shut up." I held up a hand, silencing the rest of his excuses. My chin started to quiver, my eyes welled, but I gave River no more attention as the ski patrol rolled Crew onto a stretcher board, then lifted it to the sled.

"I'm coming," I said as they loaded him onto their sleds.

"So am I." JR strode for one machine while I sat on the back of the snowmobile with Crew behind it in the sled.

The ride to the base was a blur. So was the drive into town in the back of the ambulance.

At some point on the trip, I started crying. Tears streaked down my face, pooling in the goggles I hadn't remembered to take off, while I sat in the back corner of the ambulance, trying to stay out of the way as the EMTs hovered over Crew.

Every breath seemed to cause him pain. Every dip and bump in the road made his body tense.

The moment we were parked in the emergency room loop, the doors to the ambulance flew open and the EMTs jumped out, getting Crew's stretcher to the ground. I hopped out too, trying to follow, but a nurse held up her hand, stopping me.

"You'll have to wait in the waiting room."

"Please—"

She was gone before I could finish my sentence.

So I stood in the parking lot, stuck to the snow-covered pavement, staring at the double doors that had closed behind them.

———

THE WAITING room was stifling hot, the air thick and muggy. Every chair was taken, either by a person or a pile of outerwear. My coat was in the seat beside me along with my snow pants, leaving me in my thermal leggings and long-sleeved shirt.

My face was stiff and salty from the tears that had dried on my skin hours ago.

Hours.

Two, to be exact. Two hours and thirty-nine minutes.

That's how long it had been since Weston had found me standing in the parking lot outside the ER entrance and brought me inside.

We hadn't heard from the doctor yet, and as the minutes ticked by on the waiting room's clock, the knot in my stomach twisted tighter and tighter. Was Crew in surgery? How badly was he hurt? How many bones had he broken in that fall?

River sat across from me.

For the first hour, he'd tried to talk. To make more excuses about how he'd been trying to move, and if Crew hadn't been going so fast, it wouldn't have been a problem.

I hadn't spoken a word to my brother, and finally, he'd given up talking. He still kept trying to make eye contact—I felt his stare on my face—but I kept my own gaze aimed anywhere else.

Reed and Weston were three chairs down, sitting side by side. JR, Marianne and Lewis were in the row behind mine.

Someone had needed to stay on the mountain, to make sure today's events continued, so Mark had volunteered to help Ava, maybe because he'd known that Crew would rather see his brothers than his father in a time like this.

The exhibition would have started by now.

Crew should have been there. He should have been making the crowd go *ooh* and *ahh* with his talent.

My gaze lifted to River's.

He did a double take, like he couldn't believe I was finally staring back.

I'd pandered to River enough, especially after the incident with Thayer. But I hadn't asked him to fight with Thayer. I hadn't asked him to go that far. He'd made his own reckless choices and look where it had landed us.

"Do better."

He flinched. "I'm—"

"If the next word out of your mouth isn't *sorry*, then don't speak."

He swallowed hard. "Sorry."

My chin started to quiver again. "Why?"

There was no reason he should have dropped in. There was no reason we should be here. River wasn't an amateur. He wasn't new to this level of sport and knew how badly things could go.

But he'd been high. When he'd arrived at the hospital, I'd smelled the lingering smoke and could tell he wasn't entirely focused.

"I don't know," he whispered. "It was an accident. I'm sorry."

"Figure your life out, River. Before you lose everyone who loves you." With that, I stood, walking to the windows.

There was a group of reporters outside, including the woman who'd asked Crew about the Olympics earlier.

They'd tried to stay in the waiting room, but Reed had asked the hospital staff to escort them out. So they lingered on the sidewalk, killing time by scrolling through their phones. One man had been chain-smoking cigarettes.

I dropped my forehead to the glass, desperate for the cool touch, not caring if anyone watched.

"Raven."

Mom's voice caused me to shove away from the glass, searching her face. "Is he okay?"

"He's all right. He's asking for you."

The air rushed out of my lungs.

"Come on. I'll take you back there, then come out and give everyone else an update." She led the way, walking quickly to the doors that led to the ER's patient rooms.

After passing a line of curtained rooms, almost all of them empty, she knocked on a door, pushing inside.

Crew was on the bed, his torso bare. His legs were covered with a white blanket but his feet were sticking out, so I could see he still had on his snow gear. His face was pale. He looked miserable. "Hi."

"Hi." I sighed, tears welling again, and rushed to his side to take his hand. "Are you okay?"

"He's got four broken ribs," Mom said. "We were worried he'd punctured a lung and had some internal bleeding. That's what took so long. The doctor wanted to be sure. But Crew got lucky. Though he's going to hurt for a while."

I dropped my forehead to Crew's. "I'm sorry."

"Me too."

"We're just about done here," Mom said. "We just need to finish up the discharge papers. He can't drive and probably needs someone to help."

"Me." He was coming home with me, where I'd do whatever he needed until he was healed.

"I figured you'd say that," Mom said. "We had to cut off his shirt, so let me see if I can find something for him to wear."

"I've got my coat," Crew said, his eyes heavy. "It's good enough. Besides, Raven likes my abs."

Mom laughed. "He's on some pretty heavy painkillers."

"I love you, Robin."

She shook her head, fighting a smile as she eased toward the door. "I love you too, Crew."

When she was gone, I sat on the edge of the bed, watching as his eyes drifted closed.

"I love you," he murmured.

He probably wouldn't remember saying it tomorrow. But I didn't care.

I leaned down, pressed my mouth to his and whispered, "I love you too."

"I don't want to live in Utah anymore."

"I don't want to live in Utah, period. But I will. If you need to be there, I will." The idea of moving had been rolling around my mind for the past two days. Each time I thought about leaving, my stomach would twist.

Crew had mistaken it for nerves for the exhibition. Mostly, I'd been nervous about taking this leap. For uprooting my life.

But this situation wasn't the same as my parents' marriage. Crew wasn't Dad. I wasn't Mom. We'd cut our own path.

"I bought a condo." His face lit up, like he'd forgotten I

already knew about the condo. "Two of them. Here. In Penny Ridge. We can live in 'em."

"Or we can live in my house."

He hummed. "I love your bed."

"It's a good bed."

"I love you." His brown eyes locked with mine, slightly unfocused and drowsy. "Tell me tomorrow in case I forget, okay? Tell me that I told you that I love you and then tell me that you love me too."

"Deal."

He groaned. "Lewis is going to be so pissed. So is Sydney. And Marianne. And JR."

"I think they're just worried." I brushed the hair away from his forehead, holding his gaze.

"God, I hope our kids get your eyes. And your freckles. And your hair. Let's just have mini Ravens."

"I'd prefer a mini Crew." Dimple and all.

"Meh." He lifted his arm, but it must have pinched because he frowned. "Lewis is gonna be so pissed at me."

Definitely delirious. "Yup."

"Think we can sneak out the back door?"

I laughed. "Probably not, babe."

The corner of his mouth turned up. "I love you."

"I love you."

Crew closed his eyes, for just a moment, before they popped open. "Wait. What time is it? We need to get to the exhibition."

"We're going to miss this one."

"Well, fuck." His mouth pursed. "Do you want to compete? For real?"

"Yes." I'd realized it today on my first practice run. I

loved my job, but while I was able, I wanted to see how high I could fly. That was because of Crew. He'd made me realize there was still a chance to chase my dream.

"I don't even know where to start," I said.

"I do. I'll be your coach. I think I need to retire anyway."

"You as my coach? That sounds dangerous. We might kill each other."

"Nope." He popped the *p*. "It's perfect. I've got it all figured out. Just stick with me."

I traced my thumb across his cheek. "Always."

He sighed, closing his eyes. "I love you."

"I love you too."

"Did I tell you that already?"

"Yes."

"Huh. Tell me tomorrow in case I forget, okay?"

I smiled, kissing his cheek, hoping he'd forget he told me once more just so I could hear him say it all over again. "Deal."

EPILOGUE
CREW

F *ive years later . . .*
"This place is packed," I told Weston, glancing across the sea of people at the base of the mountain.

"Reed's already talking about another development. More condos. Maybe even another hotel." Weston chuckled. "I thought after they had kids, he and Ava would slow down."

"You mean like how you and Callie have slowed down?"

Even after having two boys, Weston was as active as ever, flying his helicopter for the resort. Callie was swamped with her photography business. And this time of year, when winter events were in full swing, they took turns shuttling Sutton around the state for her competitions.

Somehow, they managed to juggle it all. So did Reed and Ava with their son and daughter. We all worked together so everyone could stay active with the resort.

"We're taking tomorrow off," he said. "That counts, doesn't it? And who the hell are you to talk anyway?"

"What do you mean? I'm retired."

"Ha." He barked a laugh. "So that hasn't been you working for months in prep for this weekend?"

I grinned. "Touché."

We were all dedicated to the mountain, but when you loved something, it didn't feel like a chore.

In the past five years, Madigan Mountain had become the newest of the elite Colorado ski resorts. People traveled across the globe to ski and snowboard on my family's slopes.

This weekend, we were hosting a competition with some of the most talented skiers and snowboarders from around the world. It was an invite-only event—as it had been for the past two years. Not a single invitee had turned us down.

Since opening the slopestyle course, five world-class athletes had made Penny Ridge their home. Barring a catastrophe, they'd all be going to the next winter Olympics.

If she wanted to go, Raven had a decent shot at making the team too.

Training would be grueling, but when it came to my wife, when she set her mind to something, there wasn't anything she couldn't accomplish.

After my wreck on the superpipe years ago, I'd taken it as a sign it was time to step back. I'd had my shoulder surgery, then spent the rest of the season healing. Then I'd given snowboarding my all for one more year, competing and retiring as a world champion.

The Olympics hadn't been in the cards, timing hadn't been right. But it hadn't been as hard as I'd expected to walk away. Not with everything I had waiting for me at home.

"There they are." Weston nudged my elbow, pointing up the hill to where a familiar hot-pink coat caught my eye.

I smiled and hiked up the hill to meet my three-year-old daughter.

Natalie, named after Mom, came skidding to a shaking stop. Her legs wobbled as the tips of her skis pointed together, her arms stretched wide.

Behind her, Dad slid to a stop.

When she spotted me jogging her way, she waved frantically like I hadn't seen her. "Daddy!"

"Hey, cutie." I dropped to my knees in the snow as Weston joined us, patting her on the helmet. "How was it?"

"Good." She beamed as I unbuckled her helmet.

Dad panted as he unclipped his own helmet, his gray hair sweaty.

"You okay?" Weston asked him.

"I'm too old for this." He bent, putting his hands on his knees. "I don't remember it being this nerve-racking teaching you boys how to ski."

Following Natalie was an adventure. She'd started skiing this year, and most of that time, we'd spent on the bunny slope. When we headed up to the beginner runs, she was strapped to a harness. But even then, it was a workout trying to keep her from crashing.

She was a bit reckless and had no fear. More than once I'd been terrified she'd slam into a tree or wipe someone out. But so far, we had yet to experience a major crash.

"Can I go again, Daddy?"

"Tomorrow."

Her shoulders slumped. Her tiny eyebrows came together in a scowl that reminded me a lot of her mother's. If my girl could spend every waking minute on the ski hill, she would.

"We've got to go watch Mommy."

"Oh yeah." Her face lit up.

I popped off her skis, pairing them together. Then I took her hand, leading her to the lodge, with Weston and Dad close behind.

We headed straight for my office, adjacent to the ski school center, where I'd stashed regular boots for Natalie, a hat and a dry pair of gloves.

Dad had left his own boots here too so he wouldn't have to trek all the way to his office in the hotel.

I'd just finished getting Natalie ready for the event when Melody came walking through the door with Delia in her arms.

"Hi." She smiled at Dad. "How was it?"

He huffed. "I'm exhausted."

Melody laughed, handing over my four-month-old daughter so I could hold her.

"How was she?" I asked.

"Perfect. She just woke up from her nap."

Raven had just finished her first full season of competitions when we'd found out she was pregnant with Natalie. It had been the year after I'd moved home to Penny Ridge, a year after our quick trip to Vegas to get married.

Maybe another woman would have let that derail her plans. Not Raven. The timing had worked out so she'd been pregnant with Natalie during the spring and summer. The same had happened with Delia. So she'd worked in training where she could, balancing motherhood and a blossoming career and making it look easy.

Raven said it was the best of both worlds. She got to be a mom and an athlete.

And I was just happy to be on this ride with her.

My place in Park City and the two condos here were investment properties now, each used as vacation rentals. Raven and I had lived in her house downtown for a few years, but after Delia was born, we'd realized we needed more space.

A month ago, we'd moved into the house we'd built on the mountain. Neither Raven nor I had to drive to work, which was awesome. We had a nanny who helped with the girls during the winter season, though Melody and Dad were always up for helping too. And Sutton never turned down babysitting, spending her earnings on new gear. With the kids all around the same age, we'd started having to reserve her a month in advance.

"Okay, we'd better get going," I said, shifting Delia to one hip so I could hold Natalie's hand. Then I nodded to Dad. "Lead the way."

Dad and I had worked hard on our relationship. It wasn't perfect, but it was improving. My girls had a lot to do with it. I didn't want old resentment clouding their relationship with their grandfather, who they adored.

"Papa." Natalie held out her free hand, waiting until he took it, then she skipped between us.

We headed out of the lodge, navigating the crowd. Conversation and laughter filled the sunny afternoon.

For the competition today, we'd brought in shuttle busses to run people from the lodge to the halfpipe and slopestyle courses. I helped load up the girls, keeping Delia in the crook of my arm, then we made our way to the event site.

Hundreds of people were waiting already. We'd hauled

in sections of bleachers for spectators, though from a glance, every seat had already been taken.

"Good thing we carved out standing room," I told Weston as we climbed out of the shuttle.

"No kidding." Weston stared at the halfpipe, where competitors were doing their practice runs. "It's nice, for a change, not to be nervous before an event. With Sutton not competing, I might actually be able to relax."

Sutton was turning heads in the big mountain competitions, already gaining notice from sponsors who'd love to claim the next up-and-coming superstar.

Just like they had for Raven.

God, I was proud of her. She'd busted her ass these past couple of months to get in shape. Her natural talent combined with her dedication and hard work were paying off. Raven had made a name for herself and had a few loyal sponsors.

Together, we managed the ski school program so that when she needed to spend the day training with JR, I had the school and instructors covered. The X Games were in Aspen in two weeks, and I had a solid feeling she'd walk away with gold.

"I'm going to go find Callie and the boys," Weston said. "See you up there?"

I nodded. "Yep. Right behind you."

Callie was probably somewhere taking photos with the boys in tow. Her camera was a constant at Sutton's competitions, a way for her to curb some of her own nerves.

"All right." I crouched down to talk to Natalie. "Nana Melody is in charge. No running off. And cheer extra loud for Mommy, okay?"

"Where is Mommy?" Natalie scanned the halfpipe, searching for Raven's pink coat.

GNU had designed them matching coats this year. Delia and I were both in yellow.

"How about some hot cocoa?" Dad asked Natalie, reaching for her hand while Melody took Delia.

"Yay!" Natalie cheered, off for the espresso hut we'd hauled in for the weekend.

I turned and strode toward the base of the halfpipe, passing the spectator area.

"Crew." River flagged me down.

"Hey." I jerked up my chin, giving him a quick hug. "Thanks for coming."

He shrugged. "Sure."

I doubted it had been his idea, but Robin's.

River hadn't changed much these past five years. After the incident on the pipe, he'd left Penny Ridge. He'd moved to Denver and taken a job working construction. He'd been fired within two weeks. But a landscaping company had hired him on, allowing him to make good money during the summer and have a more flexible schedule in winter. At least he was working and not living with Robin.

He'd made a lot of apologies after the accident, and I believed him when he said he hadn't intentionally tried to wreck me.

But our friendship was different. So was his relationship with Raven. Not strained, but stifled. My wife could hold a grudge.

"You're coming over for dinner tonight, right?" I asked. He was staying with Robin, but we'd invited them over tonight for a get-together with both of our families.

"Yep. Mom and I will be there." He hooked a thumb over his shoulder to where Robin waved from the bleachers.

"See you then. I'd better head up." I clapped him on the shoulder, then took off for the gap in the fence marked for the coaches.

"Hey, Crew." The guy stationed at the entrance jerked up his chin when I walked by.

"Hey. How's everything going?"

"So far so good. A couple of the new guys weren't sure where to go but I think we got it sorted."

We'd brought in a slew of extra staff members today, most to help with crowd control and setup. The judges were getting situated at their station. The coaches were all congregating, talking to each other.

JR was in the thick of it, everyone clamoring his direction.

He spotted me and waved. He'd be the one coaching Raven as she rode today, though I was never far away, having dubbed myself her assistant coach.

"Crew." Marianne came rushing over. "There you are."

"What's up?"

"Come with me."

Marianne and her boyfriend—now husband—had moved to Penny Ridge with me years ago. She wasn't only my assistant these days, but also Raven's. We shared everything, from a life to children to Marianne, Lewis and Sydney.

Marianne waddled more than walked at the moment, almost eight months pregnant, and though I'd told her to take today off, she'd refused.

She led the way to a group of sponsors, where I shook hands and made small talk until finally an air horn blew and the announcer for today's competition called attention over the speaker system.

"I'm going to go find JR," I told Marianne. "You go sit down."

"I need to take pictures for social media."

"Callie or someone from her team will do that today. Go sit."

"Fine," she grumbled, though I doubt she'd listen. But I'd let her husband force her into a chair.

I needed to go watch my wife.

"Ready for this?" JR asked as I joined him in the coaches' section.

A spike of nerves hit, stronger than any I'd ever felt for myself. When it came to Raven, I was always torn between worry and excitement. "She'll do great."

We didn't say much as the initial competitors did their first runs. My nerves were too rattled to talk much. And then, second to last, came my wife and that pink coat, adorned with a numbered bib pinned to the front.

A breath caught in my lungs as she stood on the lip, then after three heartbeats, she was off, racing through her tricks until she came to a stop at the bottom.

"Yes." I fist-pumped. She'd hit everything just right, even though I knew she could get more air.

Raven bent to unstrap her board, glancing up to the lighted board where her score flashed.

"First place," I whispered. Now she just had to hold it.

Raven walked over, her cheeks flushed. "Hi."

"Hi." I kissed her. "Great job, baby."

"Thanks."

God, she looked beautiful. Happy. This was her year.

I shifted out of the way so she could strategize with JR for her second run, then before she headed up for the next round, I kissed her again. "You got this."

"I got this." She nodded, then followed the path to where snowmobiles were shuttling athletes up the pipe.

Raven delivered another solid run, boosting her score by two points. But then the rider after her had a huge final frontside that pushed her far enough ahead to lead by three points.

"Damn it," I muttered. It sucked coming from behind, knowing that you had one final run to lay it all out there.

But if Raven was nervous, she didn't let it show. She talked to JR, nodded and listened to his advice, then trekked for the snowmobiles to head up for her last shot.

There were two crashes in the last round, nothing serious, but it took them out of the running. Then finally, it was Raven's turn.

"Come on, baby." I shifted from foot to foot, not able to keep still.

She dropped in, hitting her first two tricks perfectly. She angled toward the wall for her third, her knees bent and ready. Then she popped off the lip and did a massive frontside 1080.

"Yes!" I cheered, clapping as she landed, racing for her last trick. "One more. You got this. One more."

She flew.

Up into the air, she spun, once, twice, three times, adding a tail grab for back-to-back 1080s.

"Land it." I held my breath, refusing to blink as she came down, her board angled just right to sweep off the incline to the middle of the pipe.

Whoosh.

Perfect.

Her arms flew in the air.

So did mine.

The crowd roared, knowing they'd just seen greatness.

"That's it." JR clapped me on the shoulder, leaning close to yell over the noise. "That's the win."

"Oh my God." I put my hands to my cheeks, about to pass out.

Raven's smile was as bright as the sun as she unstrapped and joined us at the fence. She walked straight into my open arms.

"That was fucking awesome, baby."

"I wasn't sure if I could do it but then I was going and I could just feel it so I said screw it and went for it."

I laughed, holding her tight. "I love you."

"I love you too." She stood on her toes for a kiss, then turned, letting me keep an arm around her shoulders as we both kept our eyes glued to the scoreboard.

It flashed and my jaw dropped.

"Does that say ninety-two?" she asked.

"Fuck yes, it does." JR let out a whoop and started clapping, the sound from the crowd growing even louder.

Ninety-two. Her best score ever. That was Olympic scoring. That was what the best in the world were getting.

"There's still one more to go," Raven said.

"She's not going to beat you."

"She might."

I scoffed. "Not a chance."

And as I liked to remind my wife as often as possible, mostly because it didn't happen much, I was right.

BONUS EPILOGUE

RAVEN

The house was bursting at the seams with noise. That's the way it had been since we'd moved in ten years ago, and I wouldn't have it any other way. I smiled, walking from my home office toward the chaos in the kitchen.

Everyone had come over for dinner tonight. Reed and Ava. Weston and Callie. The kids were all running around, acting like they hadn't just seen each other at school yesterday.

Pizza boxes filled the kitchen's island. A bowl of salad had gone mostly untouched. The pitcher of margaritas was nearly empty.

Sutton was on the couch in the living room, cuddled close with the boyfriend she'd brought home from Denver. This was the first guy she'd brought home, which meant he might be serious. Weston kept sending the poor guy glares.

And Crew was looking at our daughters with this longing on his face, like he'd just realized soon they'd be bringing boys home too.

Hopefully what I had in my hand would make that pained look disappear.

"Mom, we're going in the hot tub." Natalie rushed through the living room in a swimsuit. Delia and a line of their cousins followed, slipping out the patio door.

Crew had cleared the deck of snow before everyone had arrived, assuming this would happen. The kids had inhaled their dinner and would now spend an hour in the hot tub. Then they'd all come inside and disappear to the theater room, only poking their heads out when they needed another round of snacks.

The moment the door closed behind them, the volume in the house dropped.

"Have they always been this loud?" Crew asked.

"The volume doubles every year, I swear." Reed chuckled, putting his arm around the back of Ava's chair.

I crossed the room and took my seat, patting Crew's leg beneath the table. "Since everyone is here tonight, I wanted to show you something."

"What?"

I set the envelope on the table, carefully taking out the magazine inside. "Lewis got a call about two months ago from *Snowboarder Magazine*. They asked to do a feature about you. He called me first and we thought maybe it would be a cool surprise."

"Me? Why would they want to feature me?"

"Uh, maybe because you're Crew Madigan?" Weston chuckled. "You've done a lot for the sport over the years."

Crew had spent years as a competitive snowboarder. Most who retired disappeared from the scene. But even after retirement, Crew had stayed connected to the world of snowboarding.

He'd hosted events at Madigan Mountain, getting to know athletes from around the world. He'd mentored younger athletes and even taken on some coaching. He'd leveraged his social media platforms for education and awareness. The brands he partnered with had stayed with him over the years, partly because his face was so recognizable and certainly not hard to look at.

Crew was to snowboarding what David Beckham was to soccer or Wayne Gretzky was to hockey. Just because he'd retired didn't mean he wasn't tied to the sport.

"Lewis helped with details for the article. And I gave them pictures from over the years." I slid the magazine across the table so he could take a look.

On the cover was a shot Callie had just taken this season. Crew was on top of the mountain, standing in the same spot where his mother had always asked for a season kickoff photo. A tradition we'd carried on ourselves with the girls.

Since I'd known about the article, I'd asked Callie to help me get some pictures. She'd taken this one on the sly, after me and the girls had snuck out of the way.

Crew was in profile, staring out across the mountains in the distance. His goggles were on his helmet, so you could see the crinkles at the sides of his eyes as he smiled.

Beneath the photo was the title of the article.

Legend.

My husband, the legend.

Crew stared at the photo, shaking his head. Then he looked to me, his eyes in awe. "Seriously? You did this?"

"We all pitched in." I waved a hand around the table.

Reed had uncovered some older photos from the A-frame that had been stashed in storage. There were pictures from Crew's early days on the slopes when he was a kid. Weston had found a few pictures from high school from Crew's competitions.

Photos from his professional career would have been easier to collect, but the author had wanted the piece to be all-encompassing, not simply a window in his life.

So besides a shot of Crew in the air, doing a halfpipe trick, and another of him on a podium, wearing a gold medal around his neck, everything else was from his life here, on Madigan Mountain. The article even included the story of how three brothers had come home to a small mountain ski hill and turned it into a world-class resort.

"They put in a picture of Mom." Crew gave me a sad smile, his fingers brushing the photo of him and his mom standing beside a snowman.

The table was quiet as he thumbed through the pages, turning them slowly, savoring every photo, every word. His eyes softened when he reached the last page, seeing pictures of him and the girls from their own days on the slopes.

Much to his dismay, Natalie had never given up her skis —Grandpa Mark's influence. Delia had started on a snowboard and had never looked back.

"This isn't the finished product, is it?" he asked after reaching the last page.

"It's a proof, but I think it's all ready to publish. Why?"

"They can't publish this." He frowned, shoving out of his chair to get his phone from the kitchen.

My heart dropped as he tapped the screen, then pressed it to his ear.

How could he not like this? I'd pored over every word, so had Lewis and Marianne, and we'd all thought it was so flattering. What was wrong with the article?

"Lewis," Crew said, pacing the kitchen. "Raven just showed me the article in *Snowboarder*. I need you to call them, get them to make a change."

There was chatter on the other end of the line, and though I couldn't make out what Lewis was saying, I suspected he was telling Crew no.

"Listen, I get it. But this is important to me. They left out Raven."

My jaw dropped.

No, they hadn't.

I took the magazine, scanning it for my name. "It's right here."

"There's no picture," he said to me, then focused on the call. "Lewis, I want a picture of Raven in there. Take out one of me. Add another. I don't care. But I want her in there."

Another few words from Lewis, then Crew hung up the phone.

"Crew, I don't need my picture in a magazine."

I had one, actually, in *Snowboarder*. Years ago, when I'd won my own medals.

Crew walked over, taking my hand and pulling me from the chair. Then he wrapped me in his arms, breathing in my hair. "There has to be a picture of you."

"Why?"

He leaned back, framing my face with his hands. "It's titled 'Legend,' right?"

"Yes."

Crew kissed my forehead, something he'd done countless

times in our years together. "I love the article. It's almost perfect. But not quite. Without you, there is no legend."

"Oh." Well, I was going to cry. So I burrowed into his chest, breathing in his scent. "I'm so glad I never found my clumsy nerd."

Laughter filled the room, Crew's deep chuckle rumbling against my ear. The kids burst through the door, hollering and panicked because they thought they saw a bear in the backyard.

That was our life.

A little too loud. A little too messy. A little too wild.

And utterly perfect.

PREVIEW TO INDIGO RIDGE

Enjoy this preview from Indigo Ridge, book one in the Edens series.

WINSLOW

"Could I get another . . ."

The bartender didn't slow as he passed by.

"Drink," I muttered, slumping forward.

Pops had told me that this bar was where the locals hung out. Not only was it within walking distance of my new house in case I decided not to drive, but I was a local now. As of today, I lived in Quincy, Montana.

I'd told the bartender as much when I'd asked for his wine list. He'd raised one bushy white eyebrow above his narrowed gaze, and I'd abandoned my thirst for a glass of cabernet, ordering a vodka tonic instead. It had zapped every ounce of my willpower not to request a lemon twist.

The ice cubes in my glass clinked together as I swirled

around my pink plastic straw. The bartender ignored that sound too.

Main Street had two bars—tourist traps this time of year, according to Pops. But I regretted not choosing one of those to celebrate my first night in Quincy. Given his attitude, the bartender, who must have thought I was a lost tourist, regretted my decision too.

Willie's was a dive bar and not exactly my scene.

The bartenders downtown probably acknowledged their customers, and the prices were listed on a menu, not delivered using three fingers on one wrinkled hand.

He looked about as old as this dark, dingy building. Like most small-town Montana bars, the walls were teeming with beer signs and neon lights. Shelves stacked with liquor bottles lined the mirrored wall across from my seat. The room was cluttered with tables, every chair empty.

Willie's was all but deserted this Sunday night at nine o'clock.

The locals must know of a better place to unwind.

The only other patron was a man sitting at the farthest end of the bar, in the last stool down the line. He'd come in ten minutes after I'd arrived and chosen the seat as far from me as possible. He and the bartender were nearly carbon copies of one another, with the same white hair and scraggly beards.

Twins? They looked old enough to have established this bar. Maybe one of them was Willie himself.

The bartender caught me staring.

I smiled and rattled the ice in my glass.

His mouth pursed in a thin line but he made me another

drink. And like with the first, he delivered it without a word, holding up the same three fingers.

I twisted to reach into my purse, fishing out another five because clearly starting a tab was out of the question. But before I could pull the bill from my wallet, a deep, rugged voice caressed the room.

"Hey, Willie."

"Griffin." The bartender nodded.

So he was Willie. And he could speak.

"Usual?" Willie asked.

"Yep." The man with the incredible voice, Griffin, pulled out the stool two down from mine.

As his tall, broad body eased into the seat, a whiff of his scent carried my way. Leather and wind and spice filled my nose, chasing away the musty air from the bar. It was heady and alluring.

He was the type of man who turned a woman's head.

One glimpse at his profile and the cocktail in front of me was unnecessary. Instead, I drank this man in head to toe.

The sleeves of his black T-shirt stretched around his honed biceps and molded to the planes of his shoulders as he leaned his elbows on the bar. His brown hair was finger-combed and curled at the nape of his neck. His tan forearms were dusted with the same dark hair and a vein ran over the corded muscle beneath.

Even seated, I could tell his legs were long, his thighs thick like the evergreen tree trunks from the forests outside of town. Frayed hems of his faded jeans brushed against his black cowboy boots. And as he shifted in his seat, I caught the glimmer of a silver and gold belt buckle at his waist.

If his voice, his scent and that chiseled jaw hadn't been

enough to make my mouth go dry, that buckle would have done it.

One of my mom's favorite movies had been *Legends of the Fall*. She'd let me watch it at sixteen and we'd cried together. Whenever I missed her, I'd put it on. The DVD was scratched and the clasp on the case was broken because I'd watched that movie countless times simply because it had been hers.

She'd always swooned over Brad Pitt as a sexy cowboy.

If she could see Griffin, she'd be drooling too. Though he was missing the hat and the horse, this guy was every cowboy fantasy come to life.

Lifting my glass to my mouth, I sipped the cold drink and tore my gaze from the handsome stranger. The vodka burned my throat and the alcohol rushed to my head. Ol' Willie mixed his cocktails strong.

I was unabashedly staring. It was rude and obvious. Yet when I set the glass down, my gaze immediately returned to Griffin.

His piercing blue eyes were waiting.

My breath hitched.

Willie set down a tumbler full of ice and caramel liquid in front of Griffin, then, without giving him the fingers to pay, walked away.

Griffin took a single swallow of his drink, his Adam's apple bobbing. Then his attention was on me once more.

The intensity of his gaze was as intoxicating as my cocktail.

He stared without hesitation. He stared with bold desire. His gaze raked down my black tank top to the ripped jeans

I'd put on this morning before checking out of my hotel in Bozeman.

I'd spent four and a half hours driving to Quincy with a U-Haul trailer hitched to my Dodge Durango. When I'd arrived, I'd immediately jumped into unloading, only breaking to meet Pops for dinner.

I was a mess after a day of hauling boxes. My hair was in a ponytail and whatever makeup I'd put on this morning had likely worn off. Yet the appreciation in Griffin's gaze sent a wave of desire rushing to my core.

"Hi," I blurted. *Smooth, Winn.*

His eyes twinkled like two perfect sapphires set behind long, sooty lashes. "Hi."

"I'm Winn." I held out a hand over the space between us.

"Griffin." The moment his warm, calloused palm grazed mine, tingles cascaded across my skin like fireworks. A shiver rolled down my spine.

Holy hell. There was enough electricity between us to power the jukebox in the corner.

I focused on my drink, gulping more than sipping. The ice did nothing to cool me down. When was the last time I'd been this attracted to a man? Years. It had been years. Even then, it paled in comparison to five minutes beside Griffin.

"Where are you from?" he asked. Like Willie, he must have assumed I was a tourist too.

"Bozeman."

He nodded. "I went to college at Montana State."

"Go Bobcats." I lifted my drink in a salute.

Griffin returned the gesture, then put the rim of his glass to his full lower lip.

I was staring again, unashamed. Maybe it was the

angular cheekbones that set his face apart. Maybe it was the straight nose with a slight bump at the bridge. Or his dark, bold browbone. He was no ordinary, handsome man. Griffin was drop-dead gorgeous.

And if he was at Willie's . . . a local.

Local meant off-limits. *Damn.*

I swallowed my disappointment with another gulp of vodka.

The scrape of stool legs rang through the room as he moved to take the seat beside mine. His arms returned to the bar, his drink between them as he leaned forward. He sat so close, his body so large, that the heat from his skin seeped into mine.

"Winn. I like that name."

"Thanks." My full name was Winslow but very few people ever called me anything other than Winn or Winnie.

Willie walked by and narrowed his eyes at the sliver of space between Griffin and me. Then he joined his doppelganger.

"Are they related?" I asked, dropping my voice.

"Willie Senior is on our side of the bar. His son is mixing drinks."

"Father and son. Huh. I thought twins. Does Willie Senior have the same glowing personality as Willie Junior?"

"It's worse." Griffin chuckled. "Every time I come through town, he gets crankier."

Wait. Did that mean . . . "You don't live in town?"

"No." He shook his head, picking up his drink.

I did the same, hiding my smile in the glass. So he wasn't a local. Which meant flirting was harmless. *Bless you, Quincy.*

A hundred personal questions raced through my mind, but I dismissed them all. Skyler used to criticize me for going into interrogation mode within ten minutes of meeting someone new. One of many critiques. He'd used his profession as a life coach as an excuse to tell me anything and everything I'd been doing wrong in our relationship. In life.

Meanwhile, he'd betrayed me, so I wasn't listening to Skyler's voice anymore.

But I still wasn't going to bombard this man with questions. He didn't live here, and I'd save my questions for the people who did: my constituents.

Griffin looked to the far end of the room and the empty shuffleboard table. "Want to play a game?"

"Um . . . sure? I've never played before."

"It's easy." He slid off his stool, moving with a grace that men his size didn't normally possess.

I followed, eyes glued to the best ass I had ever seen. And he didn't live here. An imaginary choir perched in the bar's dusty rafters gave a collective *yeehaw*.

Griffin went to one end of the table while I walked to the other. "Okay, Winn. Loser buys the next round of drinks."

Good thing I had cash. "Okay."

Griffin spent the next ten minutes explaining the rules and demonstrating how to slide the pucks down the sand-dusted surface toward the point lines. Then we played, game after game. After one more round, we both stopped drinking, but neither of us made a move to leave.

I won some games. I lost most. And when Willie finally announced that he was closing at one, the two of us walked outside to the darkened parking lot.

A dusty black truck was parked beside my Durango.

"That was fun."

"It was." I smiled up at Griffin, my cheeks pinching. I hadn't had this much fun openly flirting with a man in, well . . . ever. I slowed my steps because the last place I wanted to go was home alone.

He must have had the same idea because his boots stopped on the pavement. He inched closer.

Winslow Covington didn't have one-night stands. I'd been too busy wasting years on the wrong man. Griffin wasn't the right man either, but I'd learned in my time as a cop that sometimes it wasn't about choosing right from wrong. It was choosing the *right* wrongs.

Griffin. Tonight, I chose Griffin.

So I closed the distance between us and stood on my toes, letting my hands snake up his hard, flat stomach.

He was tall, standing two or three inches over six feet. At five nine, it was refreshing to be around a man who towered over me. I lifted a hand to his neck, pulling him down until his mouth hovered over mine.

"Is that your truck?"

"Shit." I cursed at the clock, then flew into action, flinging the covers off my naked body and racing for the bathroom.

Late was not how I wanted to start the first day of my new job.

I flipped on the shower, my head pounding as I stepped under the cold spray and let out a yelp. There was no time to wait for hot water, so I shampooed my hair and put in some conditioner while I scrubbed Griffin's scent off my skin. I'd mourn the loss of it later.

There was an ache between my legs that I'd think about later too. Last night had been . . .

Mind blowing. Toe curling. The best night I'd ever had with a man. Griffin knew exactly how to use that powerful body of his and I'd been the lucky recipient of three—or had it been four?—orgasms.

I shuddered and realized the water was hot. "Damn it."

Shoving thoughts of Griffin out of my head, I hurried out of the shower, frantically swiping on makeup and willing the blow dryer to work faster. Without time to curl or straighten my hair, I twisted it into a tight bun at the nape of my neck, then dashed to the bedroom to get dressed.

The mattress rested on the floor, the sheets and blankets rumpled and strewn everywhere. Thankfully, before I'd headed to the bar last night, I'd searched for bedding in the boxes and laid it out. When I'd finally gotten home after hours spent in the back of Griffin's truck, I'd practically face-planted into my pillows and forgotten to set my alarm.

I refused to regret Griffin. Kicking off my new life in Quincy with a hot and wild night seemed a little bit like fate.

Serendipity.

Maybe on his next trip through town, we'd bump into each other. But if not, well . . . I didn't have time for the distraction of a man.

Especially not today.

"Oh, God. Please don't let me be late." I rifled through a suitcase, finding a pair of dark-wash jeans.

Pops had told me specifically not to show up at the station looking fancy.

The jeans were slightly wrinkled but there was no time to find whatever box had stolen my iron. Besides, an iron meant fancy. The simple white tee I found next was also wrinkled, so I dug for my favorite black blazer to hide the worst offenders. Then I hopped into my favorite black boots with the chunky heels before jogging for the door, swiping up my purse from where I'd dumped it on the living room floor.

The sun was shining. The air was clean. The sky was blue. And I had no time to appreciate a minute of my first Quincy, Montana, morning as I ran to the Durango parked in my driveway.

I slid behind the wheel, started the engine and cursed again at the clock on the dash. *Eight-oh-two.* "I'm late."

Thankfully, Quincy wasn't Bozeman and the drive from one side of town to the police station on the other took exactly six minutes. I pulled into the lot and parked next to a familiar blue Bronco and let myself take a single deep breath.

I can do this job.

Then I got out of my car and walked to the station's front door, hoping with every step I looked okay.

One disdaining look from the officer stationed behind a glass partition at the front desk and I knew I'd gotten it wrong. *Shit.*

His gray hair was cut short, high and tight in a military style. He looked me up and down, the wrinkles on his face deepening with a scowl. That glare likely had nothing to do with my outfit.

And everything to do with my last name.

"Good morning." I plastered on a bright smile, crossing the small lobby to his workspace. "I'm Winslow Covington."

"The new chief. I know," he muttered.

My smile didn't falter.

I'd win them over. Eventually. That's what I'd told Pops last night when he'd had me over for dinner after I'd returned the U-Haul. I'd win them all over, one by one.

Most people were bound to think that the only reason I'd gotten the job as the Quincy chief of police was because my grandfather was the mayor. Yes, he would be my boss. But there wasn't a nepotism clause for city employees. Probably because in a town this size, everyone was likely related in some manner. If you added too many restrictions, no one would be able to get a job.

Besides, Pops hadn't hired me. He could have, but instead, he'd put together a search committee so that there'd be more than one voice in the decision. Walter Covington was the fairest, most honorable man I'd ever known.

And granddaughter or not, what mattered was my performance. He'd take the cues from the community, and though my grandfather loved me completely, he wouldn't hesitate to fire me if I screwed this up.

He'd told me as much the day he'd hired me. He'd reminded me again last night.

"The mayor is waiting in your office," the officer said, pushing the button to buzz me into the door beside his cubicle.

"It was nice to meet you"—I glanced at the silver name-plate on his black uniform—"Officer Smith."

His response was to ignore me completely, turning his attention to his computer screen. I'd have to win him over another day. Or maybe he'd be open to an early retirement.

I pushed through the door that led into the heart of the

station. I'd been here twice, both times during the interview process. But it was different now as I walked through the bullpen no longer a guest. This was my bullpen. The officers looking up from their desks were under my charge.

My stomach clenched.

Staying up all night having sex with a stranger probably hadn't been the smartest way to prepare for my first day.

"Winnie." Pops came out of what would be my office, his hand extended. He seemed taller today, probably because he was dressed in nice jeans and a starched shirt instead of the ratty T-shirt, baggy jeans and suspenders I'd seen him in yesterday.

Pops was fit for his seventy-one years and though his hair was a thick silver, his six-three frame was as strong as an ox. He was in better shape than most men my age, let alone his.

I shook his hand, glad that he hadn't tried to hug me. "Morning. Sorry I'm late."

"I just got here myself." He leaned in closer and dropped his voice. "You doing okay?"

"Nervous," I whispered.

He gave me a small smile. "You'll do great."

I could do this job.

I was thirty years old. Two decades below the median age of a person in this position. Four decades younger than my predecessor had been when he'd retired.

The former chief of police had worked in Quincy for his entire career, moving up the ranks and acting as chief for as long as I'd been alive. But that was why Pops had wanted me in this position. He said Quincy needed fresh eyes and younger blood. The town was growing, and with it, their problems. The old ways weren't cutting it.

The department needed to embrace technology and new processes. When the former chief had announced his retirement, Pops had encouraged me to toss my name into the hat. By some miracle, the hiring committee had chosen me.

Yes, I was young, but I met the minimum qualifications. I'd worked for ten years with the Bozeman Police Department. During that time, I'd earned my bachelor's degree and a position as detective within their department. My record was impeccable, and I'd never left a case unclosed.

Maybe my welcome would have been warmer if I were a man, but that had never scared me and it certainly wasn't going to today.

I can do this job.

I would do this job.

"Let me introduce you to Janice." He nodded for me to follow him into my office, where we spent the morning with Janice, my new assistant.

She'd worked for the former chief for fifteen years, and the longer she spoke, the more I fell in love with her. Janice had spiky gray hair and the cutest pair of red-framed glasses I'd ever seen. She knew the ins and outs of the station, the schedules and the shortcomings.

As we ended our initial meeting, I made a mental note to bring her flowers because without Janice, I'd likely fall flat on my face. We toured the station, meeting the officers not out on patrol.

Officer Smith, who was rarely sent into the field because he preferred the desk, had been one of the candidates for chief, and Janice told me that he'd been a grumpy asshole since the day he'd been rejected.

Every officer besides him had been polite and professional, though reserved. No doubt they weren't sure what to make of me, but today I'd won Janice over—or maybe she'd won me. I was calling it a victory.

"You'll meet most of the department this afternoon at shift change," she told me when we retreated back to the safety of my office.

"I was planning on staying late one evening this week to meet the night shift too."

This wasn't a large station, because Quincy wasn't a large town, but in total, I had fifteen officers, four dispatchers, two administrators and a Janice.

"Tomorrow, the county sheriff is coming in to meet you," Janice said, reading from the notebook she'd had with her all morning. "Ten o'clock. His staff is twice the size of ours but he has more ground to cover. For the most part, their team stays out of our way, but he's always willing to step in if you need help."

"Good to know." I wouldn't mind having a resource to bounce ideas off of either.

"How's your head?" Pops asked.

I put my hands by my ears and made the sound of an exploding bomb.

He laughed. "You'll catch on."

"Yes, you will," Janice said.

"Thank you for everything," I told her. "I'm really looking forward to working with you."

She sat a little straighter. "Likewise."

"Okay, Winnie." Pops slapped his hands on his knees. "Let's go grab some lunch. Then I've got to get to my own office, and I'll let you come back here and settle in."

"I'll be here when you get back." Janice squeezed my arm as we shuffled out of my office.

Pops simply nodded, maintaining his distance. Tonight, when I wasn't Chief Covington and he wasn't Mayor Covington, I'd head to his house and get one of his bear hugs.

"How about we eat at The Eloise?" he suggested as we made our way outside.

"The hotel?"

He nodded. "It would be good for you to spend some time there. Get to know the Edens."

The Edens. Quincy's founding family.

Pops had promised that the fastest way to earn favor with the community was to win over the Edens. One of their relatives from generations past had founded the town and the family had been the community's cornerstone ever since.

"They own the hotel, remember?" he asked.

"I remember. I just didn't realize there was a restaurant in the hotel these days." Probably because I hadn't spent much time in Quincy lately.

The six trips I'd taken here to participate in the interview process had been my first trips to Quincy in years. Five, to be exact.

But when Skyler and I had fallen to pieces and Pops had pitched the job as chief, I'd decided it was time for a change. And Quincy, well . . . Quincy had always held a special place in my heart.

"The Edens started the hotel's restaurant about four years ago," Pops said. "It's the best place in town, in my opinion."

"Then let's eat." I unlocked my car. "Meet you there."

I followed his Bronco from the station to Main Street,

taking in the plethora of out-of-state cars parked downtown. Tourist season was in full swing and nearly every space was full.

Pops parked two blocks away from Main on a side street, and side by side, we strolled to The Eloise Inn.

The town's iconic hotel was the tallest building in Quincy, standing proudly against the mountain backdrop in the distance. I'd always wanted to spend a night at The Eloise. Maybe one day I'd book myself a room, just for fun.

The lobby smelled of lemons and rosemary. The front desk was an island in the grand, open space, and a young woman with a sweet face stood behind the counter, checking in a guest. When she spotted Pops, she tossed him a wink.

"Who's that?" I asked.

"Eloise Eden. She took over as manager this past winter."

Pops waved at her, then walked past the front desk toward an open doorway. The clatter of forks on plates and the dull murmur of conversation greeted me as we entered the hotel's restaurant.

The dining room was spacious and the ceilings as tall as those in the lobby. It was the perfect place for entertaining. Almost a ballroom but filled with tables of varying sizes, it also worked well as a restaurant.

"They just put in those windows." Pops pointed at the far wall where black-paned windows cut into a red-brick wall. "Last time I talked to Harrison, he said this fall they'll be remodeling this whole space."

Harrison Eden. The family's patriarch. He'd been on the hiring committee, and I liked to believe I'd made a good impression. According to Pops, if I hadn't, there was no way I'd have gotten my job.

A hostess greeted us with a wide smile and led us to a square table in the center of the room.

"Which of the Edens runs the restaurant?" I asked as we browsed the menu card.

"Knox. He's Harrison and Anne's second oldest son. Eloise is their youngest daughter."

Harrison and Anne, the parents. Knox, a son. Eloise, a daughter. There were likely many more Edens to meet.

Down Main, the Eden name was splashed on numerous storefronts, including the coffee shop I wished I'd had time to stop by this morning. Last night's antics were catching up to me, and I hid a yawn with my menu.

"They're good people," Pops said. "You've met Harrison. Anne's a sweetheart. Their opinion carries a lot of weight around here. So does Griffin's."

Griffin. *Did he say Griffin?*

My stomach dropped.

No. This couldn't be happening. It had to be a mistake. There had to be another Griffin, one who didn't live in Quincy. I'd specifically asked him last night if he lived in town and he'd said no. Hadn't he?

"Hey, Covie."

So busy having my mental freak-out that I'd slept with not only a local man, but one I needed to see me as a professional and not a backseat hookup, I didn't notice the two men standing beside our table until it was too late.

Harrison Eden smiled.

Griffin, who was just as handsome as he had been last night, did not.

Had he known who I was last night? Had that been some

sort of test or trick? Doubtful. He looked as surprised to see me as I was to see him.

"Hey, Harrison." Pops stood to shake his hand, then waved at me. "You remember my granddaughter, Winslow."

"Of course." Harrison took my hand as I stood, shaking it with a firm grip. "Welcome. We're glad to have you as our new chief of police."

"Thank you." My voice was surprisingly steady considering my heart was attempting to dive out of my chest and hide under the table. "I'm glad to be here."

"Would you like to join us?" Pops offered, nodding to the empty chairs at our table.

"No," Griffin said at the same time his father said, "We'd love to."

Neither Pops nor Harrison seemed to notice the tension rolling off Griffin's body as they took their chairs, leaving Griffin and me to introduce ourselves.

I swallowed hard, then extended a hand. "Hello."

That sharp jaw I'd traced with my tongue last night clenched so tight that I heard the crack of his molars. He glared at my hand before capturing it in his large palm. "Griffin."

Griffin Eden.

My one-night stand.

So much for serendipity.

ACKNOWLEDGMENTS

Thank you for reading *A Little Too Wild*! I'm so very grateful for my incredible readers. And honored you'd choose to read one of my stories.

Thanks to my incredible editing and proofreading team: Elizabeth Nover, Julie Deaton and Judy Zweifel. Thank you to Sarah Hansen for the perfect cover. To Sarina and Rebecca, thank you for sharing the Madigan Mountain world with me. And lastly, thank you Bill, Will and Nash for supporting me through each and every book.

ABOUT THE AUTHOR

Devney is a *USA Today* bestselling author who lives in Washington with her husband and two sons. Born and raised in Montana, she loves writing books set in her treasured home state. After working in the technology industry for nearly a decade, she abandoned conference calls and project schedules to enjoy a slower pace at home with her family. Writing one book, let alone many, was not something she ever expected to do. But now that she's discovered her true passion for writing romance, she has no plans to ever stop.

Don't miss out on Devney's latest book news.
Subscribe to her newsletter!
www.devneyperry.com

Devney loves hearing from her readers.
Connect with her on social media!
Facebook
Instagram
Twitter
BookBub

CPSIA information can be obtained
at www.ICGtesting.com
Printed in the USA
LVHW032255241022
731422LV00003B/138